《昭明文选》诗歌英译选

刘贞玉　著

中国纺织出版社有限公司

图书在版编目（CIP）数据

《昭明文选》诗歌英译选：汉、英 / 刘贞玉著 . --
北京：中国纺织出版社有限公司，2021.8（2024.2重印）
ISBN 978-7-5180-8792-1

Ⅰ . ①昭… Ⅱ . ①刘… Ⅲ . ①古典诗歌—诗集—中国—汉、英②古典散文—散文集—中国—汉、英 Ⅳ . ① I212.01

中国版本图书馆 CIP 数据核字（2021）第 164840 号

责任编辑：郭　婷　　责任校对：寇晨晨　　责任印制：储志伟

中国纺织出版社有限公司出版发行
地址：北京市朝阳区百子湾东里 A407 号楼　邮政编码：100124
销售电话：010—67004422　传真：010—87155801
http://www.c-textilep.com
中国纺织出版社天猫旗舰店
官方微博 http://weibo.com/2119887771
北京兰星球彩色印刷有限公司印刷　各地新华书店经销
2021 年 8 月第 1 版　2024年2月第2次印刷
开本：710 × 1000　1/16　印张：17
字数：260 千字　定价：79.80 元

前　言

《昭明文选》是我国最早以“选”命名的文学总集，是我国现存最早的一部诗文总集，由南朝梁武帝的长子萧统组织文人编选，是一部文学巨著。这部总集收录了周代至六朝梁代七八百年间130位知名作者的七百余篇文学作品，内容丰富，风格多样，辞藻绚丽，自成体系。它流传广泛，对后世文学的发展繁荣产生过广泛而深远的影响。

《昭明文选》由于选材严谨而被视为文学的教科书。纵观中国优秀文学作品的翻译史，可以看到很多优秀的古典名著都被译成多国语言，可供海内外广大读者研读并传承，而《昭明文选》由于文体多样，注重辞藻，版本众多，至今未有大量今注今译本，译者寥寥。美国华盛顿大学亚洲语言文学系教授康达雅先生著有《昭明文选译注》，书中翻译了文选中大量的赋，对文选在海外的传播做出了卓越的贡献。还有华兹生等学者也对文选进行了翻译，这些欧美学者均比较注重文选的译介研究。我国的许渊冲教授、汪榕培教授等也翻译了文选中的大量诗歌，其翻译作品令人耳目一新。我撰写这部《昭明文选》诗歌英译选，也想为选学的传播和振兴做一份贡献。在编译的过程中，我研读了几位学者大量的译著，并从中得到很大的启发，受益颇多。

文选中的作品体裁多样，本书只节选了《昭明文选》从汉朝到晋朝的一部分诗歌进行编译，其他体裁诸如词、曲、赋均无涉猎。由于文选的版本众多，本书以吉林文史出版社出版的《昭明文选》译注为蓝本来选择所编译的内容并进行校注。在书中编者按照年代的顺序来编排作家及作品，共选取了从汉朝到梁朝30位诗人的162篇诗歌。本书的翻译作品简要介绍了所选取诗人的生平、诗歌及诗歌解析，这些内容用中英双语进行编译。希望以这本译著能推动选学的传播，向世界介绍我们中华民族的优秀传统文化，进一步促进中外文化的交流和碰撞。

本译著既是2019年吉林省社会科学基金项目《昭明文选》音注研究（项

目编号 2019c99) 的成果，也是佳木斯大学 2015 年社会科学重点项目古代诗文英译问题研究——以美国汉学家康达维教授英译《昭明文选》为例（项目编号 12SH1201501）的成果。

限于著者能力有限，书中定有很多疏漏之处，恳请读者不吝赐正。

著者

2021 年 3 月

目　录
Contents

汉朝诗歌

Poems of Han Dynasty

李陵（前134—前74），字少卿，陇西成纪（今甘肃秦安西北）人。西汉将领，名将李广之孙。少为侍中建章监，善骑射。天汉二年，武帝命李广利率骑兵三万出酒泉（今属甘肃），李陵率步兵五千出居延（在今内蒙古额济纳旗北境），以击匈奴。李陵被匈奴大军围困，连战十余日，粮尽援绝，兵败投降。居匈奴二十余年，病卒。《隋书·经籍志》著录有集二卷，已佚。

Li Ling (134BC—74BC), Shaoqing, was born in Chengji (now northwest of Qin'an, Gansu) in Longxi. He is a general of the Western Han Dynasty and the grandson of the famous general Li Guang. He is likely to serve as Shizhong Jianzhang Jian and is good at riding and shooting. In the second year of Tianhan, Emperor Wu ordered Li Guang to send 30,000 cavalry out of Jiuquan (now belongs toGansu). Li Ling led 5,000 infantry out of Juyan (in the northern border of Ejina Banner, Inner Mongolia) to attack the Huns. Li Ling was besieged by the Huns. For more than ten days of fighting, food was exhaustedand the army was defeated and surrendered. Living in Xiongnu for more than 20 years, he died of illness. In Sui Shu · Jing Ji Zhithere are two volumes, which have been lost.

《与苏武三首》诗歌赏析：

《与苏武三首》传为李陵在匈奴为苏武所作的赠别诗。锺嵘《诗品》将其列为上品，但这样成熟的五言诗不可能在苏、李时代就产生出来，加之诗中内容多与苏、李当时情事和行踪不合，故六朝时即有人怀疑此为伪托。后来学者大多认为出于伪托，推断可能是与《古诗十九首》同一时代的作品。诗在艺术上有较高成就，对后世产生了较大影响。

Three Pems to Su Wu

Three poems to Su Wu are passed down as farewell poems written by Li Ling for

Su Wu in Xiongnu. Zhong Rong's *Shi Pin* listed it as top grade, but such a mature five-character poem could not have been produced in the Su and Li era. In addition, the content of the poem was mostly inconsistent with the situation and whereabouts of Su and Li at the time, so some people suspected this during the Six Dynasties for pseudo-trust. Most of later scholars think that it is out of pseudo-trust and inferred that it may be a work of the same era as *Nineteen Ancient Poems*. The poem has a relatively high artistic achievement anda greater impact on later generations.

（一）

良时不再至，离别在须臾。

屏营衢路侧，执手野踟蹰。

仰视浮云驰，奄忽互相逾。

风波一失所，各在天一隅。

长当从此别，且复立斯须。

欲因晨风发，送子以贱躯。

There will be no good times,

The time of parting is coming.

Hesitating, I stand beside the road,

Wander in the wilderness holding hands.

When I look up, I see floating clouds running fast,

They surpass each other in a flash.

Lose their place due to the turbulence,

Each has to be far away.

From then on, I will be separated for a long time,

Stand for a while and pour out my heart.

I would like to set off with the morning breeze,

See you off one journey after another.

（二）

嘉会难再遇，三载为千秋。

临河濯长缨，念子怅悠悠。

远望悲风至，对酒不能酬。

行人怀往路，何以慰我愁。

独有盈觞酒，与子结绸缪。

It is rare to meet beautiful gatherings again in the future,

The three years together can last a thousand years.

When I came to the river and washed the long hat belt,

I felt melancholy because you were about to leave.

Looked far from the distance,

the sorrowful wind hits on his face,

But I don't want to drink at the banquet.

My friend, you only want to set off.

How to soothe the sorrow?

Only raise a full cup of wine and drink it,

May we always be affectionate.

（三）

携手上河梁，游子暮何之？

徘徊蹊路侧，悢悢不得辞。

行人难久留，各言长相思。

安知非日月，弦望自有时？

努力崇明德，皓首以为期。

Hold your hand tightly and walk up the river bridge,

Where are you going to go when it's almost dark?

Wander on the side of this small road,

No words in my heart for a while.

I know there is no way to keep you for a long time,

Part and tell each other about longing.

How do you know that we are not the moon in the sky.

I hope that we will cultivate virtue until the hair turns gray.

~~~~~~

古诗十九首《古诗十九首》最早见于《文选》，作者姓名失考，大约是东汉末年的作品。“古诗”本是六朝人对汉魏诗歌的统称。因这十九首时代风貌和艺术风格相近，萧统编《文选》时便将它们编为一组，后来《古诗十九首》便成了这组五言诗的专称。

《古诗十九首》就其题材来看，大致是游子之歌与思妇之词两类。诗歌内容多写夫妇朋友间的离愁别绪和士人的彷徨失意，有些作品表现出了追求富贵和及时行乐的思想，然而其思想内涵却极为复杂。古诗十九首的思想感情虽然复杂，但也有一点贯穿全诗的主旋律。作者通过游子怀乡、闺人怨别、游宦无成、追求享乐等的描写，流露出浓厚的人生感伤情绪，这正是一种世纪末的忧伤。东汉末年，政治黑暗，社会混乱，外出游学求仕的士人大多备尝艰辛，彷徨苦闷，发而为诗，于是便有了这许多或伤离怨别。或感叹年华虚度或悲苦人生如常或感叹知音寥寥或抱怨友情浅薄的诗作，真实反映了当时知识分子失意沉沦的心境。失意的文人倦客，对节序的推移和时间的流逝尤为敏感，反映这种思想情绪的诗句，在十九首中几乎俯拾皆是。

而在这些失意文人的思想意识中，似乎萌发着一种新的觉醒：这就是对于人和人生的觉悟。他们在对时世、人事、节物、名利、享乐的咏叹中，表现的是一种性命短暂、人生无常的悲哀。表面看来是消极、颓废、悲观的感叹，实际深藏着的恰恰是它的反面，即对于人生、生命、命运、生活的强烈的留恋和欲求。只有在对从前所宣扬和信奉的那套伦理道德、迷信经术等等规范、标准、价值的虚伪性大胆怀疑和否定的基础上，才会产生这种内在人格的觉醒和追求。他们意识到，人必然会死，短促的人生充满那么多的生离死别、哀伤不幸。那么，为什么不抓紧生活，尽情享乐呢？表面看来似乎是赤裸裸地追求贪图享乐、消极颓废，说得干脆、坦率，毫无掩饰，实质上它是在当时特定历史条件下深刻地表现了对人生、对生活的渴望
~~~~~~

追求。《古诗十九首》感情真挚，语言自然，表现委婉，形象生动，艺术上有较高成就。

《古诗十九首》标志着五言诗从以叙事为主的乐府民歌发展到以抒情为主的文人创作，显示了五言诗的成熟。它们所反映的下层文人的苦闷和愿望，在封建时代具有相当的普遍性和典型意义，极易引起共鸣；它们所创造的独特表现手法和艺术风格，适合于表现感伤苦闷情绪，更为后世封建文人所喜爱和模仿。《古诗十九首》成为文学史上五言诗成熟的标志，对后世产生了深远的影响。其最大价值就在于直接宣泄了人性的积极追求，突破了传统诗教的规范，表现了下层文人的生活境况和思想情绪。

Nineteen Ancient Poems was first seen in *Wen Xuan*. The author's name was missing, and it was probably the work of the late Eastern Han Dynasty. Ancient Poetry was originally the collective term for Han and Wei poetry by the people of the Six Dynasties. Because these nineteen poems were similar in artistic style, Xiao Tong compiled them into a group when he compiled *Wen Xuan*. Later, "Nineteen Ancient Poems" became the term for this group of five-character poems.

Nineteen Ancient Poems in terms of its subject matter are roughly divided into two categories: the songs of wandering men and the words of lovesick wife. The content of the poems is mostly about the feelings of parting between couples and friends and the hesitation and frustration of scholars. Some works show the idea of pursuing wealth and pleasure in a timely manner, but their ideological connotations are extremely complicated. Although the thoughts and feelings of the nineteen ancient poems are complicated, there is a theme that runs through the whole poem. The author reveals a strong sentimental sentiment in life through the descriptions of wandering nostalgia, grieving goodbye, wandering, and pursuing pleasure. This is exactly the sadness at the end of the century. At the end of the Eastern Han Dynasty, politics was dark and society was chaotic. Most of the scholars who went out to study and pursue official careers suffered from hardships, hesitating and depressed, and wrote poetry, so there are so many sads and farewells, or lamenting the wasted years of life, or the miserable life as usual , or lamenting the few friends, or complaining about friendship and superficial poems, truly reflect the frustration and sinking mood of intellectuals at that time. The frustrated literati, tired of visitors, are particularly sensitive to the passage of sections and the passage of time. Poems reflecting this kind of thought and emotion are almost everywhere in the nineteen poems.

And in the ideology of these frustrated literati, it seems that a new kind of awakening is emerging: this is the awareness of people and life. In their chants of time, human affairs, festivals, fame and fortune, and pleasure, what stands out is the sorrow of short life and impermanence in life. On the surface, it looks like a negative, decadent, and pessimistic sigh, but what is actually hidden is its opposite, that is, the strong nostalgia and desire for life, life, destiny, and life. Only on the basis of bold doubts and denials of the hypocrisy and denial of the norms, standards, and values of the ethics, superstitions and scriptures that have been preached and believed in the past, will the inner personality awakening and pursuit be produced. They realize that people will inevitably die, and the short life is full of so many life, parting, sorrow and misfortune. So, why not hurry up and have fun? On the surface, it seems to be a stark pursuit of pleasure and negative decadence. It is straightforward, frank and undisguised. In fact, it is a profound expression of the right under the specific historical conditions at that time. The desire and pursuit of life and life. His feelings are sincere, his language is natural, his expression is euphemistic, his image is vivid, and his artistic achievements are high.

Nineteen Ancient Poems marked the development of five-character poems from Yuefu folk songs based on narration to literary creation based on lyricism, showing the maturity of five-character poems. The depression and aspirations of the lower-class literati reflected by them are quite universal and typical in the feudal era, and can easily resonate with them; the unique expression techniques and artistic styles they create are suitable for expressing sentimental and depressed emotions, and more loved and imitated by later generations of feudal literati. *Nineteen Ancient Poems* became a symbol of the maturity of five-character poems in the history of literature and had a profound impact on later generations. The greatest value of *Nineteen Ancient Poems* is that it directly vents the active pursuit of human nature, breaks through the norms of traditional poetry education, and expresses the living conditions and thoughts and emotions of the lower-level literati.

《行行重行行》诗歌赏析:

这是一首在东汉末年动荡岁月中的相思之歌。这首诗写一位独守空房的女子对于远行异乡、许久未归的丈夫一种诚挚深切的思念之情，表达了其对丈夫真挚的爱情。结构上主要是按感情的起伏变化来陈述事实：先是述说当初的离别，倾述丈夫杳无音信带给她的思念之痛。诗人更是使用单纯优美的语言，把离别相思之苦抒发得更为深挚感人，也使这首诗具有永恒的艺术魅力。

This is a song of lovesickness in the turbulent years of the Eastern Han Dynasty. This poem writes about the sincere and deep thoughts of a woman who is alone in the vacant room for her husband who has traveled to a foreign land and has not returned for a long time, and expresses her sincere love for her husband. The structure is mainly based on the ups and downs of feelings to drive the tailoring of facts: first to tell the parting at the beginning, and to tell her the feelings of missing her husband' s lack of news. The poet uses pure and beautiful language to express the feeling of parting and lovesickness more deeply and moving, which also makes this poem possess eternal artistic charm.

行行重行行，与君生别离。

相去万余里，各在天一涯。

道路阻且长，会面安可知？

胡马依北风，越鸟巢南枝。

相去日已远，衣带日已缓。

浮云蔽白日，游子不顾返。

思君令人老，岁月忽已晚。

弃捐勿复道，努力加餐饭。

Walk forward on and on,

I separate from you alive.

Long miles apart,

Each live in one side of the sky.

The road is difficult and long,

Anyone knows when we will meet?

Huma miss the harsh north wind,

Birds fly over north to build nests with branches of south.

The parting days get longer,

Belts get looser.

The clouds in the sky obscure the sky,

The wanderer outside does not want to return.

Missing make people age very quickly,

In a blink of an eye the end of the year approaches again.

Throw away worries, not mention it again,

Hope you safe and sound.

《青青河畔草》诗歌赏析:

这也是一首用第三人称写的思妇诗，描写的是一个重演过无数次的平凡的生活片段，用的是即景抒情的手法。诗歌使用了烘托的艺术手法，将春光浪漫与娇媚佳人相互辉映，背后隐藏的却是主人公痛苦的思念和哀伤。诗歌在艺术上也很有特色，它运用极精细的笔触来描绘环境与人物，使诗的形象逐渐展开，表现得愈益明朗；该诗具有高度的语言技巧，通过语言的选择、运用、组织和安排，使诗的形象显得异常丰富生动。

This is also a poem about a yearning woman in the third person. It describes an ordinary life segment that has been repeated countless times, using an instant lyrical approach. The poem uses the artistic technique of contrast, the romance of the spring and the charming and beautiful women reflect each other, but behind it is the painful thoughts and sorrow of the protagonist. Poetry is also very distinctive in art.It uses extremely fine brushstrokes to depict the environment and characters, so that the image of the poem is gradually unfolded, and the performance becomes more and more clear; Poetry has a high degree of language skills, it uses selection, use, organization and arrangement makes the image of the poem extremely rich and vivid.

青青河畔草，郁郁园中柳。

盈盈楼上女，皎皎当窗牖。

娥娥红粉妆，纤纤出素手。

昔为倡家女，今为荡子妇。

荡子行不归，空床难独守。

Full of green grass beside the river,

Weeping willows in the lush garden.

The woman upstairs with a beautiful appearance,

White and glamorous standing at the window.

The delicate figure, with gorgeous makeup,

Hands slender and white.

She once lived on singing,

Now she is wife of a wandering man.

Wandering man go out for a long time and do not return,

The empty bed is cold and hard to stay alone.

《青青陵上柏》诗歌赏析:

这是一首忧时伤怀的感兴诗，这首诗的主旨就是感叹生命短促，劝导人们应及时行乐。前半部分从人生短促之感写到及时行乐的愿望和行动，情绪显得消极；后半部分叙述权贵享受，并以自己的郁郁不得志与之对比，在一定程度上流露了对现实的不满。

This is an emotional poem about sadness. The main theme of this poem is to lament the shortness of life and persuade people to have fun in time. The first half writes about the shortness of life to the desires and actions for timely enjoyment, and the emotions appear negative; the second half describes the enjoyment of the powerful and the rich, and contrasts with their own depression, revealing dissatisfaction with reality to a certain extent.

青青陵上柏，磊磊涧中石。

人生天地间，忽如远行客。

斗酒相娱乐，聊厚不为薄。

驱车策驽马，游戏宛与洛。

洛中何郁郁，冠带自相索。

长衢罗夹巷，王侯多第宅。

两宫遥相望，双阙百余尺。

极宴娱心意，戚戚何所迫？

Alpine cypress trees are green all year round,

Stones are piled up in the ditch for years.

Life is between this world,

Hurry is like a traveler.

Offer each other's wine to entertain each other,

Talk together intimately.

Drive the cart and horse,

Go to Wancheng and Luoyang.

The city of Luoyang is so prosperous,

Nobles visit like a shuttle.

The alleys lined on both sides of the main street,

Many residences of princes.

The north and the south opposite each other,

The two palaces far high.

Enjoy the pleasure of,

Why is sorrow so compelling?

《今日良宴会》诗歌赏析：

这是一首凭借反语抒发感愤的感怀诗。诗人借阐明曲中真意，大发人生短促、应当追求富贵、莫守贫贱的感慨。这既是感愤，亦是自嘲。反映出汉末大乱前夕人们信仰的崩溃，儒家思想已不能维系人心。诗人虽只感慨人生无常，要追求荣华富贵，追名逐利，然而这也不失其为真。并且，由于诗人诉诸情感是迸发式的强烈抒情，给人的感觉是慷慨激昂。

This is a poem that expresses indignation through irony. By clarifying the true meaning of the song, the poet expresses the feeling that life is short, and he should pursue wealth and not keep the poor. This is both indignation and self-deprecating. Reflecting the collapse of people’ s beliefs in the great chaos in the late Han Dynasty, Confucianism can no longer sustain people’ s hearts. Although the poet only sighs that life is impermanent,and wants to pursue prosperity, fame and fortune, but this is true. Moreover, because the poets resort to emotions by the burst of strong lyric, which gives people a feeling of passionate.

今日良宴会，欢乐难具陈。

弹筝奋逸响，新声妙入神。

令德唱高言，识曲听其真。

齐心同所愿，含意俱未申。

人生寄一世，奄忽若飙尘。

何不策高足，先据要路津。

无为守贫贱，轗轲长苦辛。

Banquet in high spirit,

Hard to explain all the joys.

Playing the string produces unrestrained sound,

New songs sound wonderfully fascinating.

The virtuous person sings brilliant lyrics,

Intimate person understands the true feelings.

Everyone thinks about the same truth,

Without making a sound.

Life is like a boarding for travelers,

Just like a violent wind blowing up dust.

Why not rush the horse and run quickly,

Take the road to the ferry first?

Don't keep on being poor and humble,

So suffer a hard life.

《西北有高楼》诗歌赏析：

这是一首感慨知音难遇的诗。此诗构思巧妙，虚实结合。先营造氛围，再写歌声，最后抒发感情。诗里所描绘的景象，全是诗人托化的虚拟意境。读者心理都明白，高楼上的女子，也是出于诗人的虚拟，其实也正是诗人自己。诗人借助于幻想，表达内心的寂寞与伤感，并书写政治的失意之情。

This is a poem that expresses feelings about a rare friend. This poem is cleverly conceived, combining virtual and real. The poet creates an atmosphere first, then writes a song, and finally expresses feelings. The scenes depicted in the poem are all virtual artistic conceptions entrusted by the poet. The readers understand that the woman in the tall building is also out of the poet's fiction, but in fact it is the poet himself. With the help of fantasy, the poet expresses his inner loneliness and sadness, and writes about his political frustration.

西北有高楼，上与浮云齐。

交疏结绮窗，阿阁三重阶。

上有弦歌声，音响一何悲！

谁能为此曲，无乃杞梁妻。

清商随风发，中曲正徘徊。

一弹再三叹，慷慨有余哀。

不惜歌者苦，但伤知音稀。

愿为双鸿鹄，奋翅起高飞。

A pavilion stands high in the northwest,

Rises in line with the floating clouds.

The staggered engraved window panes,

Three steps on four sides with curved eaves.

Singing and playing come from above,

Sound full of infinite sadness!

Who sing such a tune,

Could it be the wife of Qiliang?

The tunes of the Qing Shang melody radiate with the breeze,

Music reciprocates in the middle.

After a piece of music, then play repeatedly,

The frustration leaves inexhaustible sorrow.

I don’t deplore the pain in the singer’s heart,

But for the singer has few friends.

I would like to be a pair of crowing cranes,

Struggling to spread wings and fly high towards the sky.

《涉江采芙蓉》诗歌赏析:

这是一首写游子思念故乡和亲人的诗，描写了远方游子的思乡之情。此诗的主人公是一位女子，诗中所书写的是游子怀念远在家乡的妻子，还有妻子思念丈夫的深切忧伤。诗歌结构本身的回环曲折，正反映了诗中主人公内心深处那种相思难耐、苦闷忧伤的情绪，诗人的失望之情溢于言表。此诗借物咏怀，繁花似锦的自然景色与诗人内心的痛苦形成鲜明的对比，使诗歌意境深邃，表达了诗人内心的忧伤和凄苦，加重了诗歌的悲剧色彩。

This is a poem about a wanderer who misses his hometown and relatives. It describes the homesickness of a wanderer from afar. The protagonist of this poem is a woman. What is written in the poem is that the wanderer misses his wife who is far away in his hometown, and his wife misses her husband with deep sadness. The twists and turns of the structure itself reflect the feelings of lovesickness and sadness deep in the protagonist’s heart, and the poet’s disappointment is beyond words. This poem borrows objects to chant.The blossoming natural scenery in it forms a sharp contrast with the poet’s inner pain, which makes the poetry profound in artistic conception, expresses the sadness and misery in the poet’s heart, and adds to the tragedy of the poetry.

涉江采芙蓉，兰泽多芳草。

采之欲遗谁，所思在远道。

还顾望旧乡，长路漫浩浩。

同心而离居，忧伤以终老。

I wade in the river to pick lotus flowers,

Pick a lot of bluegrass in Lanze.

Who do you want to give the flowers to?

To the person miss far away.

Looking back at the long-lost hometown,

Only see an endless road.

So intimate, but separated for long,

Fear the grief until old age.

《明月皎夜光》诗歌赏析:

这是一首失意之人写的感怀诗，抒发了诗人的悲秋之情和对于世态炎凉的怨愤。诗人从描绘秋叶景写起，由景入情，全诗似乎与主旨没有关联，却与作者的情感紧密相连，抒发了诗人在月下徘徊的哀伤和感叹，全诗笼罩着悲秋的气氛。后四句是由悲秋转入作者对自身境遇的感慨，通过比喻抒发感慨，形象生动，抒发得淋漓尽致。写景从目见到耳闻，从耳闻到想象，从客观事物过渡到主观心情，为我们描绘了一位被同门好友欺骗的落魄之人。在最后一句中诗人仰天长叹，饱含着无尽的辛酸，以悲愤的心情结束了全诗。这叹息和感慨，包含着诗人的伤痛和悲哀。

This is a poem written by a frustrated person, expressing the poet's sadness of autumn and his resentment towards the hot world. The poet starts from depicting the scenery of autumn leaves, then goes from the scenery into the emotion. The whole poem seems not related to the main theme, but is closely connected with the author's emotions. It expresses the sadness of the poet wandering under the moon, and envelopes the atmosphere of sad autumn. The last four sentences are transferred from the sad autumn to the author's feelings about his own situation, expressing his feelings through metaphors. The image is vivid, and the expression is incisively.

From seeing to hearing, from hearing to imagining, and from objective things to subjective mood, the depiction of scenery portrays us a deceived person who is deceived by fellow friends. The last sentence of the poet looked up to the sky and sighed, full of endless bitterness, and ended the whole poem with grief and indignation. This sigh and emotion contained the pain and sorrow of the poet.

明月皎夜光，促织鸣东壁。
玉衡指孟冬，众星何历历。
白露沾野草，时节忽复易。
秋蝉鸣树间，玄鸟逝安适？
昔我同门友，高举振六翮。
不念携手好，弃我如遗迹。
南箕北有斗，牵牛不负轭。
良无盘石固，虚名复何益？

Bright moon glowed brightly at night,
Crickets crowed endlessly by eastern wall.
Yuheng pointed out deep winter night,
Stars shine bright and distinct.
The white dew descended from the sky, wet the weeds,
Seasons changed in turn.
Cicadas screamed in the bushes,
Where would the swallow fly south to rest?
A friend who used to read together,
Now rises to fame.
Regardless of old friendship,
Like abandoning footprints.
Southern and Northern Stars don’t pick rice and scoop wine,

Altair not actually pull the cart to yoke.

If not be as firm as a rock,

What good is it to have a name?

《冉冉孤生竹》诗歌赏析:

这是首思夫诗，此诗一说为女子埋怨新婚久别之作，一说为女子埋怨婚迟之作。前半部分追忆新婚的情景，后半部分写思念的情怀。新婚后的远别、久别，而且会面难期，对于一位年轻少妇来说，除了殷切地怀念之外，更为敏锐的，便是描述了女子顾影自怜的心情和青春不再的自伤自怜。本诗正是抓住这一心理特征，从而突出了描写的重点。

This is a poem about a woman missing her husband. This poem has two interpretation one is that complains about a woman’s long goodbye to a newlywed, and the other is that complains about a woman’s late marriage. The first half recalls the newly-married scene, and the second half writes the feelings of missing. The farewell and long-term goodbye after the wedding, and the difficult time to meet, for a young woman, besides ardent remembrance, what is more acute is the description of the woman’s self-pity feelings of being no longer young. This poem captures this psychological feature, thus accentuating the focus of the description.

冉冉孤生竹，结根泰山阿。

与君为新婚，兔丝附女萝。

兔丝生有时，夫妇会有宜。

千里远结婚，悠悠隔山陂。

思君令人老，轩车来何迟！

伤彼蕙兰花，含英扬光辉。

过时而不采，将随秋草萎。

君亮执高节，贱妾亦何为？

A weak and lonely bamboo,

Pierce the roots deep in the nest of Mount Tai.

Husband and I become a couple,

Like doddar tightly entwining vine.

There is a certain time limit for the blooming doddar.

Husband and wife should take advantage of the bloom of youth to get together.

Get married far away,

Unexpectedly stay apart so long.

Missing husband makes me old,

The husband's cart arrive too late!

Poor cypresses and orchids,

The flowers are exuding dazzling brilliance.

If not pick in time,

They wither along with the autumn grass.

I believe in my husband,

Why should I bitterly grieve?

《庭中有奇树》诗歌赏析:

这是一首思妇怀念游子的诗，抒发了强烈的相思之情。诗歌描述了妇女对远行丈夫的深切怀念。全诗共八句，可分为两个部分。前四句诗从庭树开花说到攀枝折花、欲寄远人，后四句语气一转，发生转折，再说到路远难至，最后却说此物不足以献给远人，不过因为久别思深，而生痴想罢了，是诗人无可奈何的自我解脱。全诗只就“奇树”一意写到底，中间却有千回百转。在诗中诗人用花来衬托人物，写出人物的内心世界。最后两句点明了全诗的主题——借奇花寄相思感离愁。

This is a poem about a woman who misses her husband, expressing strong lovesickness. The poem describes a woman' s deep nostalgia for her husband on a journey. There are eight sentences in the poem, which can be divided into two parts. The first four lines of poems start from the blossoming of the garden tree and talk about picking flowers and wanting to send flowers to her husband. The tone of the last four lines is changed, and there is a turning point, and the road is far and difficult, but at the end it says that this little thing is not enough to be dedicated to her husband, justbecause of the long absence of deep missing. It is the poet who has no choice but to free himself. The whole poem is only written to the end with "Qishu" , but there are thousands of twists and turns in it. In the poem, the poet uses flowers to set off the characters and writes the inner world of the characters. The last two sentences clarify the theme of the whole poem—send lovesickness through strange flowers.

庭中有奇树，绿叶发华滋。
攀条折其荣，将以遗所思。
馨香盈怀袖，路远莫致之。
此物何足贵？但感别经时。

A rare tree grows in the courtyard,
With green leaves and flowers blooming prosperously.
Climb a branch to fold a flower,
Give it to the person who I miss.
The fragrance of flowers fills sleeves,
Far away, impossible to send.
This flower originally not worth sending,
Just because we talk lovesickness.

《迢迢牵牛星》诗歌赏析:

这首诗描写了天上的一对夫妇——牛郎和织女隔银河遥望的离别之苦，实际上是从女子的哀怨入手，借天上牵牛星和织女星相爱的民间故事传说，把牵牛和织女说成夫妇，并把他们之间的爱情染上了一层悲剧色彩，使之更加优美动人，写出人间的男女离别，抒发强烈的相思之情。此诗大约完成于东汉末年。就现存历史文献看，本诗是最早而又最完整的关于牵牛星和织女星的记录。在十九首中这首诗是最为突出的一篇。

This poem writes about the parting pains of a couple in the sky, the Cowherd and the Weaving Maid looking across the Milky Way. It actually starts from the woman' s grievances and uses the folktale of the love between Altair and Vega in the sky. The Cowherd and the Weaving Maid are described as couples, and the love between them has been dyed with a layer of tragedy, making this love story more beautiful and moving. The poem writes the parting of men and women on earth and expresses strong lovesickness. This poem was completed around the end of the Eastern Han Dynasty. Judging from the existing historical documents, this poem is the earliest and the most complete version about the legend. Among the nineteen poems, this poem is the most outstanding one.

迢迢牵牛星，皎皎河汉女。

纤纤擢素手，札札弄机杼。

终日不成章，泣涕零如雨。

河汉清且浅，相去复几许？

盈盈一水间，脉脉不得语。

Altair hangs far in the sky,

Opposite is a bright Vega.

The Weaver Girl wiggles slender hands,

Busy weaving with a shuttlecock.

Never knit cloth even after busy all day long,

Tears only because of lovesickness.

The Milky Way so clear and shallow,

How far can it be between each other?

The clear and shallow river in the middle,

Only look at each other with affection.

《回车驾言迈》诗歌赏析:

这是一首说理诗，诗歌从客观景物的更新联系到人生的短暂，从而转到当及时努力，建功立业的人生态度。自警自励的语气中，包含着一种凄惨的情绪。这首诗从写景到抒情说理，诗人借景抒情，抒发对人生失意的感叹。结尾表现出诗人对荣禄声名的迫切向往，但全诗却流露出一种无可奈何的消极情绪。

This is a reasoning poem. The renewal of the scenery in the poem is related to the shortness of lifespan, and thus it is transferred to the life attitude of working hard in time and making contributions. There is a miserable mood in the tone of self-alert and self-motivation. This poem goes from description of scenery to lyrical reasoning. The poet uses scenery to express his emotions and express his disappointment in life. The end shows the poet’s eager yearning for glory and fame, but the whole poem reveals a helpless negative emotion.

回车驾言迈，悠悠涉长道。
四顾何茫茫，东风摇百草。
所遇无故物，焉得不速老？
盛衰各有时，立身苦不早。
人生非金石，岂能长寿考？
奄忽随物化，荣名以为宝。

Turn around and drive the carriage for a long distance,
Mountains and rivers far away all the way.
Look around the boundless wilderness,
Spring breeze blows the green weeds.
What see in eyes is nothing in the past,
So how can people never age quickly?
There is a certain time for the rise and fall,
I only hate that I can’t succeed early.
Life is not a solid gold and stone,
How can one stay healthy and immortal forever?
In a blink of eyes, everything dies,
Only glory can be regarded as a treasure.

《东城高且长》诗歌赏析:

这是一首描写士人感叹年华易逝，而思为荡涤情志的感怀诗。这首诗主张人们摆脱拘束，采取放任情志的生活态度。前半部分所写内容，无非是岁月易逝，应尽情游乐的思想；后半部分则是诗人的纪实。

This is a poem depicting scholars lamenting the passing of years, but thinking about swaying their emotions. This poem advocates that people get rid of constraints and adopt a laissez-faire attitude towards life. The first half of the writing is nothing more than the thought that the time passes by and one should have fun; the second half is the real reflection of the poet.

东城高且长，逶迤自相属。

回风动地起，秋草萋已绿。

四时更变化，岁暮一何速！

《晨风》怀苦心，《蟋蟀》伤局促。

荡涤放情志，何为自结束！

燕赵多佳人，美者颜如玉。

被服罗裳衣，当户理清曲。

音响一何悲！弦急知柱促。

驰情整中带，沉吟聊踯躅。

思为双飞燕，衔泥巢君屋。

The eastern wall erects long,

Stretch continuously to the distance.

Looking at the whirlwind from afar,

Autumn grass turned into a yellow color.

Seasons change alternately,

How quickly time exhaust in a year!

The sentiment in *Morning Wind* is too sad,

Cricket is not too restrictive.

Get rid of worries and indulge emotions,

So why bother to restrain tightly.

More beauties in Yanzhao since ancient times,

Beautiful faces are like jade.

Dressed in silk, soft and gorgeous,

Play Qingshang music to the door.

Clearer and more sorrowful, moving,

The tune is high and urgent.

Unconsciously fascinated,

Stop for a while.

Hope we become two swallows,

Hold mud and build nests to be together forever.

《驱车上东门》诗歌赏析:

这是一首宣扬及时行乐的感怀诗，反映了诗人身逢乱世的凄凉心态和消极颓废心理。诗歌从叙事写起，写景、抒情、议论融为一体。这首诗是诗人的直抒胸臆之作，诗歌表现了东汉末年大动乱时期一部分文人的颓废思想和悲凉心态，反映当时人们的精神状态。“生命无常，及时行乐”，是《古诗十九首》中最常见的思想，而在这首诗里表现得最为深透。

This is a poem that promotes timely enjoyment, reflecting the poet’s desolate mentality and negative decadence in troubled times. The poem begins with narrative writing, combining scene description, lyricism, and discussion. The poem is a direct expression of the poet’s thoughts. It expresses the decadent thoughts and sad mentality of some literati during the turmoil in the late Eastern Han Dynasty, reflecting the mental state of some people during the social turmoil in the late Han Dynasty. The impermanence of life and timely enjoyment are the most common thoughts in *Nineteen Ancient Poems*, especially in this poem.

驱车上东门，遥望郭北墓。

白杨何萧萧，松柏夹广路。

下有陈死人，杳杳即长暮。

潜寐黄泉下，千载永不寤。

浩浩阴阳移，年命如朝露。

人生忽如寄，寿无金石固。

万岁更相送，贤圣莫能度。

服食求神仙，多为药所误。

不如饮美酒，被服纨与素。

I drive out of the upper eastern gate,

Look at the graves on the Beimang Mountain.

White poplars shake in the wind,

Pine and cypress trees line with tomb roads.

People dead for long buried below,

Long night is always dark.

Lying in silent sleep,

Never asleep once again.

The circulation of seasons never ceases,

Life is as short as morning dew.

Life is like a journey,

The life span is not as strong as a golden stone.

Since ancient timeslife and death have been circled,

Even sages will also die.

Swallowing the pill to beg for immortality,

Many people died from it.

Better to have a good drink,

Wear silk and satin to be comfortable at present .

《去者日以疏》诗歌赏析：

这是一首描写游子因经过墓地而思乡的诗歌，此诗哲理性强，全诗充满了感伤的情调。这首诗与《驱车上东门》的思想内容基本相同。但前篇归结为及时行乐，本篇则归结到乡土之思。诗人在城郊的路上，看到了坟墓，有感于世事艰难，人生如寄，愤慨地抒发了内心对于世态无常、危机重重的伤痛之情。篇章的结构自然浑成，通过具体景象抒情，写景、说理、抒情融为一体，层次鲜明生动。

This is a poem about a wanderer who is homesick after passing through the cemetery. This poem is philosophical and the whole poem is full of sentimental meaning. This poem has basically the same ideological content as *Driving to the East Gate*. But the poem boils down to timely enjoyment, and this poem boils down to the thinking of the countryside. On the road on the outskirts of the city, the poet saw the tomb. He felt that the world was difficult and life was short. He expressed indignantly the sadness in his heart for the impermanence and crisis of the world. The structure of the poem is naturally integrated. Through concrete scenery the poem is lyrical, scene description and reasoning. They are integrated, and the levels are vivid.

去者日以疏，生者日以亲。

出郭门直视，但见丘与坟。

古墓犁为田，松柏摧为薪。

白杨多悲风，萧萧愁杀人。

思还故里闾，欲归道无因。

The days of death get estranged,

The days of life are closer.

Walk out of the outer gate to look around,

I see a mound of graves lined up.

The ancient tomb are plowed into fields,

Pines and cypresses next are for firewood.

The white poplars sweep through the sorrowful winds,

Leaves rustle sharply.

I want to return to my hometown,

But how should I do.

《生年不满百》诗歌赏析：

这是一首感怀诗，诗歌感叹人生短暂，劝人及时行乐。在这首诗中，诗人用不同的人生态度作对比，语言平淡自然，但语意却动人心弦。诗歌的本意是以放浪之语，劝诫人们要及时行乐，不要把人生有限的享乐，拖延到遥远的未来。但如果说人生的价值就在于纵情享乐，也不是一种积极的人生态度。事实上，这种心态，大抵是由于汉末社会动荡不安，人们对于人生毫无出路的痛苦和对于未来的担忧及苦闷生活的抗议。

This is a poem of feelings, lamenting the shortness of life, and persuading people to have fun in time. In this poem, the poet uses different attitudes to life for comparison. The language is plain and natural, but the meaning is touching. The original intention of the poems is to use stray language to exhort people to have fun in time and not to delay the limited enjoyment of life into the distant future. But if the value of life lies in indulgence, it is not a positive attitude towards life. In fact, this mentality is largely due to the social turmoil in the late Han Dynasty, people' s pain of no way out in life, and the worry about the future and the protests of the boring life.

生年不满百，常怀千岁忧。

昼短苦夜长，何不秉烛游？

为乐当及时，何能待来兹？

愚者爱惜费，但为后世嗤。

仙人王子乔，难可与等期。

Men live no more than one hundred years,

But worry about what will happen for long.

They hate short days and long nights,

Why not light a candle and travel all night long?

People should hurry up,

How can we delay waiting for the coming year?

People reluctant to spend money,

Finally ridiculed and embarrassed by posterity.

Wang Ziqiao went to Songshan and became an immortal,

Others couldn't follow suit.

《凛凛岁云暮》诗歌赏析:

这是一首女子思念丈夫的诗。全诗以梦境为核心，层次清晰。由于是梦境，诗人不得不以细致而曲折的笔触、精炼的语言，来刻画这种迷离恍惚、深刻复杂的相思心情，给诗的形象染上了一层奇丽的梦幻色彩。此诗借景抒情，情景交融，借梦境表达情思，构思巧妙。其表现形式和内容完全贴合，让人感觉如梦如幻。

This is a poem about a woman missing her husband. The whole poem is centered on dreams, with clear levels. Because it is a dreamland, the poet has to use meticulous and tortuous brushstrokes and refined language to portray this vague, profound and complex lovesickness, and to dye the image of the poem with a wonderful and dreamy color. This poem uses scenes to express emotions, blends scenes, expresses mood through dreams, and is cleverly conceived. Its form and content are completely suitable, making people feel dreamlike.

凛凛岁云暮，蝼蛄夕鸣悲。

凉风率已厉，游子寒无衣。

锦衾遗洛浦，同袍与我违。

独宿累长夜，梦想见容辉。

良人惟古欢，枉驾惠前绥。

愿得常巧笑，携手同车归。

既来不须臾，又不处重闱。

亮无晨风翼，焉能凌风飞?

眄睐以适意，引领遥相睎。

徒倚怀感伤，垂涕沾双扉。

In the cold weather the end of the year draws near,

Crickets cry at night in sadness.

Cool breeze became stern and violent,

The wanderer had no winter clothes yet.

Broidered quilt has probably been sent the goddess of Luoshui,

Far away from me.

How many long nights spent sleeping alone,

I suddenly dreamed that my husband looked radiant.

He still loved me so much,

Drove me to the carriage.

Said “May you often laugh,

Hold hands and come home together”.

After the husband came, he only stayed for a moment,

Not even sleep in this boudoir.

I have no flying wings,

How can I follow him and fly high in the wind?

Look around and relax your mind,

Far away to find my husband.

Wander around the door, infinitely sentimental,

The door leaf is wet with my tears.

《孟冬寒气至》诗歌赏析:

这仍是一首描写妻子思念丈夫的诗。全诗共十四句，诗歌的前八句写这位思妇在寒冷漫长的冬夜里孤独寂寞，怀人念远的心情无所寄托，只有怅望星空以寄托其离愁别绪。丈夫久别，自己凄然独处，对于季节的变化和气候的转换非常敏感，人物的内在心情及其外在表现完全是通过季节环境的气氛衬托出来的。诗歌接下来的八句则是追述三年前曾接到丈夫寄来的一封书札，自己一直珍藏爱护，表明自己对丈夫的拳拳钟爱之情。这中间两句自然地从现在的心情过渡到以往的事件。读到最后，越来越理解主人公的悲惨遭遇和对丈夫归来的期盼，对她产生同情，引起共情。此诗借景抒情，借事抒情，情、景、事融为一体，淋漓尽致地表达了女子缠绵的感情。语言自然质朴，委婉含蓄。

This is also a poem about a wife missing her husband. In the fourteen sentences of the whole poem, the first eight sentences write that this woman is lonely in the cold and long winter night. Her husband has been away for a long time, and she is alone and very sensitive to the changes of the seasons and climate. The inner mood and outer performance of the characters are completely brought out by the atmosphere of the seasonal environment. The last eight sentences are a recall of a letter She received from her husband three years ago. She has always cherished and cared, showing her love for husband. The middle two sentences naturally transition from the current mood to the past events. At the end of the poem, we became more and more aware of the protagonist' s tragic experience and the expectation of her husband' s return, and sympathized with her, which aroused everyone' s mutual encouragement. This poem uses scenes and things to express emotions. The poet's feelings, scenes, and things are integrated together, expressing the lingering feelings of the woman vividly. The language of poem is natural and simple, euphemistic and implicit.

孟冬寒气至，北风何惨栗！

愁多知夜长，仰观众星列。

三五明月满，四五蟾兔缺。

客从远方来，遗我一书札。

上言长相思，下言久离别。

置书怀袖中，三岁字不灭。

一心抱区区，惧君不识察。

The cold air of early winter came in waves,

North wind blew so sternly.

The night was long, sad,

Look up to see the stars.

Every fifteenth I see the round moon,

Every twentieth I see the moon wane.

A guest from afar came to my home,

Brought me a letter from my husband.

It says that he misses me often,

In the back it says the couple's long-term parting.

Conceal the letter in the underwear,

The writing will not be dim in three years.

I love my husband wholeheartedly,

Afraid my husband will not know.

《客从远方来》诗歌赏析:

这是一首民歌风格浓厚的思妇诗。诗歌描写了主人公收到远方丈夫送的礼物后的意外喜悦和一片痴情。此诗所描述的意外喜悦，实则蕴含着夫妇别离的无尽酸楚；痴情的思念，伴随着苦苦相思的无声抽泣。此诗语言自然质朴，婉转含蓄。诗歌淋漓尽致地表达了主人公对丈夫深沉的痴情和美好的期待。

在《古诗十九首》中，这首诗最具有浓厚的民歌气息。诗中多用双关隐语，独具特色，具有浓郁的民歌风味。这种双关隐语，也是比喻的一种，它是人民口头语，往往通过某些日常习见的事物，表现了曲折达意的功能。此外如“双鸳鸯”“合欢被”的象征比喻，都极富民歌风味，写出了女子对夫君的一往情深。

This is a poem of lovesick woman with a strong folk song style. The poem describes the unexpected joy and infatuation of the protagonist after receiving a gift from her distant husband. The unexpected joy described in this poem actually contains the endless sorrow of the couple's parting; infatuation accompanied by the silent sobbing of bitter love. The language of this poem is natural and simple, tactful and subtle. The poem vividly expresses the protagonist's deep infatuation and beautiful expectation for her husband.

In *Nineteen Ancient Poems*, this poem has the strongest folk song flavor. In the poems, puns are often used, which are unique and have a strong folk song flavor. This kind of pun is also a kind of metaphor. It is the people's spoken language that often expresses the tortuous function of expressing meaning through certain things that are commonly used in daily life. In addition, symbolic metaphors such as "Double Mandarin Duck" "Acacia Quilt" are all very flavorful of folk songs, and they describe a woman's deep affection for her husband.

客从远方来，遗我一端绮。

相去万余里，故人心尚尔。

文彩双鸳鸯，裁为合欢被。

著以长相思，缘以结不解。

以胶投漆中，谁能别离此。

A guest came from afar,

Brought me a roll of satin.

My husband is far away from me,

He always misses me so much.

Mandarin ducks are embroidered on the silk,

Cut it into a silk quilt.

Install in the silk floss symbolizing endless love,

Edges embellished with insoluble silk knots.

Put glue into the paint, stick them together,

Who can separate us apart?

《明月何皎皎》诗歌赏析:

这是一首写女子闺中思夫的诗。诗歌描写女子睹月思人，长夜难眠，细腻刻画了主人公孤寂悲凉的心情。开篇两句描述了在月明之夜，皎洁的月光透过罗帐照到了床上，引起了女主人公如潮愁思，不能入眠。诗人接连用动词描写具体的行动，而这些行动是一个接一个，中间没有穿插其他任何情节，层次井然，却又具有千回百折之势。因而这些具体描写所构成的便是女主人公内心的忧伤形象，说明本诗对心理状态的刻画是极其细致的。

This is a poem about a woman missing her husband in her boudoir. It describes the woman who sees the moon and reminded of her husband, and can't sleep in the long night. It delicately portrays the protagonist's lonely and sad mood.The opening two sentences describes that in the moon night bright moonlight shone through the Luo tent on the bed, caused the heroine such as tide of melancholy, can not sleep. The poet uses verbs to describe specific actions, and these actions are one after another, without any other plot in between, neatly arranged, but with the tendency of a thousand twists and turns. Therefore, the complete image constituted by these specific descriptions is the image of the heroine's inner sadness, and the description of the psychological state is extremely meticulous.

明月何皎皎，照我罗床纬。

忧愁不能寐，揽衣起徘徊。

客行虽云乐，不如早旋归。

出户独彷徨，愁思当告谁。

引领还入房，泪下沾裳衣。

How bright the moon is,

Shine on my silk bed.

I can't fall asleep in sadness,

But get up and wander in contemplation.

Journey also has fun outside,

Better to get home early.

Wander around alone, full of sorrow,

Who can I talk to?

Look up and go back to the room,

Tears wet the clothes on chest.

魏朝诗歌
Poems of Wei Dynasty

王粲（177—217），字仲宣，山阳高平（今山东邹城）人，建安时期的著名文学家。他年轻时就很有才名，十四岁即受到当时著名文学家蔡邕的器重。西京扰乱，王粲避难荆州，依附刘表，未被重用。后归曹操，先任丞相掾，赐爵关内侯。由于他亲历变乱，目睹战争的残酷和人民苦难的深重，加上自己长期流离南方时仕途很不得意，故前期的作品内容真实深刻，情调慷慨悲凉，富于现实主义精神。王粲在“建安七子”中成就最高。四十一岁时随曹操征吴，途中病故。共遗赋、诗、论近六十篇。他擅长辞赋，在严可均《全后汉文》中共收入他的作品四十八篇，辞赋最多，其中以《登楼赋》最为人所称道。

Wang Can (177-217), Zhongxuan, was born in Gaoping, Shanyang (now Zoucheng, Shandong Province). He was a famous litterateur in the Jian' an period. When he was young, he was very talented and famous. At the age of fourteen, he was highly regarded by Cai Yong, a famous writer at that time. When the Western Capital was disturbed, Wang Can took refuge in Jingzhou and attached himself to Liu Biao. After return to Cao Cao, first as prime minister, later was appointed asGuannei Hou. Because he experienced the chaos, witnessed the cruelty of the war and the people' s suffering, and he was not satisfied with his official career when he lived in the south for a long time, his early works were true and profound, generous and sad, and full of realistic spirit, and he achieved the highest among the " Seven Jian' an Scholarss" . At the age of 41, he accompanied Cao Cao to march to Wu, but died of illness on the way. He has a total of nearly 60 odes and poems. He was good at Ci Fu. Yan Kejun's *Quan Hou Han Wen* collected forty-eight of his works, among which *Deng Lou Fu* was the most well-known.

《杂诗》诗歌赏析：

“杂诗”其名，最早见于《文选》。这首诗传为曹植《赠王粲》诗的答诗。建安末期，曹丕与曹植争太子之位，双方各植党羽，明争暗斗得异常激烈。王粲深恐卷入漩涡，故在诗中表达了一种既想亲近曹植，但又不敢与之公开交往的心情。但也有人认为，这不过是一首追求爱情的诗，其中是否有所借喻，尚难确定。该诗在艺术上颇具特色。

A Miscellaneous Poem

The name was first seen in *Wen Xuan*. This poem is the answer to the poem *To Wang Can* by Cao Zhi. At the end of the Jian' an period, Cao Pi and Cao Zhi fought for the crown prince. Wang Can is deeply afraid of being involved in the whirlpool, so he expresses in his poem a feeling of wanting to get close to Cao Zhi, but not daring to communicate with Cao Zhi publicly. But some people think that this is just a poem pursuing love, and it is difficult to determine whether there is a metaphor in it. Poetry is quite distinctive in art.

日暮游西园，冀写忧思情。

曲池扬素波，列树敷丹荣。

上有特栖鸟，怀春向我鸣。

褰衽欲从之，路险不得征。

徘徊不能去，伫立望尔形。

风飙扬尘起，白日忽已冥。

回身入空房，托梦通精诚。

人欲天不违，何惧不合并。

In the evening, I came to the West Garden to roam alone,

Want to relieve inner sadness.

White water waves rolled in the pond,

Red flowers bloomed like clouds on the rows of trees.

A lonely bird on it,

Love is sprouting and wailing at me.

Lift his clothes and wanted to meet,

But the road was too difficult to make a trip.

Wandering back and forth, unwilling to leave here,

Stand for a long time looking at your figure.

The whirlwind suddenly lifted up clouds of dust,

The day became groggy in an instant.

Turn around and return to the vacant room,

Let the dream convey the sincerity of love to you.

God will not go against people's wishes,

We are not afraid that we will not get married at last.

《七哀诗》二首诗歌赏析：

王粲《七哀诗》共三首，并非同时所作。《文选》选录二首。第一首作于汉献帝初平三年（192），是时董卓专权，屠戮朝臣，王粲离开长安，往投荆州刘表处避乱。诗作描写了路途所见。由于战乱，白骨蔽野，饿殍遍地，难民成群，亲人离散。尤其令人触目惊心的是，母亲不忍见孩子饿死在怀中，不得不强忍悲痛，将嗷嗷待哺的婴儿弃置草丛。深刻地反映了当时人民所遭受到的灾难和痛苦。

Two Poems on Seven Sorrows

Wang Can' s "Poems on Seven Sorrows" consist of three poems, which were not written at the same time. Two selected poems are from *Wen Xuan*. The first work was in the third year of Emperor Xianping of the Han Dynasty (192). It was when Dong Zhuo had the power to slaughter courtiers. Wang Can left Chang' an and went to Liubiao in Jingzhou to avoid wars. The poem describes what he saw along the way. As a result of the war, bones were left in the wild, starvation was everywhere, refugees were in groups, and relatives were separated. What is particularly shocking is that the mother could not bear to see the child starving to death in her arms, so she had to endure her grief and abandon the baby waiting to be fed into the grass. It profoundly reflects the disaster and suffering suffered by the people at that time.

（一）

西京乱无象，豺虎方遘患。

复弃中国去，远身适荆蛮。

亲戚对我悲，朋友相追攀。

出门无所见，白骨蔽平原。

路有饥妇人，抱子弃草间。

顾闻号泣声，挥涕独不还。

未知身死处，何能两相完？

驱马弃之去，不忍听此言。

南登霸陵岸，回首望长安。

悟彼《下泉》人，喟然伤心肝。

Xijing was in chaos,

Jackals, tigers and leopards indiscriminately caused disaster.

I had to leave the prosperous capital,

Far away to Jingzhou to escape the disaster.

Relatives felt sad for me far away from home,

Friends were difficult to say goodbye.

Out of the gate, there was nothing to see,

But piles of bones covered the plain.

On the way I saw a hungry woman,

With her child lying in the weeds.

Several times back to listen to the child cry,

But had to leave in tears.

I don't know where I'm going to die,she said.

How can I keep both mother and son alive?

I hastened to drive the horse away,

Really could not bear to listen.

Going south, I boarded the Baling Heights,

Looked back at the West Capital, Chang ’an.

I understood the mood of the author in *Xia Quan*,

I couldn’t help sighing deeply and breaking my heart.

（二）

第二首诗歌作于诗人客居荆州之时，主要抒写思念乡井之情。这种乡井之思与王粲在荆州遭到的冷遇和漠视有十分密切的联系，其同时所作的《登楼赋》对此有明显的反映，可以参看。

The second poem was written when the poet was living in Jingzhou, mainly expressing his feelings of missing hometown. This kind of feeling is closely related to the coldness and indifference of the author in Jingzhou, which can be clearly reflected in his *Deng Lou Fu* written at the same time, for reference.

荆蛮非我乡，何为久滞淫？

方舟溯大江，日暮愁我心。

山岗有余映，岩阿增重阴。

狐狸驰赴穴，飞鸟翔故林。

流波激清响，猴猿临岸吟。

迅风拂裳袂，白露沾衣衿。

独夜不能寐，摄衣起抚琴。

丝桐感人情，为我发悲音。

羁旅无终极，忧思壮难任。

Jingzhou is not my hometown,

Why should I stay here for a long time?

Two boats tied up along the river,

The sunset added to my homesickness.

There was still a glimmer of sunset over the hills,

In the hollow it grew darker.

The fox hurried back to his den,

Bird flew home to the wood where it dwelt.

The torrent of the river made a roaring noise,

The monkey's voice came from the cliff near the river.

The wind stirred my clothes,

The night dew soaked the skirts of my clothes.

Hard to sleep in the lonely night,

I get up to dress and fiddle with the strings.

My beloved stringed lute is so considerate,

It sends out a sad sound of missing my hometown for me.

Infinite period in foreign land,

Only heavy worry that people cannot bear.

~~~~~~

曹植（192—232）：字子建，三国魏文学家，诗人。曹操第三子，封陈王，谥思，世称陈思王。曹植在年轻时就很有文学才华，才思敏捷，又有建功立业的强烈愿望，颇受曹操喜爱，一度欲立为太子，后失宠。后来曹丕称帝，曹植备受猜忌与迫害，屡遭贬爵、改换封地，终于在41岁时郁郁死去。

曹植是建安时期成就最高的作家，他的文学成就是多方面的，诗、赋、文兼善，现存其诗八十多首，辞赋、散文四十余篇。他的辞赋既继承了前人的优秀传统，又充分体现了时代气息和自己的独特风格，代表了建安时期辞赋发展所到达的新高度。其诗赋均善用比兴手法，语言精炼，辞采华茂。

Cao Zhi (192-232): Zijian, writer and poet of the Three Kingdoms Wei Dynasty. Cao Cao's third son,was named King Chen, posthumously named King of Chensi. When he was young, he had great literary talents, quick thinking, and a strong desire to make contributions. He was quite popular with Cao Cao. He once wanted to become a prince, but fell out of favor. When Cao Pi became emperor, Cao Zhi was subject to suspicion and persecution. He was repeatedly demoted and changed fiefs, and finally died depressed when he was 41 years old.
~~~~~~

Cao Zhi is the most accomplished writer during the Jian' an period, and his literary achievements are multifaceted. Poems, Fus and essays are good, and there are more than 80 poems and more than 40 Cifus and proses. His Cifus not only inherited the excellent traditions of predecessors, but also fully embodies the atmosphere of the times and his own unique style, and represents the new height of the development of Cifu during the Jian' an period. His poems and verses all make good use of Bi Xing(a kind of figures of speech), refined language, and luxuriant diction.

《杂诗》六首诗歌赏析：

《杂诗》六首大体上是曹植后期的作品，始载于《文选》。第一首为登高怀远之作，所怀之人可能是诗人的异母弟曹彪。第二首以“转蓬”喻游子，实以“转蓬”、游子自喻，倾诉自己迁徙不定、生活困顿的苦衷。第三首写女子对久戍不归的丈夫的思念，不一定有什么寄托。第四首写佳人不为世俗所累。第五、第六首写甘赴国忧的壮志及壮志不能实现的苦闷和愤慨。六首诗在艺术上深受《楚辞》和《古诗》的影响，但自抒怀抱，风骨与丹采并重。

Six Miscellaneous Poems

The six miscellaneous are basically Cao Zhi' s later works, which were first published in *Wen Xuan*. The first one is a work of yearning, and the person may be Cao Biao, the poet' s half brother. The second song uses “Zhuanpeng” as a metaphor for wanderers, and in fact uses “Zhuanpeng” and wandering man to describe himself, telling himself about his difficulties in migration and difficult life. The third poem writes about the woman' s longing for her husband who has not returned for a long time, which may not have any sustenance. The fourth song is about a beautiful lady who is not burdened by common customs. The fifth and sixth poems are about the aspirations of going to the country and the distress and indignation that the aspirations cannot be realized. The six poems are deeply influenced by *Chu Ci* and *Ancient Poems* in art, but they express the poet' s ambitionsand emphasize both vigor and salvation.

（一）

高台多悲风，朝日照北林。

之子在万里，江湖迥且深。

方舟安可极，离思故难任。

孤雁飞南游，过庭长哀吟。

翘思慕远人，愿欲托遗音。

形影忽不见，翩翩伤我心。

A stern wind blew constantly on the high platform,

Morning sun shone on the northern forest.

The person I miss was miles away,

The distance between us was far and deep.

How could reach destination even if there was an ark?

Parting sorrow was particularly unbearable.

The lone wild goose lost, flew to the south alone,

Utter a long cry as it flew over the courtyard.

Looked up and missed the distant person again,

Wanted to beg goose to send a message.

It disappeared in a blink of eye,

So fast, I am in grief.

（二）

转蓬离本根，飘飖随长风。

何意回飙举，吹我入云中。

高高上无极，天路安可穷。

类此游客子，捐躯远从戎。

毛褐无掩形，薇藿常不充。

去去莫复道，沉忧令人老。

Zhuanpeng dried up and left the root,

Drifted along with the far-away wind.

Unexpectedly, a whirlwind suddenly came,

It blew me into the clouds.

The sky was high and endless,

How could I find the road end to heaven?

Like the wanderer outside,

Dedicated life for the country and served in the army.

The coarse woolen cloth was not enough to cover,

Wild vegetable bean leaves hardly made me full.

Put aside all of it.

Much sadness makes me older.

（三）

西北有织妇，绮缟何缤纷。

明晨秉机杼，日昃不成文。

太息终长夜，悲啸入青云。

妾身守空闺，良人行从军。

自期三年归，今已历九春。

飞鸟绕树翔，噭噭鸣索群。

愿为南流景，驰光见我君。

A woman wasweaving silk in the northwest,

How dazzling the silk weaving!

Woke up early in the morning with a shuttle,

At sunset she hadn't stopped.

She sighed again and again all night,

A long, sad sigh floated on the blue clouds.

She stayed alone in this empty boudoir,

Husband went out to be a soldier in the distance.

When left, he thought he would be back in three years,

Now nine winters and springs have passed.

The birds were flying around the woods,

Chirping and looking for the birds.

She would like to turn into sunlight flowing southward,

Fly to the south to see husband.

（四）

南国有佳人，容华若桃李。

朝游江北岸，日夕宿湘沚。

时俗薄朱颜，谁为发皓齿。

俛仰岁将暮，荣耀难久恃。

There is a young and beautiful girl in Jiangnan,

Her face is like a peach and plum blossom in full bloom.

She was still on the north bank of the Yangtze River in the morning,

But at night she slept on the small island of Xiangshui.

Nowadays, the customs don't value beauty,

Who is going to sing the song for?

In a blink of eyes, the cold winter is approaching,

Difficult for the glorious beauty to last long.

（五）

仆夫早严驾，吾将远行游。

远游欲何之？吴国为我仇。

将骋万里涂，东路安足由？

江介多悲风，淮泗驰急流。

愿欲一轻济，惜哉无方舟。

闲居非吾志，甘心赴国忧。

The servant prepared the chariots and horses,

I leave for a long journey.

Where do I be on the long journey?

To defeat enemy in Wu.

I will gallop on a long road,

How can I return east to City Juancheng peacefully?

The Yangtze River often has stern winds,

The Huaishui and Sishui rapids surges and churns.

I want to fly over at once,

Unfortunately no ship to carry me.

It is not my wish to live at home,

I am willing to sacrifice for the country anytime.

（六）

飞观百余尺，临牖御棂轩。

远望周千里，朝夕见平原。

烈士多悲心，小人媮自闲。

国仇亮不塞，甘心思丧元。

拊剑西南望，思欲赴太山。

弦急悲声发，聆我慷慨言。

Watchtowers stand high in the sky,

I am leaning on the railing facing the window.

Look around miles away,

What I see is always a broad plain.

Lofty People worry about the country,

Mediocre people only care about own peace.

The country's enemies have not yet been wiped out,

I am willing to go conquer.

Looking at the west and the south with my sword,

I want to give my life on the battlefield.

The sound of the string is so rushing and tragic,

Listen to my passionate rhetoric.

《情诗》诗歌赏析：

《情诗》写游子远役思归之叹，可能寓有作者身世的感慨。全诗情真意切，意象生动，音节流美，色彩明丽。

A Love Song

A Love Song writes about the wandering men' s thinking about returning home. The poem may contain the feelings of the author' s life experience. The whole poem is full of affection, vivid images, beautiful syllables, and bright colors.

微阴翳阳景，清风飘我衣。

游鱼潜渌水，翔鸟薄天飞。

眇眇客行士，遥役不得归。

始出严霜结，今来白露晞。

游子叹《黍离》，处者歌《式微》。

慷慨对嘉宾，凄怆内伤悲。

Thin clouds blocked the sun,

Breeze moved my clothes.

Fish roamed in the clear water,

Birds flew high in the sky.

The wanderer serves in a distant foreign land,

Nostalgic for hometown but cannot return.

The field was full of frost when I left home,

Now the white dew has dried up.

The wanderer sighed"Shu Li",

His family sang "Shi Wei" in anticipation of his return.

I was extremely excited towards the guests,

Cherished strong sorrow in heart.

《七哀诗》诗歌赏析：

七哀，是魏晋乐府诗题之一。除本篇外，王粲、张载皆有《七哀诗》，内容都是反映社会动乱，抒发悲伤的感情。

A Poem on Seven Sorrows

A Poem on Seven Sorrowsis one of the titles of the Wei and Jin Yuefu poem. In addition to this article, both Wang Can and Zhang Zai have *A Poem on Seven Sorrows*, which all reflect social unrest and express sad feelings.

明月照高楼，流光正徘徊。

上有愁思妇，悲叹有余哀。

借问叹者谁，言是客子妻。

君行逾十年，孤妾常独栖。

君若清路尘，妾若浊水泥。

浮沉各异势，会合何时谐。

愿为西南风，长逝入君怀。

君怀良不开，贱妾当何依。

The bright moon is shining on this tall building,

Moonlight is pouring down like water all night.

A sad woman upstairs,

Full of sorrow with a sigh.

I would like to ask: Who are you?

Answer: I am a wanderer's wife.

My husband has been out for more than ten years,

Leave me alone in the vacant rooms.

He is like the dust on the road flying with the wind,

I am sinking deeply like mud in the water.

The situation of floating and sinking is very different.

Who knows when we'll meet?

I am willing to become the southwest wind,

Blow from afar until my husband's arms.

If my husband has never opened his arms,

Then where should I depend on.

《赠丁仪》诗歌赏析：

丁仪（？—220），字正礼，沛郡（今安徽濉溪北）人。曹操与曹植亲善。曹操原打算立曹植为太子，丁仪竭力赞助，故被曹丕忌恨。曹丕即位后就杀了丁仪。此诗大约写在曹丕即位后不久。诗中安慰丁仪，让他不要因为没有得到封赏而不安。

A Song to Ding Yi

Ding Yi (?-220), Zhengli, was born in Peijun County (the north of Suixi in present-day Anhui). Cao Cao was kind to Cao Zhi. When Cao Cao originally planned to make Cao Zhi the prince, Ding Yi tried his best to support. So He was hated by Cao Pi. After Cao Pi came to the throne, he killed Ding Yi. This poem was written shortly after Cao Pi came to the throne. The poem comforted Ding Yi and told him not to be upset because he didn' t get the reward.

初秋凉气发，庭树微销落。

凝霜依玉除，清风飘飞阁。

朝云不归山，霖雨成川泽。

黍稷委畴陇，农夫安所获。

在贵多忘贱，为恩谁能博？

狐白足御冬，焉念无衣客。

思慕延陵子，宝剑非所惜。

子其宁尔心，亲交义不薄。

In early autumn, the climate gradually became cold,
Trees in front of the court had begun to wither slightly.
Frost condensed on the steps in front of the hall,
Breeze drifted over the towering pavilions.
The clouds were so dense that the sky would never dissipate,
The ground had become a river, the rain still kept on.
The crops had died in the fields,
How can farmers expect to have a harvest.
How can therich know the plight of the poor,
Who can grant a boon all over without any omission?
Wearing a fox fur coat is enough to withstand the cold,
How can you think of people who are without clothes?
I admire the ancient Yanling Jiza's character,
Not hesitate to Present his beloved sword to Xu Jun.
Rest assured, my friend, that you and I are dear friends.

《赠王粲》诗歌赏析：

吴淇认为此诗作于王粲投奔曹氏后，曹操欲易换储君之际。黄节则认为王粲有《杂诗》一首，或为曹植所发，曹植此诗就是对王粲诗的回赠之作，故诗中多模拟王粲诗句。

To Wang Can

Wu Qi believes that this poem was written after Wang Can defected to Cao Cao and Cao Cao wanted to change the prince. Huang Jie believes that Wang Can has *A Miscellaneous Poem*, which may have been written by Cao Zhi.This poem is an answer poem to Wang Can' s poems. Therefore, the poems mostly imitate Wang Can' s poems.

端坐苦愁思，揽衣起西游。
树木发春华，清池激长流。

中有孤鸳鸯，哀鸣求匹俦。

我愿执此鸟，惜哉无轻舟。

欲归忘故道，顾望但怀愁。

悲风鸣我侧，羲和逝不留。

重阴润万物，何惧泽不周。

谁令君多念，自使怀百忧。

Sit in a daze, think of friends, full of sorrow,

Tidy up clothes and stroll west.

Trees have spit out spring flowers,

Clear pond are rippling with the long stream.

A lonely mandarin duck in the pool,

Cry sadly for a spouse.

I want to capture this mandarin duck,

But unfortunately no canoe to cross the water.

I want to go back, but forget the way I come.

Looking back, my heart is full of sorrow.

The wind blow past me mournfully,

Days fade away quickly and refuse to stay.

The dense clouds and rain nourish everything,

No need to worry about the omissions.

Who makes you miss so much,

Fill your heart with endless sorrow.

《又赠丁仪王粲》诗歌赏析：

丁仪因位卑禄薄，而对朝廷有怨言。王粲崇尚恬淡清玄、避世无争的生活。曹植认为二人均有所偏失，故作此诗，赞颂帝业弘美，劝勉二人当持中和的态度，努力效命王业。

To Ding Yi and Wang Can

Ding Yi had a grudge against the court because of his humble position and poor salary. Wang Can advocates a life of tranquility and seclusion. Cao Zhi thinks the two are biased, so he writes this poem and praises the king's prosperous cause, and exhort the two to maintain a neutral attitude and strive to serve the king.

从军度函谷，驱马过西京。

山岑高无极，泾渭扬浊清。

壮哉帝王居，佳丽殊百城。

员阙出浮云，承露概泰清。

皇佐扬天惠，四海无交兵。

权家虽爱胜，全国为令名。

君子在末位，不能歌德声。

丁生怨在朝，王子欢自营。

欢怨非贞则，中和诚可经。

Join in the army to go through Hangu Valley,

Drive the horses through Chang'an.

The towering mountain peaks can't be seen,

Rivers make great waves.

Chang'an is the majestic city where the king lives,

Far more beautiful than others.

Yuanque Mansion towers above the floating clouds,

The sky is picked up on a fairy tray on the copper pillar.

The emperor's ministers interpret mighty virtue,

No one to fight in the world.

Although military strategists like victory in battle,

Most praised for preserving the enemy's country and getting it to submission.

It's a pity that you two are in low positions,

Fail to write the article topraise the king's merits and virtues.

Ding complained to the imperial court,

Wang advocated nothingness and standing aloof from worldly strife.

Complaining and being indifferent have their own deviations,

The way of neutralization is the most worthy of life.

《赠丁翼》诗歌赏析：

丁翼，字敬礼。丁仪之弟，官任黄门侍郎。兄弟俩俱与曹植友善，后同被曹丕所杀。本诗勉励丁翼不要拘于世俗，不做为礼教束缚的腐儒。

To Ding Yi

Ding Yi, Jingli, Ding Yi' s younger brother, Huangmen Shilang. The brothers were friendly to Cao Zhi, and later were both killed by Cao Pi. This poem encourages Ding Yi not to stick to the common customs, and not to be a corrupt Confucian who is bound by ethics.

嘉宾填城阙，丰膳出中厨。

吾与二三子，曲宴此城隅。

秦筝发西气，齐瑟扬东讴。

肴来不虚归，觞至反无余。

我岂狎异人，朋友与我俱。

大国多良材，譬海出明珠。

君子义休偫，小人德无储。

积善有余庆，荣枯立可须。

滔荡固大节，世俗多所拘。

君子通大道，无愿为世儒。

The guests were sitting in the turret of the city,
Rich meals came from the skillful hands of the royal chefs.
I set up a private banquet with close friends,
In the watchtower on the corner of the city.
Qin Zheng played the western tune,
Qi Se raised the eastern music.
The dishes were not for decoration,
The wine in the glass was drunk without any drops.
How could I get along with other people,
Here were friends and relatives.
So many outstanding talents in a big country,
Just like a bright pearl in the sea.
The gentleman was rich in virtues,
But the villain never kept virtues.
Prosperity soon showed signs of prosperity,
Decline went down later generations.
Being unruly and unrestrained was a virtue of human beings,
Secular views only kept small knots in check.
A gentleman should know the great principles,
I hope you won't be a corrupt scholar.

~~~~~~

刘桢（？—217），字公干，东平（今山东寿光县）人，汉末文学家。与王粲、陈琳、徐干、阮瑀、应玚、孔融相友善，号称“建安七子”。有《毛诗义问》十卷，集四卷，已失传。明人张溥《汉魏六朝百三家集》辑有《刘公干集》。

Liu Zhen (?-217), Gonggan, was born in Dongping (now Shouguang County, Shandong Province). He is a writer at the end of Han Dynasty. He is friendly with Wang
~~~~~~

Can, Chen Lin, Xu Gan, Ruan Yu, Ying Yan and Kong Rong. They are known as the "Seven Scholars of Jian' an" . There are ten volumes of *Mao Shi Yi Wen* and four volumes, which have been lost. In *Three Hundred Collections in the Six Dynasties of Han and Wei*(Ming Dynasty), Zhang Pu complied *Liu Gonggan Collection*.

《杂诗》诗歌赏析：

刘桢其人，"建安七子"之一。曹操当丞相的时候，他被征为丞相的属官。这首诗写他整日忙于公务，累得昏头昏脑的情况，表达了他希望摆脱这些俗务归返自然的心情。刘桢对功名事业的渴望与追求远不如大多数建安诗人那么强烈，诗中又极少歌功颂德，故得与徐幹结为至交。

A Miscellaneous Poem

Liu Zhen is one of the Seven Scholars of Jian' an. When Cao Cao was the prime minister, Liu Zhen was conscripted as a subordinate official of him. This poem writes about how he was busy with official duties all day, expressing his desire to get rid of these mundane affairs and return to nature. Liu Zhen' s desire and pursuit of fame is far less than that of most Jian' an poets. In his poems, there are very few praises of virtues, so he was a close friend of Xu Gan.

职事相填委，文墨纷消散。

驰翰未暇食，日昃不知晏。

沉迷簿领书，回回自昏乱。

释此出西城，登高且游观。

方塘含白水，中有凫与雁。

安得肃肃羽，从尔浮波澜。

Things are piled up in front,

The case slip is always chaotic.

I keep swiping and have no free time,

The sun is not to be idle in the west.

I plunged my head between the official documents,

Dizzy all day long.

Let me go of work and come to the outskirts,

Go up to the heights to have a fun tour.

The pond is filled with clear water,

Wild ducks and geese are playing in the water.

How can I grow a pair of wings,

Swim among the clear waves and waters.

《赠五官中郎将》四首诗歌赏析：

曹丕初为五官中郎将、副丞相，刘桢染疾，前往探视。去后，刘桢赋诗以赠。诗作叙述与曹丕初识，以及蒙曹氏父子厚遇的情形，感激之情溢于字里行间。第一首回忆昔日与曹丕共同游乐，亲密无间，难舍难分。第二首描述别后自己久病，曹丕亲自慰问的情景，诗人表达了对挚友的依恋与良好的祝愿。第三首抒发对即将远征在外的挚友的深沉留恋之情。诗人终夜不寐，以见留恋之深，清风白露，更增凄凉之感。这首诗歌表现出作者忧虑征战中挚友的安危祸福。第四首描写诗人与曹丕离别时彼此赋诗的情景，赞扬曹丕诗作的文雅壮思。

Four Poems to Cao Pi

Cao Pi was Wuguan Zhonglang Jiang and deputy prime minister. Liu Zhen was sick and Cao Pi went to see him. After Cao Pi' s leaving, Liu Zhen wrote poems as a gift. The poem narrates the first acquaintance with Cao Pi and the encounter between father and son of Cao family. The gratitude is overflowing between the lines. In the first song, he remembered playing together with Cao Pi in the past, and they were intimate and hard to separate. The second song describes the scene of Cao Pi coming to condolences Liu Zhen after he has been sick for a long time. The poet expresses his attachment and good wishes to his close friend Cao Pi. The third song expresses deep missing for his close friend who is about to expedition. The poet stays awake all night, showing the deep friendship. The breeze and the white dew adds a sense of desolation. The poem shows the poet' s worries about the safety of his close friend in the battle. The fourth song describes the scene of the poet and Cao Pi composing poems when they parted, and praises Cao Pi' s poems for the elegant and grandiose thoughts.

（一）

昔我从元后，整驾至南乡。

过彼丰沛都，与君共翱翔。

四节相推斥，季冬风且凉。

众宾会广坐，明灯熺炎光。

清歌制妙声，万舞在中堂。

金罍含甘醴，羽觞行无方。

长夜忘归来，聊且为大康。

四牡向路驰，叹悦诚未央。

I think back I followed Cao Gong and purged the cart to the south.

Just when I passed through the rich capital,

I forged a deep friendship with you.

Four seasons replace each other in turn,

The wind in winter is still so cold.

Many guests gathered at the grand banquet,

The lights were shining brightly.

The crisp voice sings a wonderful song,

The dance in the nave is very spectacular and charming.

The golden wine glass was full of sweet wine,

The wine glass flew round after round.

After a long night, I forgot to return,

So I was in peace for the time being.

I drove a four-horse carriage and galloped on the road,

Full of joy and feel that it was not over yet.

（二）

余婴沉痼疾，窜身清漳滨。

自夏涉玄冬，弥旷十余旬。

常恐游岱宗，不复见故人。

所亲一何笃，步趾慰我身。

清谈同日夕，情盼叙忧勤。

便复为别辞，游车归西邻。

素叶随风起，广路扬埃尘。

逝者如流水，哀此遂离分。

追问何时会，要我以阳春。

望慕结不解，贻尔新诗文。

勉哉修令德，北面自宠珍。

I was entangled by a serious illness,

I came to the Qingzhang River, living alone.

From the scorching summer to the gloomy winter,

I was sick for more than a hundred days.

I often worry that my soul will return to Mount Tai,

I will never be able to see friends and family again.

How deep is your affection for me,

Come to me personally to comfort.

We talked from morning to night,

You asked me affectionately.

Finally, you said goodbye to me,

Drove back to Luoyang to the west.

The dead leaves of the trees drifted with the wind,

The wide roads raised dust.

Time goes by like flowing water,

The years are ruthless and make us sad.

I am asking when I can see you again.

You invite me to meet in spring next year.

My yearning is stuck in my heart,

So I can only make this poem for you to comfort my heart.

I hope you are diligent in politics and your virtue is increasing day by day,

You will cherish yourself in serving the monarch for the sake of the country.

（三）

秋日多悲怀，感慨以长叹。

终夜不遑寐，叙意于濡翰。

明灯曜闺中，清风凄已寒。

白露涂前庭，应门重其关。

四节相推斥，岁月忽欲殚。

壮士远出征，戎事将独难。

涕泣洒衣裳，能不怀所欢！

Autumn often makes people feel sad,

Sighs with emotion.

I didn't sleep all night,

I put all my thoughts in brush and ink.

Bright lights illuminate the bedroom,

The cold autumn breeze has revealed bursts of cold night.

White dew had already condensed on the road in the vestibule,

The door had to be closed tightly.

The four seasons converge one after another,

A year will pass in a hurry.

It is so difficult for a strong man to travel far and engage in warfare.

It is so difficult for you to support the military alone.

I couldn't help but wet my clothes with tears,

How did long-term friendship tell me not to miss it!

（四）

凉风吹沙砾，霜气何皑皑。

明月照缇幕，华灯散炎辉。

赋诗连篇章，极夜不知归。

君侯多壮思，文雅纵横飞。

小臣信顽卤，僶俛安能追！

The cold wind blows off the sand and gravel,

The thick frost condenses the white light in the wild.

The bright moon was shining on the yellow military curtain,

The lanterns radiated mild and bright lights.

You and literary friends happily gather to compose poems and sing peace,

All night you forgot to return to the camp.

You are full of pride and thoughts,

Your witty words express your lofty ambitions.

We are really stubborn, no matter how hard we try,

We still can't catch up with you.

《赠徐幹》诗歌赏析：

徐幹，字伟长，与刘桢同为“建安七子”。这首诗既是刘桢表达对徐幹的思念之情，也是抒发自己的怀才不遇之感。诗作抒发了虽与友人近在咫尺，却无由相见的感叹。二人本来并不处于天涯海角，却不得相见而一叙衷肠。这是因为他们的地位使他们不能逾越“西掖垣”之隔，这已表露出政治上不如意的心情；而眼中景物的轻叶、孤鸟，也未尝不是自己身世的象征，因而涕下沾襟就不仅是思念之情了。诗的最后，更以日光比喻当权者的恩泽，以自己独不能得到日光的照耀比喻自己仕途上的冷落处境。

To Xu Gan

Xu Gan, Wei Chang. Together with Liu Zhen, he is one of the "Seven Schlors of Jian' an" . Liu Zhen not only expresses his longing for Xu Gan in the poem, but also expresses his disappointed asfeelings. The poem also expresses the sigh of being close with friends, but they are unable to meet. They are not at the end of the world, but they couldn' t meet each other. This is because their status prevent them. This has revealed a politically unsatisfactory mood. The leaves and lone birds in sights are a symbol of their own life experience, so tears are not only a feeling of longing. At the end of the poem, the daylight is used as a metaphor for the blessings of those in power, and the political indifference is compared with the inability to receive the sunlight alone.

谁谓相去远？隔此西掖垣。

拘限清切禁，中情无由宣。

思子沉心曲，长叹不能言。

起坐失次第，一日三四迁。

步出北寺门，遥望西苑园。

细柳夹道生，方塘含清源。

轻叶随风转，飞鸟何翻翻。

乖人易感动，涕下与衿连。

仰视白日光，皦皦高且悬。

兼烛八纮内，物类无颇偏。

我独抱深感，不得与比焉。

Who said that we are so far apart ?

Separated from each other by a palace wall.

Just because the detention is limited to the solemn and strict imprisonment,

The feelings in my heart cannot confess to you.

Missing you makes me feel heavy,
I can't speak with a long sigh.
The restless actions lost normality,
Wander around three or four times a day.
Stroll out of the gate of the North Temple,
Look at the Xiyuan Garden from a distance.
The tender willows grow in the middle of the road,
The clear spring water in the pond is clear.
The leaves flutter lightly with the wind, how light the birds fly freely.
It's always easy to touch things and feel sad when I'm away,
My clothes are wet with tears.
Look up at a round of daylight in the sky,
Hang high in the middle of the sky to brighten up the light.
The sun is shining throughout the entire circle,
Benefit everything without any eccentricity.
But I am alone and deeply sad, not as joyful as all things.

《赠从弟三首》诗歌赏析：

从弟，指堂弟。诗作以藻、青松、凤凰喻其从弟，有赞美和勉励之意，其实也是作者自况。三首诗全用比兴，造语清新自然，毫无当时赠答诗客套做作之弊。

Three Songs toMy Cousin

Cong di, refers to the cousin. In this poem, algae, green pines and phoenix are used to refer to the poet' s younger brother, expressing praise and encouragement, which is also the poet' s own situation. The three poems are all written by Bi Xing, and the language is fresh and natural, without the disadvantage of the affectation of the poems presented at that time.

（一）

泛泛东流水，磷磷水中石。

蘋藻生其涯，华纷何扰弱。

采之荐宗庙，可以羞嘉客。

岂无园中葵，懿此出深泽。

The river drifted eastward,

Clear and visible.

Algae grew by the river,

Ripple with flowers and leaves.

Pick it to present to ancestral temple,

To entertain guests.

It is not that there is no garden sunflower available,

Just to enjoy algae out of the deep.

（二）

亭亭山上松，瑟瑟谷中风。

风声一何盛，松枝一何劲！

冰霜正惨凄，终岁常端正。

岂不罹凝寒？松柏有本性。

Tall and straight pine grow on the mountain,

The valley blows a cold wind.

The whistling of the wind seemed so fierce,

Pine branches were still so firm.

The climate is harsh and cold,

The pine tree stands tall and green all year round.

Had it not suffered from the cold?

Pines and cypresses have a hardy nature of their own.

（三）

凤凰集南岳，徘徊孤竹根。

于心有不厌，奋翅凌紫氛。

岂不常勤苦，羞与黄雀群。

何时当来仪？将须圣明君。

Phoenix perches in the south of the Dan cave mountain,

Wander in the pavilion independent of the bamboo.

It is not satisfied with the mediocrity of life,

The vigorous exhibition of wings in the sky flys far.

To fly is so hard,

But it is ashamed to live together with the yellow sparrows.

When are you going to fly?

That will be until there is a sovereign.

~~~~~~

阮籍(210—263)，字嗣宗，陈留（今河南）人，三国魏著名诗人，“竹林七贤”之一。魏晋之交竹林七贤的代表人物。其父阮瑀，“建安七子”之一，颇受曹氏礼重。籍生于汉末，长于曹魏，政治思想当然倾向曹魏。所处时会，适值曹魏由盛转衰之期。司马懿父子以辅政进而擅权，屡行废弑。魏之宗族亲信及天下名士，多遭杀戮，人人自危。阮籍则终日酣饮，因得自保。

阮籍是有名的玄学家，代表了魏晋易代之际的思想主潮。他耽游山水，嗜酒善琴，尤好老庄之学。他反对名教礼法，言行常与传统相悖，痛恨伪君子、阴谋家。内心主张自然无为，追求宁静真朴超然物外的人格理想。对曹魏王室的腐败无能深怀不满；迫于司马氏集团的专横残暴，鄙弃轻蔑其黑暗统治，纵酒佯狂，绝不合作。

由于诗人所处的社会与文化背景的特殊性，诗人既对司马氏集团及黑暗现实不满，又不敢公开反抗，想抗争又不敢明白地表露心迹，于是诗人在诗中大量使用比兴和隐喻的手法抒发感情。这就使得《咏怀诗》诗意曲折隐晦。
~~~~~~

阮籍在文学上的最高成就为《咏怀诗》。这些诗皆为慨叹人生、表达心志、讥刺时政、随事偶感的记录。其内容暴露了当时社会政治的黑暗恐怖，抨击了虚伪的礼教和伪君子，抒写了自己抱负无法施展的苦闷，也流露出人生无常、消极避世的思想。阮籍继承了《诗经》《楚辞》和建安文学的优良传统，对五言诗的发展颇有贡献，是“正始文学”的代表作家之一。陶渊明的《饮酒》、李白的《古风》都明显受他的《咏怀诗》的影响。原有集十卷，已佚。明人辑有《阮步兵集》。其传载入《晋书》。

Ruan Ji (210-263), Sizong, was born in Chenliu (now in Henan Province Province). He is a famous poet of Wei Dynasty in the Three Kingdoms, and one of the “Seven Scholars of Zhulin” at the turn of the Wei and Jin Dynasties. His father Ruan Yu, one of the Seven Scholars of Jian’an, was highly respected by the Cao family. Ruan Ji was born in the late Han Dynasty and grew up in Cao Wei. So his political thoughts were of course inclined to Cao Wei. It was the time when Cao Wei turned from prosperous to decline. Sima Yi and his son dominated power by assisting in the administration and killed people. Many of Wei’s close clan members and famous scholars sufferedslaughters. People were in danger. Ruan Ji was drinking all day to protect himself.

Ruan Ji is a well-known metaphysician who represents the main trend of thoughts during the Wei and Jin Dynasties. He enjoyed the landscape and was addicted to drinking and playing the strings. He was especially good at the studies of Zhuangzi. He opposed famous teachings and rituals. His words and deeds often went against the tradition, and he hated hypocrites and conspirators. In wardly he advocated nature and inaction and pursued the ideal of personality that was quiet, simple and transcendent. He was deeply dissatisfied with the corruption and incompetence of the Cao Wei royal family. Forced by the tyrannical brutality of the Sima group and contemptuous of its dark rule, he indulged in drinking and pretended to be mad, and would never cooperate.

Due to the particular social and cultural background, the poet was not only dissatisfied with the Sima group and the dark reality, but also dare not openly resist. He wanted to resist but didn’t dare to express his thoughts clearly. The poet used Bi Xing and metaphors in the poem to express his feelings. This made the meaning of *Chanting Poems obscure*.

The highest achievement of Ruan Ji in literature is the *Chanting Poems*. These poems are all the records of lamenting about life, expressing mind, ridiculing the current politics and random feelings. Its contents exposed the darkness and terror of social politics at that time, attacked the hypocritical ethics and hypocrites, expressed the frustration that one could not fulfill his ambition, and also revealed the thoughts of impermanence of life and negative seclusion from the world. Ruan Ji inherited the fine tradition of *The Book of Songs*, *ChuCi* and Jian' an Literature, and made great contributions to the development of five-character Poetry. He is one of the representative writers of "Zhengshi Literature" . Tao Yuanming' s *Drinking* and Li Bai' s *Ancient Style* were all obviously influenced by his *Chanting Poems*. The original set of his ten volumes has lost. In the Ming Dynasty there is The *Collection of Ruan Bubing*. His autobiography is in *The Book of Jin*.

《咏怀诗》六首诗歌赏析：

阮籍《咏怀诗》共八十二首,《文选》只载十七首,各首原无题目,以首句标之。"咏怀"是阮籍生平诗作的总题。歌咏的内容广泛，从多方面形象而深刻地反映了魏晋易代时期社会的黑暗和恐怖，或隐或显地抒发了封建专制统治下正直的知识分子的愤懑。这些诗作的内容主要表现诗人在生活中的各种感慨。

Six Chanting Poems

There are eighty-two pieces in Ruan Ji' s *Chanting Poems*, but only seventeen poems is in *Wen Xuan*, each of which has no title and is marked by the first sentence. "Chanting" is the general theme of Ruan Ji' s poems. The content of the poem is extensive, and it vividly and profoundly reflects the darkness and terror of the society in the Wei and Jin Dynasties from many aspects, and expresses the resentment of the righteous intellectuals under the feudal autocracy implicitly or explicitly. The content of these poems mainly shows the poet' s various feelings in life.

这首诗歌是《咏怀诗》的第一首，抒发了诗人处于当时社会黑暗统治下的苦闷，实际上点出了"咏怀"的主题。魏末司马氏专权施虐，铲除异己。诗人深感危殆，疑虑祸难将临。

This is the first poem in *Chanting Poems*. It expresses the poet' s distress under the dark rule of the society at that time, and points out the theme of "Chanting" in fact. At the end of the Wei Dynasty, Sima group exercised power and abolished their dissidents. The poet was in deep danger and had doubts of impending disaster.

（一）

夜中不能寐，起坐弹鸣琴。

薄帷鉴明月，清风吹我衿。

孤鸿号外野，朔鸟鸣北林。

徘徊将何见，忧思独伤心。

In midnight I still can't fall sleep,

Sit up and play the harp to relieve boredom.

Bright moonlight shed from the thin curtain into the room,

The breeze gently blows my clothes.

The lonely swan wails beyond the countryside,

Birds of the north cry in the woods of the north.

What do you want to see?

Lonelyand sad.

（二）

这首诗歌以郑交甫与江上神女偶遇相欢的传说，讥讽司马氏始忠于魏后竟篡逆的现实。在诗歌的末尾诗人向现实发问，昔日曹魏与司马氏情义坚如金石，如何今朝变故终至离伤？可见诗人对背信弃义者的愤恨是很强烈的。

The poem starts ith the legend of Zheng Jiaofu and the goddess on the river meeting and having a love affair, the poem ridicules the reality that Sima had usurped the rebellion after being loyal to Wei. In the last two lines of the poem, the poet asks the reality: How can the friendship between Cao Wei and Sima in the past be as strong as stone? How did the current changes end up from injury? We can see that the poet' s anger against the renegade is strong.

二妃游江滨，消遥顺风翔。

交甫怀环佩，婉娈有芬芳。

猗靡情欢爱，千载不相忘。

倾城迷下蔡，容好结中肠。

感激生忧思，谖草树兰房。
膏沐为谁施，其雨怨朝阳。
如何金石交，一旦更离伤。

Concubine Jiang Fei wandered in Jianghan shore,
Walk leisurely along the river wind.
The ring is presented as a gift to show love,
Young beauty is amorous in first love.
Endless hope and love for the beloved,
Love each other for thousands of years and never forget.
The beauty is rare and admired by thousands of people.
The love of beloved comes from heart.
The feeling of love so deep and affectionate,
Solve worries I plant day lilies in my boudoir.
Tired and uninterested in washing up,
Like looking forward to rain but the sun rises.
Who could have imagined passion is as solid as stone,
It would be sad to break off.

（三）

此诗是《咏怀诗》的第三首，诗歌借助时序的变化、草木的荣枯，引起世事兴亡的感慨，抒发了忧国忧民的情怀。诗歌运用比喻、象征、对比等手法，婉转表达主旨。诗人以情观景，以景喻意，使主旨的表达，既隐晦又清晰。论者多以为诗人忧感曹魏将亡，司马氏篡逆之危，曲折地表现主题，表达弃乱世避祸患的心志。但是，诗意尤含阮籍对人生世态所做的玄学体验，即祸福倚伏，人生无常，当以超脱物欲追求宁静真朴的人格理想为尚。

It is the third poem in *Chanting Poems*. With the help of the change of time sequence and the rise and fall of plants and trees, the poem evokes feelings of the rise and fall of the world affairs and expresses the feelings of concern for the country and the people.

The poem uses metaphors, symbols, contrasts and other techniques to express the theme tactfully. The poet enjoys the scenery with emotions and conveys the meaning by the scenery description, so that the expression of the theme is both obscure and clear. Most theorists think that the poet is worried about the imminent death of Cao Wei and the danger of Sima's usurpation, so he presents the theme in twists and turns and expresses the intension of abandoning the troubled times and avoiding the calamity. However, the poem contains Ruan Ji's metaphysical experience of the world of life, that is, fortune depends on misfortune and life is uncertain. People should be detached from material desires and pursue the tranquil and simpleideal.

嘉树下成蹊，东园桃与李。

秋风吹飞藿，零落从此始。

繁华有憔悴，堂上生荆杞。

驱马舍之去，去上西山趾。

一身不自保，何况恋妻子。

凝霜被野草，岁暮亦云已。

Under fruit trees are countless fruit,

The peach and plum in Dongyuan.

But when the autumn wind blows leaves to fall,

From now on the peach and plum drift desolate.

The prosperity comes to an end,

The thorns grow in the desolate palace.

Better to gallop home,

At the foot of the western mountain to escape the world.

If you can't protect yourself,

How can you take care of wife and children?

Thick frost covers the weeds,

The end of the year drops near.

（四）

这首诗歌描写古时两个幸臣，以其色相取宠君王的行径。结尾写幸臣对君恩的忠贞不渝，是以正语出反意。言外之意则在于，幸臣尚能忠贞不渝，尽心君王；晋文王（司马昭）受魏厚恩，却将篡逆。魏晋是人格意识空前觉醒的时代，阮籍即其主要代表之一。那种媚事强横之徒，正是其反面。本诗是此类人的绝好写照。

The poem describes the behavior of two minions of the king in ancient times who sought favor from the king by appearances. The ending of the poem is about the minions' loyalty to the king's grace. They are positive words with negative meanings. The implication lies in the fact that the minions can still be faithful to the king. King Wen of Jin (Sima Zhao) received the favor of Wei, but would usurp the rebellion. Wei and Jin Dynasties was an era of unprecedented awakening of personality consciousness, and Ruan Ji was one of its main representatives. It is the opposite of those who flatter. The poem is a good portrayal of this kind of people.

昔日繁华子，安陵与龙阳。

夭夭桃李花，灼灼有辉光。

悦怿若九春，磬折似秋霜。

流眄发姿媚，言笑吐芬芳。

携手等欢爱，宿昔同衾裳。

愿为双飞鸟，比翼共翱翔。

丹青著明誓，永世不相忘。

In the past, there were two minions as beautiful as flowers.

Anling of the State of Chu and Longyang of the State of Wei.

Like the spring peach in blossom,

Sparkling radiant light.

Smiling face is like spring warm breeze,

Bow to ingratiate like grass meet frost.

The flow of the eyes looks charming,

Laughter is full of sweet fragrance.

Hand in hand with the king with joy,

Wearing nigh dress to keep out the cold.

Like the birds into a pair with the king,

Fly together in the sky.

Vows are as vivid as pictures,

Love will kept in mind as long as they live.

（五）

这首诗歌表达诗人的忧生之叹。全诗皆用比兴手法。“清露转凝霜，少年变丑老”皆显示世事易变，人生无常，当珍惜生命。不信仙道，听任自然，因而忧生并非厌世，本质上是现实的、乐观的。

The poem expresses the poet’s sorrow and worry. The whole poem uses the technique of Bi Xing. “Clear dew turns to thick frost. The young becomes ugly and old.” These show that the world is fickle and life is impermanent. We should cherish life itself. Don’t believe in the fairy. Let nature take its own course. Therefore, worrying about life is not misanthropy, but realistic and optimistic in nature.

天马出西北，由来从东道。

春秋非有托，富贵焉常保。

清露被皋兰，凝霜沾野草。

朝为媚少年，夕暮成丑老。

自非王子晋，谁能常美好。

The holy horse originally grew up in the northwest,

But came to eastern road.

Spring is always replaced by the sad autumn,

How can wealth and nobility forever be kept?

Is spring clear dew moistens the bank of the orchid,

Suddenly the autumn frost destroyed the grass.

In the morning he was a good-looking boy,

While in the evening he was ugly and old.

We are not the kind of immortals like Wang ZiJin,

Who can always maintain a beautiful face?

（六）

诗歌描写诗人登高北望，满目坟茔，从而慨叹生命无常，为人生不得永恒而悲。诗歌的后四句引出福祸相依的感触，将贪取功名的李斯、苏秦终而亡身同鄙弃功名的伯夷、叔齐相对照，暗示自隐可安。这是诗人身处魏晋之交的乱世所做的人生思索。

The poem describesthe poet's climbing high to look at the north. What he see are graves, thus lamenting the impermanence of life, for life is not eternal and sad. The last four sentences of the poem point out the feeling of fortune and misfortune depend on each other. The comparison between the death of Li Si and Su Qin who were greedy for fame, and Bo Yi and Shu Qi who despised fame, suggests that it is safe toseek seclusion. This is what the poet living in the troubled times between Wei and Jin thinks about life.

登高临四野，北望青山阿。

松柏翳冈岑，飞鸟鸣相过。

感慨怀辛酸，怨毒常苦多。

李公悲东门，苏子狭三河。

求仁自得仁，岂复叹咨嗟！

Climb high to look downthe countryside,

Look to the north to see the hills covered with tombs.

Shade of pine trees by the tomb covered the hill,

Birds fly with continuous cries.

Seeing this scene I sigh with bitterness,

Sorrow is like a heavy burden in heart.

Li Si lamented before the execution,

It was difficult for him to return back home,

Su Qin disliked Sanhe and sought post out of greed.

If you donate your life for benevolence like Bo Yi and Shu Qi,

No one will sigh deeply when facing death!

晋朝诗歌

Poems of Jin Dynasty

傅玄（217—278），字休奕，泥阳（今陕西铜川耀州区东南）人。西晋大臣、文学家，仕魏、晋两朝。性刚直，在朝多有针对时弊的谏议。博学能文，精通音律。著《傅子》数十万言，评论诸家学说，已散佚，今存辑本五卷。诗以乐府见长，内容大多描写儿女情事和女性痛苦，善用比兴，情致委婉。

Fu Xuan (217-278), Xiuyi, was born in Niyang (now southeast of Yaozhou District, Tongchuan, Shaanxi Province). He was Minister of the Western Jin Dynasty and a litterateur. During the Wei and Jin dynasties, he served as official. He was rigid and had many admonitions against current malpractices. He was knowledgeable and proficient in melody. He wrote *Fu Zi* with thousands of words and commented on the doctrines of various schools. It has been scattered and lostand there are only five volumes in existence. *Fu Xuan* was good at Yuefu Poems, and most of his Poems described love affairs and women's lovesickness. He made good use of Bi Xing and his poems were euphemistic.

《杂诗》诗歌赏析：

这首诗通过对一夜中不同时分的不同物象的捕捉和描写，表现了"愁人知夜长"的诗旨，抒发了一种轻淡的人生倏忽孤寂之感，实际上是诗人在政局翻覆多变时代的一种忧危悲凄情绪的反映。诗人善于描摹景物，景物自然清丽，具体可感。

A Miscellaneous Poem

Through the capture and description of different objects at different times of a night, this poem expresses the theme of "sorrowful people know the night is long", expressing loneliness in life. In fact, it is a reflection of sadness of the poet in the ups and downs of an era of always-changing political situation. The poet is good at describing scenery. The scenery is natural and beautiful, concrete and sensible.

志士惜日短，愁人知夜长。

摄衣步前庭，仰观南雁翔。

玄景随形运，流响归空房。

清风何飘飖？微月出西方。

繁星依青天，列宿自成行。

蝉鸣高树间，野鸟号东箱。

纤云时仿佛，渥露沾我裳。

良时无停景，北斗忽低昂。

常恐寒节至，凝气结为霜。

落叶随风摧，一绝如流光。

Lofty person lamented that the day was short,

Sad people knew that the night was long.

Picking up clothes, strolling in the front yard,

Looked up at the wild goose fly towards the south.

The black shadow gradually moved forward with the geese,

Honks continued to enter the vacant room.

The breezeswiftly blew everywhere,

Moonlight appeared faintly in the west sky.

The blue night sky was dotted with dense stars,

Stars were naturally arranged in rows.

Cicadas cried among tall trees outside the house,

Wild birds wailed in the east wing.

Floating clouds looked faintly,

Dew drops heavily wet my clothes.

Good times did not stop for a moment,

Beidou was constantly falling and rising.

I often worry that when the cold season comes,

Cold air condense into thick hoarfrost.

The leaves fall in the cold wind,

Sweep away like the passing time.

~~~~~~

卢谌（284—350），字子谅，范阳涿郡（今河北涿州）人。东晋文学家。有才思，善文章。洛阳沦陷，北依刘琨，为刘粲所虏。粲败，复归刘琨，任从事中郎。刘琨死后，至辽西，流寓近二十年。原有集十卷，已散佚。今存诗八首，以《文选》所录《览古》《赠刘琨》《赠崔温》《答魏子悌》较有名。卢谌身处祖国分裂、山河破碎的时代，故诗中多有感慨凄怆之词，并通过对蔺相如、李牧、赵奢等古代英雄的歌颂，抒发了自己的抱负和期望。

Lu Chen (284-350), Ziliang, was born in County Zhuo, Fan Yang(now Zhuozhou, Hebei Province). He was a litterateur in Eastern Jin Dynasty. He was talented and good at writing. When Luoyang fell in ruins, he went to Liu Kun' s court and was captured by Liu Can. After Liu Can was defeated, he returned to Liu Kun' s court and took up the post of Congshi Zhonglang. After Liu Kun died, he lived in the west of Liao for nearly 20 years. The original ten volumes have been scattered and lost. There are eight poems in existence today, which are famous as *Looking to the Ancients, To Liu Kun, To Cui Wen* and *Reply to Wei Ziti,* recorded in *Wen Xuan*. Lu Chen was in an era when the motherland was divided and the territory was broken. Therefore, there are many sad lines in his poems, and he expressed his ambition and expectations by praising ancient heroes such as Lin Xiangru, Li Mu, and Zhao She.

《时兴》诗歌赏析：

这是一首因时感兴的诗。诗歌的前半部分描写大自然的运转变化，抒写感慨，要存养本性，恬淡自然。诗歌反映了诗人在为人处事上力求淡泊的一种考虑，实际上是在复杂多变的社会政治环境中力求安宁自适的一种考虑。诗人谈玄多直接从理性入手，形成枯燥的说理诗。这首诗却能将理性的东西同感性的形象的东西结合起来，在阐发玄理时，以物象的刻画为依托，具有诗的意境，这是其在艺术上成功的地方。
~~~~~~

On Time

This is a poem inspired by the times. The front part of the poem describes the movement and changes of nature, and expresses feelings. Human beings should preserve their nature, stay calm and natural. This poem reflects the poet' s consideration of striving to be indifferent when it comes to dealing with things. In fact, it strives for peace and comfort in a complex and changeable social and political environment. Generally the poets directly started from reason and formed a boring reasoning poem to talk about the mystical theory. However, this poem emphasizes and combines the rational things with the perceptual image things.When elucidating the mystical theory, it relies on the depiction of objects and has the artistic conception of poetry.This is where its artistic success lies.

亹亹圆象运，悠悠方仪廓。

忽忽岁云暮，游原采萧藿。

北逾芒与河，南临伊与洛。

凝霜沾蔓草，悲风振林薄。

摵摵芳叶零，蕊蕊芬华落。

下泉激洌清，旷野增辽索。

登高眺遐荒，极望无崖崿。

形变随时化，神感因物作。

澹乎至人心，恬然存玄漠。

The celestial bodies keep moving around,

The earth looks wide.

In a flash, one year will pass again,

I come to the wilderness to pick mugwort hummus.

I crossed the Mang Mountain and the Yellow River to the north,

Came to Yishui and Luohe Rivers to the south.

Severe frost wet the trailing weeds,

The desolate wind blew the grass and trees back and forth.

The fragrant leaves withered, chuckling,

The fragrant flowers fell in the sound of pistil.

The stream spring at the lower part is cold and clear,

The wilderness looks extremely remote and desolate.

Ascend to the height and look into the distance,

Empty without cliffs and steep slopes.

The shape of everything changes with the seasons,

The spirit is moved by foreign objects.

To keep human nature, we should be tranquil and quiet,

Stay indifferent to leisure.

~~~~~~

张华（232—300），字茂先，范阳方城（今河北固安）人。西晋文学家，少时孤贫，曾以牧羊为生。但其好学不倦，学业优博。张华才华横溢，博闻强识，工于诗赋，辞藻华丽。诗以五言见长，多言儿女之情。张华写过《励志诗》以自勉。初未知名，著《鹪鹩赋》以自寄，由是名声始著。惠帝时，历任太子少傅、中书监、右光禄大夫等要职。后因拒绝参与赵王伦和孙秀的篡权阴谋而被害。《隋书•经籍志》著录有集十卷，已散佚。明人辑有《张司空集》。

Zhang Hua (232-300), Maoxian, was born in Fangcheng, Fanyang (now Gu' an, Hebei Province). He is a litterateur in the Western Jin Dynasty.When he was young, he was poor and made a living as a shepherd. But he was eager to learn and had excellent academic performance. Zhang Hua is talented, knowledgable and well-remembered. He is good at poems and Fu, which has beautiful rhetoric.He is known for five-character poems thatmainly talks about love. He is tireless in learning and has written *Inspirational Poems* to encourage himself. At the beginning as an unknown writer, he wrote *The Wren Fu*, afterwards he won his fame. In the reign of Emperor Hui, he served successively as the Taizi Shaofu, Zhongshu Jian, YouGuanglu Dafu and other important positions. He was later killed for refusing to participate in the usurpation of King of Zhao(Sima Lun) and Sun Xiu. He has ten volumes in *Sui Shu · Jing Ji Zhi*, which have been scattered and lost. In Ming Dynasty there is The *Collection of Zhang Sikong*.
~~~~~~

《情诗二首》诗歌赏析：

《情诗二首》选自张华《情诗》五首，诗歌或写闺中离妇思夫，或写远游旷夫恋妇、深情绵邈，哀艳动人，历来颇为选家注目。这里所选的是其三与其五。第三首写独守幽闺的女子思念远方的丈夫，第五首写游子对家中妻子的思慕。两诗刻画细致，情调凄回，哀艳动人，历来为读者所青睐。能将儿女之情摹写得精妙入微，自有其存在的价值，诗歌百花园中是少不得这一朵奇葩的。

Two Love Poems

Two Love Poems are selected from five *Love Poemsby* Zhang Hua. The poems write about wives in their boudoirs, or about traveling far away from their beloved ones. Affectionate and moving, they have always attracted the attention. The selections here are the third and the fifth poems in *Love Poems*. The third one writes about the woman who keeps missing her husband from afar, and the fifth one writes about the wanderer's longing for his wife at home. The two poems are meticulously portrayed. The sentiment is mournfuland the sadness is moving. They have always been favored by readers. Portraying love in a subtle way, the poems have their own value. This wonderful flower is indispensable in the garden of poetry.

（一）

清风动帷帘，晨月照幽房。

佳人处遐远，兰室无容光。

襟怀拥虚景，轻衾覆空床。

居欢惜夜促，在慼怨宵长。

拊枕独啸叹，感慨心内伤。

The breeze stirred the curtains,

Morning moon shone upon the quiet boudoir.

The husband is far away,

So he cannot be seen in the boudoir.

With the empty light and shadow in bosom,

The quilt only cover the empty bed.

When happy, I'm afraid the night is too short.

When sad, I hate that the night is too long.

Cuddling the pillow and sigh,

I feel infinite sadness in heart.

（二）

游目四野外，逍遥独延伫。

兰蕙缘清渠，繁华荫绿渚。

佳人不在兹，取此欲谁与？

巢居知风寒，穴处识阴雨。

不曾远别离，安知慕俦侣？

Look around in the open field,

Stand alone for a long time.

Orchid hues flourish along the stream,

Green banks are covered with flowers.

Unfortunately she is not here,

Whom I pick orchid and give to?

Nesting birds can predict cold,

Ants in the hole can predict the rain.

How can we understand this?

When we have never experienced departing?

《杂诗》诗歌赏析：

这首诗写诗人冬夜不眠情景，并揭示了不眠原因：一因气候严寒，二因思虑太多，而思虑太多是起决定作用的内因。诗歌不仅表现了对时光流逝的焦虑，更表现了对于生命和时局的一种消逝感和危惧感。

A Miscellaneous Poem

This poem writes about sleepless nights in winter and reveals the reasons for sleeplessness: one is because of the cold weather, the other is because of too much thinking. Too much thinking is the internal cause of the decisive effect. The poem not only expresses the anxiety about the passing of time, but also expresses a sense of passing and fear of life and the current situation.

晷度随天运，四时互相承。

东壁正昏中，涸阴寒节升。

繁霜降当夕，悲风中夜兴。

朱火青无光，兰膏坐自凝。

重衾无暖气，挟纩如怀冰。

伏枕终遥昔，寤言莫予应。

永思虑崇替，慨然独抚膺。

The shadow of the sun moved with the movement of the celestial bodies,

Four seasons replaced each other.

At dusk, Dongbi star hanged in the southern sky,

Freezing cold winter drew near.

The thick frost descended at night,

A miserable wind blowed in midnight.

The candlelight and blue smoke lingered in the darkness,

Fragrant oil condensed without noticing it.

There was no heat under the thick quilt,

Wearing a cotton coat was like holding ice.

He lay down on the pillow all night, sleepless.

Talk but no one agreed.

Repeatedly thought and worried about the eternal passage of time,

Chanted and pounded chest with infinite groaning.

《答何劭》二首诗歌赏析：

张华与何劭友善，曾一道为官，故以“同僚”相称。告老辞官家居，二人庐舍田园比邻，极便密切往来，常在一起理琴、读书、赏析诗文，互相慰藉，结伴安度晚年。张华生活俭朴，何劭尚奢华。何劭赠诗给张华，约其春游，诗中流露出年老退归之意，同时也劝张不必自苦其身，张华作诗以答。《文选》入选了他们三首赠答诗，都是晚年辞官归隐期间所作。

比勘诗意，何邵《赠张华》与这首诗正是互相唱和之作，当对照阅读。这首诗记叙以前仕途烦苦、拘束，称赞何邵赠诗所含美德、文采，怀念好友深厚情谊，昔日同僚今日一同归田，成为邻居，抒发志趣相投、结伴安度晚年的喜悦心情。全诗写得从容自然，富有真情实感。

Two Reply Poems to He Shao

Zhang Hua and He Shao are friendly and once served as officials together, so they are colleagues. When they resigned from office, they lived in the countryside and stayed in close contact with each other. They often played strings, read and appreciated poems together. They comforted each other and spent their old age together. Zhang Hua lives a simple life while He Shao enjoys luxury. He Shao gave a poem to Zhang Hua to make an appointment for a spring outing. The poem showed the meaning of seclusion in old age. At the same time, he also persuaded Zhang not to suffer himself. Zhang Hua then wrote a poem to answer. In *Wen Xuan*, there are three of their reply poems, all of which were written during the resignation in the seclusion years.

Comparing the poetic meaning, He Shao's *To Zhang Hua* and this poem are just harmony poems between each other and should be read in contrast. This poem recounts the trouble and constraints of the previous official career. It praises the virtues and literary talents in the poem given by He Shao, and misses their deep friendship. The former colleagues return to the fields together and become neighbors, expressing the joy of similar interests and spending their old age together. The whole poem is written calmly and naturally, full of true feelings.

（一）

吏道何其迫？窘然坐自拘。

缨绶为徽纆，文宪焉可逾？

恬旷苦不足，烦促每有余。

良朋贻新诗，示我以游娱。

穆如洒清风，奂若春华敷。

自昔同寮寀，于今比园庐。

衰夕近辱殆，庶几并悬舆。

散发重阴下，抱杖临清渠。

属耳听莺鸣，流目玩儵鱼。

从容养余日，取乐于桑榆。

How busy as an official,

No idle time for self-restraint.

The crown belt is like a rope,

How dare to violate the laws and regulations?

I often suffer from lack of quiet and leisure,

Cumbersome and urgent things come one after another.

A good friend gave me this new poem,

Invite to travel in spring to relieve trouble.

Friendship is as gentle as the breeze,

Speech is as bright as the spring flowers.

In the past we were officials together,

At present we live close to each other.

Being old officials are nearly humiliated,

Hope to retire and no longer serve in court.

Take off crown and rest under the forest,

Wander on the clear stream with a cane in hand.

Listen to crisps singing and watch the fish frolicking.

Spend the rest of the day calmly,

Happily enjoy the old age of life.

（二）

洪钧陶万类，大块禀群生。

明暗信异姿，静躁亦殊形。

自予及有识，志不在功名。

虚恬窃所好，文学少所经。

忝荷既过任，白日已西倾。

道长苦智短，责重困才轻。

周任有遗规，其言明且清。

负乘为我戒，夕惕坐自惊。

是用感嘉贶，写心出中诚。

发篇虽温丽，无乃违其情。

The heaven has nurtured all things,

The earth gives them life.

Whether light or dark,

It is really in a variety of poses,

Dynamic or static, each has a different shape.

Since I first gain knowledge,

My own ambition is not to gain fame.

Tranquility is what I pursue,

I also study literature when I was young.

Undertaking the task has exceeded my ability,

Not to mention I am too old now.

Often feel that there is a long way to go,

I'm afraid I'm not smart enough to take on the responsibility,

Zhou Ren once said he should resign if he can't do his utmost.

This statement is clear and must be followed.

Reluctantly taking on responsibilities makes me inevitably cautious,

Thinking at night, frighteningly.

I am grateful to my old friend for the poem,

The answering expresses the sincerity out ofheart.

Despite of the poem's grace and tenderness,

It is against my wishes and cannot be followed.

~~~~~~

何劭（236—301），字敬祖，夏阳（今陕西韩城南）人。武帝即位，为散骑常侍。惠帝初为太子太师，永康初，迁司徒。永宁元年（301）卒。博学多闻，善属篇章。现存诗四首。

He Shao (236-301), Jingzu, was born in Xiayang (now South of Hancheng, Shaanxi Province). When Emperor Wu ascended to the throne, He Shao took up the post of Sanqi Changshi. In the early period of Emperor Hui, he was the prince' s first master. At the beginning of Yongkang, he was appointed as Situ. He died in the first year of Yongning (301). Learned and well-informed, he was good at writing. There are four existing poems.

《杂诗》诗歌赏析：

这首诗所表达的意思是很平常的，但语言平易，层次清晰，意境空灵，在写作上颇具特色。其时诗坛藻饰之风渐起，而何劭也有较重藻饰之作，这首诗却别具一格。

A Miscellaneous Poem

The meaning of this poem is very ordinary, but the language is easy, the structure is
~~~~~~

clear, the artistic conception is ethereal, and the writing feature is quite distinctive. At that time, decoration in the poetry world gradually got popular, and He Shao also had poems with algae decorations. But this poem is unique.

秋风乘夕起，明月照高树。
闲房来清气，广庭发晖素。
静寂怆然叹，惆怅出游顾。
仰视垣上草，俯察阶下露。
心虚体自轻，飘摇若仙步。
瞻彼陵上柏，想与神人遇。
道深难可期，精微非所慕。
勤思终遥夕，永言写情虑。

The autumn breeze is blowing in the evening,
Bright moon is shining on the tall trees in the courtyard.
The room is quietly bubbling with fresh air,
The courtyard is wide and covered with moonlight.
Feeling the silence, I can't help but sigh,
I go out and roam around in infinite melancholy.
Look up at the grass on the wall,
Look down at the white dew under the steps.
My heart is empty and quiet,
I feel light and refreshed, swaying as if taking a fairy step.
Looking at the lush cypress trees on the grave,
I hope to meet the gods.
The way of immortals is profound and hard to expect,
Its principles are subtle and faint.
The whole night passed by thinking about this,

So I write down my thoughts in poetry.

《游仙诗》诗歌赏析：

游仙诗为诗体之一种，《文选》单独列为一类，收何劭、郭璞二人游仙诗八首。其内容主要是对功名富贵及世俗生活的蔑视和对隐逸生活的歌颂，当然也流露出逃避现实的消极思想。

Immortals

Poems about immortals are a type of poetry, and in *Wen Xuan* they are classified as a separate category, including eight poems about immortals by He Shao and Guo Pu. The content is mainly contempt for fame, wealth and secular life, and praises for life in seclusion. Of course, they also reveal the negative thoughts of escaping from reality.

青青陵上松，亭亭高山柏。

光色冬夏茂，根柢无凋落。

吉士怀贞心，悟物思远托。

扬志玄云际，流目瞩岩石。

羡昔王子乔，友道发伊洛。

迢递陵峻岳，连翩御飞鹤。

抗迹遗万里，岂恋生民乐？

长怀慕仙类，眩然心绵邈。

There are lush mausoleums with pines,

Towering mountains with cypresses.

Luster without winter and summer,

The roots are deep and leaves are not scattered.

An upright person has an honest mind,

His eyes are on the pines and cypresses.

Determined to reach far and wide,

The rock is so strong.

I am envious of the fairy prince Wang Ziqiao,

Make friends with Dao as Yi and Luo.

No matter how high the mountain is,

I ride a flying crane and soar.

Go for miles with noble deeds,

Do you love the joy of the world?

I often hold immortal wishes in my heart,

Confused and unconscious.

《赠张华》诗歌赏析：

诗人在诗歌中劝说好友张华要珍惜身体，不要过度勤苦，并约同张华一起退休安享晚年。

To Zhang Hua

The poet advised his friend Zhang Hua to cherish his body and not to be overly diligent. He also expressed his wish of enjoying old age with Zhang Hua after their retirement.

四时更代谢，悬象迭卷舒。

暮春忽复来，和风与节俱。

俯临清泉涌，仰观嘉木敷。

周旋我陋圃，西瞻广武庐。

既贵不忘俭，处有能存无。

镇俗在简约，树塞焉足摹？

在昔同班司，今者并园墟。

私愿偕黄发，逍遥综琴书。

举爵茂阴下，携手共踌躇。

奚用遗形骸？忘筌在得鱼。

Four seasons of the year alternate,

The sun and the moon rise one after another.

The late spring comes in a hurry,

The spring breeze blows.

Look down at the clear springs,

Look up at the trees and flowers blooming.

Wander in the rudimentary flowerbeds,

Look westward at Guangwuhou Mansion.

Rich but frugal, life is still plain and simple.

The restraint of luxury is in simplicity,

Guan Zhong's luxury is not worthy of imitation.

In the past, we were officials together,

But now we live in near houses.

I would like to retire with you in old age,

Read and enjoy with ease.

Toast under the thick shade,

Take a leisurely stroll hand in hand.

If we don't care about health,

How can we be spiritually satisfied?

~~~~~~

张载，生卒年不详，字孟阳，安平武邑（今属河北）人，西晋文学家。曾任著作郎、弘农太守等职位。后因世乱托病告归，卒于家。其文以《剑阁铭》为代表。其诗甚重辞藻，成就不及其文。与其弟张华、张协号称“三张”。原有集七卷，已散佚，明人辑有《张孟阳集》。《晋书》有传。

Zhang Zai, whose birth and death year is unknown, Mengyang, was born in Wuyi, Anping (now Hebei Province). He is a writer in Western Jin Dynasty. He took up the post
~~~~~~

of Zhuzuo Lang，Hongnong satrap and so on. Later he returned home for the excuse of his illness because of the chaos of the world and died at home. His poem is represented by *Jian Ge Inscription*. His poems emphasize on rhetoric and his achievements in poems are not as good as his articles. He is known as the "Three Zhangs" with his younger brothers Zhang Hua and Zhang Xie. The original seven-volume collection has been scattered and lost. In Ming Dynasty there is *The Collection of Zhang Mengyang*. In *Book of Jin* there is a biography of him.

《拟四愁诗》诗歌赏析：

本篇拟张衡《四愁诗》(载《文选》卷第二十九)，原共四首，此处选第四首。诗作情韵辞藻，颇得神似。亦借怀人愁思的抒发表达自己的伤时忧世之情，不无寄寓之意。

A Imitation Poem on Four Sorrows

This poem is intended to be Zhang Heng's four *Poems on Four Sorrows* (in *Wen Xuan* Volume 29). There are four original poems, and this selection is the fourth one. This poem is emotional rhetoric, quite alike the original poem. The poem may express feelings of sadness and worry about the world through the expression of sadness, which has the meaning of implication.

我所思兮在营州，欲往从之路阻脩。

登崖远望涕泗流，我之怀矣心伤忧。

佳人遗我绿绮琴，何以赠之双南金。

愿因流波超重深，终然莫致增永吟。

The person I miss is in Yingzhou in the north,

I want to follow him despite the long and hard road.

I couldn't help but flow down tears when I walk on the shore,

Deep missing makes me feel sad.

The beauty gives me a Luqi Baoqin.

How should I return? A pair of southern gold.

It is hoped as the flowing waves cross the deep mountains and valleys,

They finally fail to reach the disciples and sigh.

《七哀诗》二首诗歌赏析：

这两首诗，前一首描写汉代帝王陵墓的毁坏和荒废，抒发了对帝室衰微的感慨。后一首写时光易逝，令人触景伤情。由此可见，两诗次序原来可能正好相反。

（一）

第一首诗描写东汉末年，长期诸侯割据，东汉帝王陵墓也惨遭破坏、洗劫，通过死人亦不能幸免于难的典型事例，愤怒谴责罪魁祸首诸侯和豪强。写法上，诗歌通过描写东汉皇陵的厄运，从一个侧面反映了战乱带来的深重灾难。诗人借古讽今，影射西晋统治阶级争权夺利的纷乱给经济、文化都带来的极大破坏。

Two Poems on Seven Sorrows

The first one of the two poems describes the destruction and desolation of the tombs of the emperors in the Han Dynasty, expressing feelings about the decline of the imperial family. The latter one of the poems writes that time goes by easily, which is touchy and sad. It can be seen that the order of the two poems may be exactly the opposite.

The first poem writes about the long-term warlords fighting in the late Eastern Han Dynasty. The tombs of the emperors of the Eastern Han Dynasty were also brutally destroyed and looted. Through the typical examples that the dead were not spared, the poem angrily condemns the warlords and bullies who are the culprits. In terms of writing, by describing the doom of the Eastern Han Dynasty imperial mausoleum, the poet reflects from one aspect that the profound disasters are brought about by the war. The poet uses the past to satirize the present and alludes to the turmoil of the ruling class in the Western Jin Dynasty fighting for power and profits, which caused great damage to economy and culture.

北芒何垒垒，高陵有四五。

借问谁家坟，皆云汉世主。

恭文遥相望，原陵郁膴膴。

季世丧乱起，贼盗如豺虎。

毁壤过一抔，便房启幽户。

珠柙离玉体，珍宝见剽虏。

园寝化为墟，周墉无遗堵。

蒙笼荆棘生，蹊径登童竖。

狐兔窟其中，芜秽不复扫。

颓陇并垦发，萌隶营农圃。

昔为万乘君，今为丘山土。

感彼雍门言，凄怆哀往古。

There are many tombs on Beimang Mountain,

Four or five high tombs that are particularly eye-catching.

If you ask who's tomb it is,

It is said that the monarch of the Han Dynasty is buried there.

Gong mausoleum and Wen mausoleum face each other,

The original tomb is covered with lush vegetation.

At the end of the Han Dynasty disasters arose one after another.

The robbers are unscrupulous like wolfs and tigers,

The tomb soil has been severely damaged,

The dark door in the tomb has been dug.

The jewellery box next to the emperor's body has been stolen,

All the treasures buried with him have been taken into captivity.

The temple in the cemetery has been in ruins,

Even the walls of the temple are not left.

The ruins were covered with thorns,

Children stepped out of the path to chop wood and graze.

The fox and rabbit are hiding in the nest in the mausoleum,

The dirt has not been cleaned up long.

The decayed grave has been reclaimed into land,

Farmers planted vegetables and grains on it.

The majestic and dignified king of the past,

Has now become dirt in hills.

I think of what Yong Men Zhou said,

It is hard to help but be full of misery to heal the wounds of the past.

（二）

这首诗侧重写墓地萧条凄凉，令人悲伤不已，诗歌抒发了人生无常的悲观情调，表现了士大夫文人常有的感伤。诗歌描写深秋时节傍晚的景物，西风萧瑟，霜寒凄冷，树术光秃，鸟虫无声，太阳阴沉，孤鸟高栖，呈现一片死寂景象。诗歌后半部分重在抒情，诗人向长风宣泄幽思，愁苦无法解脱。表现手法注重铺陈词藻，词句工整。

This poem focuses on the desolation of the cemetery, which is very sad. It expresses the pessimistic sentiment of life' s impermanence, and expresses the sentimentality that literati and scholars often have. The poem describes the scenery in the late autumn evening. The west wind is bleak and the frost is cold. Trees are bare and birds and insects are silent. The sun is gloomyand the lone bird roosts high, presenting a silent scene. The latter part of the poem focuses on lyricism. The poet vent sorrow to the wind, but his sorrow cannot be relieved. The expression technique focuses on laying out words and phrases, and the words and sentences are neat.

秋风吐商气，萧瑟扫前林。

阳鸟收和响，寒蝉无余音。

白露中夜结，木落柯条森。

朱光驰北陆，浮景忽西沉。

顾望无所见，惟睹松柏阴。

肃肃高桐枝，翩翩栖孤禽。

仰听离鸿鸣，俯闻蜻蛚吟。

哀人易感伤，触物增悲心。

丘陇日已远，缠绵弥思深。

忧来令发白，谁云愁可任。

徘徊向长风，泪下沾衣衿。

The cold autumn wind swept across the woods,

With waves of murderous air.

The migratory birds no longer screamed crisply in the forest,

Chilling cicada disappeared with its last wailing.

The crystal dew dropped into frost in the midnight,

Bald branches with withered leaves are deserted.

The sun moved north and winter came,

The shadow of the sun hurriedly set in the west.

Looking around, there was no other sight in sight,

But the pines and cypress at the head of the tomb revealed gloom.

The bare paulownia trees stand tall,

Only the lonely birds come to inhabit.

Look up and hear the call of the southern wild goose,

Look down and hear the low moan of the cricket among the grass.

People who are full of sorrow are easy to feel sad,

Touchings add to the sadness.

The ancestors in the tomb have already left us,

But my lingering thoughts gets deeper and deeper.

Too much worry will make people's hair gray early.

Who say sorrow is so easy to bear?

I was lingering in the endless wind,

Couldn’t help but soak my clothes with tears.

~~~~~~

潘岳（247—300），字安仁，荥阳中牟（今属河南）人，晋代文学家。少时即以文章而闻名。在文学上，潘岳工于诗赋，与陆机齐名。潘岳的作品，皆以辞藻华丽、才思妍巧名世。有《悼亡诗》三首，是其代表之作。

Pan Yue (247-300), Anren, was born in Xingyang Zhongmu (now part of Henan Province). He is a litterateur of the Jin Dynasty. When he was young, he was famous for his articles. In literature, Pan Yue was as famous as Lu Ji for his work in poetry and Fu. Pan Yue’s works are famous for its flowery rhetoric and brilliant wit. There are three mourning poems, which are his representative works.

《悼亡诗》三首诗歌赏析：

《悼亡诗》一组，凡三首，为潘岳代表作。这三首诗是潘岳为悼念亡妻而作。一般认为皆写于为亡妻服丧一年期满之时。根据古代礼制，妻死，丈夫服丧一年。这三首诗写得哀婉缠绵，有较高的艺术价值。后世悼念亡妻之作便专以“悼亡”为题。

三首诗有共同特点：通过对亡妻生前一系列生活琐事和行止的描写，寄托无限哀思，抒发真挚深厚的夫妻感情。能够融叙事、写景、抒情为一体，读来缠绵悱恻，具有感人的艺术力量。还应该看到，三首诗各有侧重，没有雷同之感。能从多角度着笔，互相补充，更加强烈地表达了悼念亡妻的深情。

Three Mourning Songs

Poems for the Dead, contains a group of three poems, are Pan Yue’s representative works. These three poems were composed by Pan Yue to mourn the death of his wife. It is generally believed that they were written in the autumn after the one-year mourning period for his dead wife. According to the ancient etiquette, the husband was in mourning for a year after his wife died. These three poems are sad and touching and have high artistic value. Later generations’ work that mourns the death of one’s wife always use “mourning” for the title.

The three poems have a common feature: through the description of a series of life
~~~~~~

trifles and actions of the deceased wife, they express infinite grief and sincere feelings of the couple. Poems integrated narrative, depiction of scenery and lyrical as one, which are sentimental with touching artistic power. It should also be noted that each of the three poems has its own emphasi. The poet can write from multiple angles, complement each otherand express more strongly deep feelings of mourning for his dead wife.

（一）

这是《悼亡诗》其一，从诗中看，这首诗当作于诗人爱妻去世一周年，这首诗写的就是诗人周年祭毕时的所思所见所感，表现了他对亡妻的深切怀念。就全诗而言，诗人的感情浓烈而深沉。在感情的表达上，寓情于景，以景托情，显示了诗人深厚的艺术功力。同时，恰当的比喻，层次分明的结构，也为诗歌增添色彩。

爱妻亡故已满一年，潘岳为之服丧一年，转眼期满，不得不遵从王命，准备重新返回原官任所。但是诗人禁不住黯然神伤，抒发物是人非的悲哀之情。这是本首诗的核心部分。诗人沉浸在长久忧伤之中不能自拔，孤独的感觉，哀伤的情绪，不但不能随着时光的流逝而淡薄，而且越积越深。时光的流逝抹不掉他对亡妻的怀念，诗人期望能像庄子一样达观，能够解脱永恒的哀伤。

This is one of the mourning poems. From the perspective of the poem, this poem is regarded as the first anniversary of the death of the poet' s beloved wife. This poem is about what the poet thought, saw and felt at the end of the anniversary festival, showing his deep yearning for his dead wife. As far as the whole poem is concerned, the poet' s emotions are strong and deep. In the expression of emotion, he combines emotion with scene, and describes emotions with descriptions of scenery, which shows the poet' s profound artistic skill. At the same time, appropriate metaphors and layered structures add luster to the poem.

It had been a year since his beloved wife died. Pan Yue had been in mourning for her for a year, but he had to obey the emperor' s order and was ready to return to his official post. However, the poet could not help feeling sad, expressing the sad feeling that things had changed. This is the core of the poem. The poet is immersed in long-term sadness and cannot extricate himself. The feeling of loneliness and sadness not only cannot fade with the pass of time, but also accumulate more deeply. The pass of time does not erase the memory of his dead wife. The poet wishes to be as philosophical as Zhuangzi, freeing himself from eternal grief.

荏苒冬春谢，寒暑忽流易。
之子归穷泉，重壤永幽隔。
私怀谁克从，淹留亦何益。
僶俛恭朝命，回心反初役。
望庐思其人，入室想所历。
帷屏无仿佛，翰墨有余迹。
流芳未及歇，遗挂犹在壁。
怅恍如或存，周遑忡惊惕。
如彼翰林鸟，双栖一朝只。
如彼游川鱼，比目中路析。
春风缘隙来，晨溜承檐滴。
寝息何时忘，沉忧日盈积。
庶几有时衰，庄缶犹可击。

Seasons gradually change,
Another year comes in a hurry.
Beloved wife buried in tomb,
Heavy loess cut off the couple.
Who can sympathize with the sadness in my heart?
Stay at home can hardly relieve the sadness.
Had to reluctantly listen to the royal court's orders,
Endure sorrow to return to the original post.
Look at this room, I think of the beautiful image of my dead wife.
When I enter the room, I miss the past situation even more.
Although her figure disappeared between the curtains and the screen,

Her poetry was left on the bookcase.
Between the lines still radiates her fragrance,
Calligraphic work still hangs on the wall.
In my trance it seemed to me that she was alive,
But when I awoke, I felt only horror and sorrow.
Like the birds of the forest that perch on both sides,
How desolate the only one is.
Or like the flounder swimming together in the river,
Suddenly separated midway swimming alone.
The cold spring breeze from the gap bursts of penetration,
Water drops until dawn.
I cannot forget my dead wife in my sleep,
My sorrow grows deeper every day.
I hope one day sorrow will be relieved,
I will be as philosophical as Chuang Tzu.

（二）

这首诗抒发了诗人对亡妻的深深怀念和永恒的哀伤。诗歌的开始诗人叙述了亡妻已去世一周年，秋天又到，严寒在即，谁和诗人一起熬过寒冬呢？人去床空，孤独难眠，远望愁云和月亮，空荡荡的房间里，凄厉的寒风袭人。诗人盼望亡妻能再现仪容，宽慰孤寂之心。诗人哀叹难以自我解脱，不忘亡妻音容笑貌。面对不幸命运，他深感无可奈何。

The poem expresses the deep remembrance and eternal grief for his dead wife. One year after the death of his wife, autumn comes againand the severe cold draws near. Who will endure the cold winter together with the poet? The poet goes to the empty bed. He feels lonely and hard to sleep. Looking at the distant clouds and the moon, the empty room is cold and bitter. He hopes his dead wife reappear to comfort him. The poet laments that it is difficult to relieve from sorrow. He could not forget the voice and appearance of his dead wife. Facing the unfortunate fate, he is deeply helpless.

皎皎窗中月，照我室南端。

清商应秋至，溽暑随节阑。

凛凛凉风升，始觉夏衾单。

岂曰无重纩？谁与同岁寒？

岁寒无与同，朗月何胧胧。

展转眄枕席，长簟竟床空。

床空委清尘，室虚来悲风。

独无李氏灵，仿佛睹尔容。

抚衿长叹息，不觉涕沾胸。

沾胸安能已？悲怀从中起。

寝兴目存形，遗音犹在耳。

上惭东门吴，下愧蒙庄子。

赋诗欲言志，此志难具纪。

命也可奈何？长戚自令鄙。

The moon shone brightly through the window,

At the southern end of my bedroom.

The cold autumn wind arrived at the right time,

Sent away the humid summer.

The chill in the autumn wind grew heavier day by day,

I began to feel the thinness of summer quilt.

No thick was available?

Only for no one to share the cold years with me.

In cold age no one lived together with me,

But only the moon shone the curtain.

Tossing and turning to sleep, I stared at the pillow beside,
No trace of her was on the long empty seat.
Only fly dust was on the lonely bed,
Cool autumn wind flowed into empty bedroom.
Why can't you be like Mrs. Li?
Even if your figure was faintly blurred.
I could not help but sigh aloud,
Imperceptibly tears soaked the clothes.
How deep was the sorrow in the heart,
Burning emotion couldnot be quelled by tears.
Whenever I was asleep or wake up, there was your shadow in front of my eyes,
Your voice was always lingering in ears.
Only ashamed that I was not tough guy like Dongmen Wu,
Ashamed that I could not be as broad-minded as Zhuangzi.
I wrote poems to express feelings in my heart,
But poems were not enough to convey.
Fate was so helpless,
I was sad for a long time, it was hard to let it go.

（三）

这首诗写诗人即将复职，临行前再一次向亡妻告别，抒发他悲伤不已的沉痛心情。诗歌的前十四句描写日月如梭，他转眼守丧一年已满，祭奠亡妻的活动已经终止，诗人不得不脱去丧服，不得不悲叹：此后将如何对亡妻表达哀思呢？启程复职前他再度看望长眠地下的亡妻，描写自己徘徊坟墓前的状态，抒发诗人不忍离去的哀伤。诗人着意渲染坟地凄凉、萧索，哀叹孤魂寂寞，心有余悲。

In this poem, the poet is about to return to his job. Before he leaves, he once again bids farewell to his dead wife, expressing his sad feelings. As the sun and the moon circle, he had spent a year in mourning and the activities of mourning had ceased. The poet had to take off his mourning clothes, and he had to lament: how would he express his mourning for his dead wife after that? He visits his dead wife in the grave before returning to post. The poem describes his state of wandering before the grave and expresses his sadness before leaving. The poet focuses on rendering the desolate and bleak of cemetery. He feels lonely and sad.

曜灵运天机，四节代迁逝。
凄凄朝露凝，烈烈夕风厉。
奈何悼淑俪，仪容永潜翳。
念此如昨日，谁知已卒岁。
改服从朝政，哀心寄私制。
茵帱张故房，朔望临尔祭。
尔祭讵几时？朔望忽复尽。
衾裳一毁撤，千载不复引。
亹亹期月周，戚戚弥相愍。
悲怀感物来，泣涕应情陨。
驾言陟东阜，望坟思纡轸。
徘徊墟墓间，欲去复不忍。
徘徊不忍去，徙倚步踟蹰。
落叶委埏侧，枯荄带坟隅。
孤魂独茕茕，安知灵与无？
投心遵朝命，挥涕强就车。
谁谓帝宫远？路极悲有余。

The sun rises and sets every day,
Seasons replace each other throughout a year.
The morning dew has gradually congealed into frost,

Night wind has grown harsher day by day.

Deeply miss my beautiful wife,

But She has long been buried in the grave.

Recall the past scene as if it's yesterday,

Who knows it has been a year in a hurry.

Take off the mourning clothes into royal clothes,

Difficult to give up sorrow in heart.

The screen of mourning still hangs on the old house,

The first day and the fifteenth of the lunar month it is time for the sacrifice.

Mourning hasn't been long,

A month has passed in a blink of eyes.

Once the mourning clothes are removed,

They will never be worn again.

Time will not stay for another month,

My sorrow grows deeper.

The sadness in heart often rises,

It's difficult to restrain, with tears down.

Drive on the carriage, step on the east hill,

I see the grave and feel pain.

Wander around the tomb of my wife,

How hard it is to leave.

It's really hard to separate,

Stop and go with thoughts in mind.

Falling leaves are piled up on either side of the tomb,

Grass roots are strewn about.

A lonely soul alone in the desert,

Whether people have soul?

I ask the heaven!

I have no choice but to obey the order,

Dry my tears reluctantly and set off.

Who said it is a long way to the capital?

To the end I could not hold back my grief.

~~~~~~

潘尼（约 250—约 311），字正叔，荥阳中牟（今属河南）人。西晋文学家。太康中，举秀才。官至太常卿。与叔父潘岳同以文学著名，世称“两潘”。其诗注重文采，多为应酬赠答之作。原有集十卷，已散佚。明人辑有《潘太常集》。

Pan Ni (approx 250-311), Zhengshu. He was born in Zhongmu, Xingyang (now in Henan Province). He is a litterateur in Western Jin Dynasty. In Taikang periodhe，he was a scholar and then took up the post of Taichang Qing. Together with his uncle Pan Yue, he is famous in literature, and they are both known as “Two Pans” . His poems focus on literary talent and are mostly written for entertainment. The original ten volumes have been scattered and lost. In Ming Dynasty, there is *Pan Taichang Collection* for him.

《赠河阳》诗歌赏析：

河阳，故地在今河南孟州。潘岳为河阳令，潘尼写诗赠之。此诗以古代贤才喻潘岳，但求德行美誉流播，何必奢求高官厚禄，表达了诗人安慰之意。

To Pan Yue

Heyang is now in Mengzhou, Henan. Pan Yue took up the post of Heyang Ling and Pan Ni wrote the poem for him. The poem compares an ancient wise man to Pan Yue. He encourages Pan Yue that he seeks the reputation and virtue. So why does he bother to ask high position and salary? The poem expresses Pan Ni’s comfort.

密生化单父，子奇莅东阿。

桐乡建遗烈，武城播弦歌。
~~~~~~

逸骥腾夷路，潜龙跃洪波。

弱冠步鼎铉，既立宰三河。

流声馥秋兰，摛藻艳春华。

徒美天姿茂，岂谓人爵多？

Mi Sheng took control of Shan Fu,

Ziqi's management of Dong'a deeply won the hearts of people.

The people of Tongxiang built ancestral temples for Zhuyi,

Ziyou governed the city of Wucheng gently.

The horse runs faster on a smooth road,

The dragon in water will be vigorous in the flood.

You were a subordinate official of the Zaifu in years of grown-up,

You were ordered to serve as the magistrate of Heyang County at thirty.

Your reputation is far-reaching and fragrant is better than orchid,

Your writing is colorful like spring flowers.

People only praise the virtues,

How can they be regarded as a high-ranking official?

《赠侍御史王元贶》诗歌赏析：

王元贶，生平未详。曾任侍御史，负责举劾非法，督察郡县等职务。王元贶从尚书郎转任侍御史，均系卑官，潘尼此诗以为慰勉。

To Wang Yuankuang

Wang Yuankuang, his life is unknown. His official position is Shi Yushi. He is responsible for impeaching illegal affairs, inspecting counties and other duties. Wang Yuankuang was transferred from Shangshu Lang to Shiyu Shi. Both of the posts were low-ranking positions. Pan Ni comforted him with the poem.

昆山积琼玉，广厦构众材。

游鳞萃灵沼，抚翼希天阶。

青兰孰为销？济治由贤能。

王侯厌崇礼，回迹清宪台。

蠖屈固小往，龙翔乃大来。

协心毗圣世，毕力赞康哉！

Kunlun Mountain is rich in beautiful jade,

The mansion is made of good materials.

Wandering dragons gather in a beautiful lake,

The phoenix spreads wings and flies towards the sacred heaven.

Candles and incense burn themselves for the benefit of others,

Just like talented people assisting in political affairs and serve the court,

Prince disgusted with the position of Shangshu Lang,

Turned around and came to the Yushitai to take the post.

The inchworm bends itself as a stopgap measure,

The dragon flys to show its excellence.

Loyally assisting on your pilgrimage to wise emperor,

Do your utmost to praise the prosperous customs and customs.

~~~~~~

左思（约 250—305），字太冲，临淄（今属山东）人。西晋时期的诗人和辞赋家。他出身寒门，自幼勤奋好学。虽然其貌不扬，却富有才华。后其妹左芬被选入宫，遂迁居洛阳。为秘书郎，得以博览群书。为作《三都赋》，他广集资料，深入调查。十年赋成。名人皇甫谧、张载、刘逵、卫权等为之作序和注释，于是东都豪贵竞相传写，洛阳为之纸贵。

左思因出身寒微，受门阀制度的限制，但在文学上成就很高。他的《咏史》诗笔力矫健，情调高亢，气势宏大，《诗品》称之为“左思风力”，当是“建安风骨”的继承和发展。他著有《左太冲集》，今存《白发赋》《三都赋》《齐都赋》和诗十四首。

Zuo Si (approx. 250-305), Taichong, was born in Linzi (now in Shandong Province). He is a poet and Cifu writer in the Western Jin Dynasty. Born in a poor family, Zuo Si
~~~~~~

was diligent since he was a child, he is Plain-looking but very talented. Later his sister Zuo Fen was selected into the royal palace and he moved to Luoyang. As Mishu Lang, he read a variety of books. In order to make *Sandu Fu*, he collected materials and conducted in-depth investigations. He finished it after ten years of endowment. Celebrities such as Huangfu Mi, Zhang Zai, Liu Kui, and Wei Quan all wrote prefaces and annotations for it. The rich man of the Eastern Capital competed to write it down. So paper in Luoyang was expensive.

Zuo Si was born from a humble background and was restricted by the clan system. But he achieved high literary achievements. His *Chanting History* has a vigorous writing style, a high-pitched mood and full of vigor. In *Shi Pin* it says "Zuosi Fengli", which is the inheritance and development of "Jian' an Style". He wrote The *Collection of Zuo Taichong*. There are fourteen poems and *Bai Fa Fu,San Du Fu* and *Qi Du Fu* to be saved now.

《杂诗》诗歌赏析：

这是一首秋夜感怀之作。从时节变换写起，后直陈感慨，表达了对人生失意的悲愤。诗篇表明诗人直到晚年也并没有从早年强烈的功名之心中超脱出来，虽曾写过《招隐》等诗，但并非真想绝意仕宦，归隐田园。诗歌在表现上，前以景写起，后以情作结。由外物而内心，步步深入，可谓深具匠心，很好地达到了述志抒怀的目的。

A Miscellaneous Poem

This is a poem about autumn night. The poem starts from the change of seasons and expresses feelings, grief and indignation for the frustration of life. The poem shows that the poet did not detach from the strong fame of his early years until his old years. Although he had written poems such as *Poem of Seclusion*, he did not really want to return to the pastoral. In terms of performance, the poem starts with a scene description, and expresses emotion as the ending. The poem writes from the external object to the heart and changes step by step. It can be described as ingenious and greatly achieves the purpose of expressing thoughts and aspirations.

秋风何洌洌，白露为朝霜。

柔条旦夕劲，绿叶日夜黄。

明月出云崖，皦皦流素光。
披轩临前庭，嗷嗷晨雁翔。
高志局四海，块然守空堂。
壮齿不恒居，岁暮常慨慷。

The autumn wind is so cold,
The white dew in the morning turns into thick frost.
The weak branches are strong,
Green leaves wither day by day.
The bright moon appear in the high clouds,
Bright and clear, emit a white glow.
Open the door and walk into the courtyard,
Look at the geese wailing and flying.
Lofty ambitions cramped by the world,
I stand alone in this empty hall.
The vigorous years never stay long,
I often feel infinite sadness when the years come.

《招隐诗》二首诗歌赏析：

汉代淮南小山的《招隐士》，是召唤隐居山林之士出山之作。时至魏晋，隐逸之风大盛，招隐诗的寓意则变为招人归隐，与淮南小山寓意恰恰相反。

Two Songs of Seeking Seclusion

Recruiting Hermits written by Huainan Xiaoshan in the Han Dynasty is a work of summoning those who live in the mountains and forests in seclusion. At the time of Wei and Jin Dynasties, the ethos of seclusion was flourishing, and the meaning of the poems was changed to persuade people to hermit, which was exactly the opposite of the meaning of Huainan Xiaoshan.

（一）

本诗第一首即写前去招隐士出山之人反而被隐士居处幽雅自然的山林美景所吸引，也要弃官隐居了。这实际上是一首山林隐居生活的赞美诗。

The first of this poem is that people who went to recruit hermits to go out of the mountains were attracted by the elegant and natural scenes where the hermits lived, and they wanted to abandon officials and live in seclusion. This is actually a hymn about retiring in the mountains and forests.

杖策招隐士，荒涂横古今。
岩穴无结构，丘中有鸣琴。
白雪停阴冈，丹葩曜阳林。
石泉漱琼瑶，纤鳞亦浮沉。
非必丝与竹，山水有清音。
何事待啸歌，灌木自悲吟。
秋菊兼糇粮，幽兰间重襟。
踌躇足力烦，聊欲投吾簪。

Walk hard with a cane to recruit hermits,
No one on the mountain road with thorns.
I have never seen houses in the caves,
But hear the sound of the strings from the mountains.
White clouds surround on the north hill,
Red flowers in the southern forest are shining brightly.
The jade-like stones flow from the clear spring,
Little fish float and sink repeatedly.
Why should I comfort myself with the string pipe,
Listen to the clear sound of the green hills and waters.
Why should I sing to express feelings,
Listen to the sorrow songs of woods.

Pick chrysanthemums for accompaniment.

Pick orchids to decorate elegant clothes.

Why bother in the Vanity Fair,

Throw away the officialdom with a hairpin.

（二）

第二首诗歌是诗人闲居洛阳时所作。史载左思迁居洛阳，闭门十年，乃成《三都赋》。而《三都赋》起初并不为时人看重，左思名亦不著，诗作即抒发了自己怀才不遇的慨叹与洁身自好的情怀。

The second poem was written while the poet lived in Luoyang. It is recorded that Zuo Si moved to Luoyang and closed doors for ten years. Then he wrote *Sandu Fu*. However, at the beginning Sandu Fu was not valued by people of the time, and Zuo Si didn' t get his fame. The poem expresses feelings of his unrecognized talent and aspirations of self-cleanliness.

经始东山庐，果下自成榛。

前有寒泉井，聊可莹心神。

峭蒨青葱间，竹柏得其真。

弱叶栖霜雪，飞荣流余津。

爵服无常玩，好恶有屈伸。

结绶生缠牵，弹冠去埃尘。

惠连非吾屈，首阳非吾仁。

相与观所尚，逍遥撰良辰。

Since I came to Dongshan thatched cottage,

Saplings has yielded and is still buried.

Fortunately, there is a cold spring and deep well,

Let me use it to clean my heart.

There are lush forests in the mountains and wilds,

Only bamboos and cypresses are evergreen throughout a year.

Peach and plum, even though gorgeous, is intolerant to frost and snow,
Flowers and leaves are withered by the cold wind and flow with river.
The majesty of the official uniform is rare,
People in the world have their own comments.
There are too many vulgar duties to be an official,
It is difficult to tackle.
Why not go back to the vulgar dust?
Do not imitate the bird,
Do not follow the example of Bo Yi and Shu Qi perishing for benevolence.
Everyone has aspirations,
Do what you want and choose a good time at ease.

~~~~~~

嵇康（224—263），字叔夜，三国魏晋著名文学家、哲学家、音乐家。少孤贫，聪颖好学，有奇才，远迈不群。官拜中散大夫，世称嵇中散，“竹林七贤”之一。嵇康性情刚直，政治上反对司马氏集团，后为司马昭的心腹钟会所陷害，遭司马昭杀害。嵇康诗歌以四言诗见长，现存五十四首，着重表现一种清逸脱俗的境界。散文语言犀利，飘逸洒脱。

Ji Kang (224-263), Shuye. He is a famous writer, philosopher and musician in the Wei and Jin Dynasties of The Three Kingdoms. He was poor when he was young, but he was smart, diligent and talented. He was appointed as Zhongsan Dafu, known as Ji Zhongsan, and was one of the "Seven Scholars of Zhulin" . Ji Kang had an upright temperament and was politically opposed to the Sima group. He was later framed by Sima Zhao' s confidant Zhong Hui and killed by Sima Zhao. Ji Kang' s poems are known for their four-character style. There are 54 existing poems. He emphasizes on expressing a state of cleanliness and elegance. The language of his prose is sharp and elegant.

《赠秀才入军》五首诗歌赏析：

这是一组赠别诗。嵇康之兄嵇喜，曾举秀才。有学者认为此诗是嵇喜从军，嵇
~~~~~~

康作诗相赠。组诗共十八首或写送别情形，或写兄弟之情，或写军旅生活，内容不拘一格。本诗即是以兄长从军后的生活为想象对象，表达了诗人对兄长的敬佩之情，抒发了诗人对狂浪不羁人生境界的向往。

Five Poems to My Brother for Joining the Army

This is a series of farewell poems. Ji Xi, brother of Ji Kang, was once a scholar. Li Shan believes that this poem was written to Ji Xi as a gift for his joining the army. The eighteen poems in the group are either about the farewell situation, or about the love of brotherhood, or about the life in the army, and the content is not limited to one pattern. Based on his brother' s imaginative life after joining the army, the poem expresses the poet' s admiration for his brother and yearning for the realm of unruly life.

（一）良马既闲

诗人从马入题，想象嵇喜的军中之威：战马驰骋，戎装生辉，左右开弓，顾盼生姿。诗人烘托了战马主人的不同凡响。嵇喜一意磅礴，神勇毕肖。诗歌描写了畋猎之乐。古代畋猎并非单纯的游乐，而与军旅生活有关，是练武的一种形式。但毕竟属游乐，故笔意舒缓，其乐无穷。骑射者策马狂奔，风驰电掣，驰骋中原。由此寥寥数语，就形象地勾勒出一位英雄的矫健身姿。比喻等艺术手法的运用，使诗歌更加生动传神。

The poet starts from the horse and imagines Ji Xi' s military power: the war horse gallops, the uniform is shining, the bow is shot left and right, and he looks forward to his posture. The poet highlights the extraordinary of the horse master. Ji Xi is majestic and brave. The poem writes about the joy of hunting. Ancient horse hunting was not simply a amusement, but was related to military life and was a form of martial arts training. But it was an amusement after all,so the writing style is soothing and fun. Riders rode horses and galloped across the central plains. A few words vividly outline the righteous posture of a hero. The use of artistic techniques such as metaphors makes the poem more vivid.

良马既闲，丽服有晖。

左揽繁弱，右接忘归。

风驰电逝，蹑景追飞。

凌厉中原，顾盼生姿。

携我好仇，载我轻车。

南凌长阜，北厉清渠。

仰落惊鸿，俯引渊鱼。

盘于游田，其乐只且。

Ride a well-trained horse,

Wear a beautiful military uniform.

The left hand holds the bow,

The right hand holds an arrow that never returns.

The steed gallops like the wind and electricity,

It can chase the birds and the shadows.

The horse is leaping in the Central Plains ,

Look around, valiant and brave.

Bring close friends,

Drive forward together in my cart.

Ascend the long hillside to the south,

Cross the clear river to the north.

Shoot the wild geese flying in the sky from above,

Swoop down to fish in the abyss.

Seek amusement in the field hunting,

It is endless fun and never thinks returning.

（二）轻车迅迈

诗歌描述了诗人春游时思念故人的情怀。这首诗歌用词清新，描绘了一幅春光明媚、生机盎然的景色。

The poem describes the poet's feelings of missing his elder brother when he goes for a spring outing. This poem is fresh in language and depicts a bright and vibrant scene of spring.

轻车迅迈，息彼长林。
春木载荣，布叶垂阴。
习习谷风，吹我素琴。
咬咬黄鸟，顾俦弄音。
感悟驰情，思我所钦。
心之忧矣，永啸长吟。

Drive forward quickly in cart,
Rest in the lush long forest.
The trees in spring are blooming,
Green leaves are hanging down shade.
The gentle breeze of the valley is blowing slowly,
It flicks elegant strings.
A yellow bird sings a song,
Miss partner and sing happily.
I can’t help feeling agitated,
Think of the friend I admire.
It is inevitable to feel depressed,
Only utter high howls and long chants.

（三）浩浩洪流

诗歌叙述了诗人与兄长的别离之情。诗歌虽然语调伤感，但格调昂扬，辞藻华丽。

The poem narrates the parting feelings between the poet and his elder brother. Although the poem is written in a sad emotion, it has an exciting style and gorgeous rhetoric.

浩浩洪流，带我邦畿。
萋萋绿林，奋荣扬晖。

鱼龙瀺灂，山鸟群飞。

驾言出游，日夕忘归。

思我良朋，如渴如饥。

愿言不获，怆矣其悲。

The mighty river surrounds the capital like a belt.

The lush and verdant woods are full of brilliance.

Fish appears in the water and swim happily,

Flocks of mountain birds fly high together.

My friend drove out and still forget to return at dusk.

How I miss my dear friend!

Like a hungry man looking forward to food.

I miss friend and we cannot meet,

My heart is full of infinite sadness.

（四）息徒兰圃

嵇康的诗歌，将道理蕴含于意象，议论中饱含激情，发人深思，耐人寻味。

Ji Kang's poems embed the truth in image. The discussion of the poem is full of passion, thought-provoking and intriguing.

息徒兰圃，秣马华山。

流磻平皋，垂纶长川。

目送归鸿，手挥五弦。

俯仰自得，游心泰玄。

嘉彼钓叟，得鱼忘筌。

郢人逝矣，谁与尽言？

Rest in the garden full of Orchid,

Graze horses in the mountains full of flowers.

Fly upside down on the flat ground by the water poultry,

Hang down a fishing rod leisurely by the long river.

Watch the wild goose return to fly,

Open the Suqin and play the strings.

Every move is so contented, supernatural,

Intoxicated in nature.

I really envy the fisherman by the river,

Who forgets to catch the bamboo tongs when got the fish.

The confidant leaves me far away,

Whom can I talk to?

（五）闲夜肃清

诗人在诗中描写了离别的缠绵，诗歌意境清雅，读了诗歌仿佛置身于清丽静谧的月夜之中，会引起人们的种种遐想。

The poet described the lingering parting in the poem, and the poetic mood is elegant. It seems that we are in a quiet and beautiful moon night after reading the poem, which will arouse kinds of reveries.

闲夜肃清，朗月照轩。

微风动袿，组帐高褰。

旨酒盈樽，莫与交欢。

鸣琴在御，谁与鼓弹。

仰慕同趣，其馨若兰。

佳人不在，能不永叹。

The peaceful night is quiet and clear,

The bright moon shines from the windows of the pavilion.

The breeze blows my sleeves,

The curtain is hung high in the room,

Even more deserted.

Fill the cup with wine,

Who drinks with me happily.

The zither should be played,

But there is no confident to play together.

What a longing for like-minded friends,

Life was as warm as an orchid at that time.

Now you are not by my side,

How can I not lament sadness.

~~~~~~

司马彪（约 246—约 306），字绍统，河内温县（今属河南）人，西晋史学家。晋王室宗族，魏末任骑都尉，入晋历任秘书郎、秘书丞、散骑侍郎。曾著《续汉书》，记述东汉史事。后纪、传散佚，仅存八志三十卷，北宋后配合范晔《后汉书》刊行。原有集四卷，已佚。《晋书》有传。

Sima Biao (approx. 246-306), Shaotong, was born in Wen County (now Henan Province). He was a historian of the Western Jin Dynasty and was from a royal family. At the end of the Wei Dynasty, he took up the post of Jidu Wei, and then Mishu Lang, Mishu Cheng, and Sanqi Shilang in Jin Dynasty. He once wrote *The Book of the Continued Han Dynasty* which describes the historical events of the Eastern Han Dynasty. Later the records and biography are lost. There are only eight records thirty volumes left. In the Northern Song Dynasty, The Book of the Continued Han Dynasty and Fan Ye's Hou Han Shu were both published. The four collections have been lost. There is his biography in *Book of Jin*.

《赠山涛》诗歌赏析：

山涛（205—283），字巨源，“竹林七贤”之一。热衷名利，攀附司马氏集团。魏时曾任尚书吏部郎。入晋，任吏部尚书。当时司马彪因品行问题未入仕，故赠诗于山涛以求荐举。
~~~~~~

To Shan Tao

Shan Tao (205-283), Juyuan, one of the "Seven Scholars of Zhulin" . He was passionate about fame and fortune and clinged to Sima Group. In Wei Dynasty he took up the post of Shangshu Libu Lang. In Jin Dynastyhe took up the post of Libu Shangshu. At that time, Sima Biao did not enter the official position due to his personality issues, so he presented the poem to Shan Tao for recommendation.

苕苕椅桐树，寄生于南岳。

上凌青云霓，下临千仞谷。

处身孤且危，于可托余足？

昔也植朝阳，倾枝俟鸾。

今者绝世用，倥偬见迫束。

班匠不我顾，牙旷不我录。

焉得成琴瑟，何由扬妙曲？

冉冉三光驰，逝者一何速？

中夜不能寐，抚剑起踯躅。

感彼孔圣叹，哀此年命促。

卞和潜幽冥，谁能证奇璞？

冀愿神龙来，扬光以见烛。

The tall and straight paulownia tree,

Grow on the rugged Hengshan Mountain.

The upper is above the clouds,

The bottom is next to the abyss.

In this isolated and dangerous situation,

What do you rely on to protect yourself?

It used to grow on the sunny flat land,

With branches stretching out to wait for the phoenix to inhabit.

Now he was abandoned by the world,
Feeling depressed in a difficult situation.
Skilled craftsmen refused to look at me,
Musicians and luthier refused to choose me.
How can it be made into a good player?
How can it make a wonderful music?
The sun, moon and stars keep moving,
How quickly the time passes.
Less sleep in the midnight,
Get up and walk with a sword.
Sage Confucius lamented the passing of time,
Also lamented the shortness of life.
Bian He, who knows jade, has gone forever.
Who has the insight to prove the rare jade?
How I hope that the dragon's coming,
Bright light will make me stand out.

~~~~~~

张翰，生卒年不详，字季鹰，吴郡（今江苏苏州）人，西晋诗人。有清才，善属文，时人号为“江东步兵”。张翰见天下祸难未已，有不安意。见秋风起，乃思念家乡，遂辞官归家。年五十七卒。

Zhang Han, whose birth and death year is unknown, Jiying. He was born in Wu Jun(now Suzhou, Jiangsu Province). He was a poet of the Western Jin Dynasty, was talented and good at writing. People called him “Jiangdong Bubing” . Zhang Han saw that the world was plagued with disaster, he was worried and uneasy. When the autumn wind was blowing, he missed his hometown. So he resigned and returned home. He was fifty-seven years old when he died.
~~~~~~

《杂诗》诗歌赏析：

从这首《杂诗》看来，诗人虽陶醉于家乡的风物之美，但也并未忘怀世事，内心仍然翻腾着荣辱贵贱、生老病死的矛盾，就像归隐田园的陶渊明一样。

A Miscellaneous Poem

From the miscellaneous poem, although the poet is fascinated by the beauty of his hometown, he has not forgotten the worldly affairs. His heart is still churning with the contradictions of honor and disgrace, birth and death, just like Tao Yuanming who has retired to the pastoral.

暮春和气应，白日照园林。

青条若总翠，黄华如散金。

嘉卉亮有观，顾此难久耽。

延颈无良途，顿足托幽深。

荣与壮俱去，贱与老相寻。

欢乐不照颜，惨怆发讴吟。

讴吟何嗟及，古人可慰心。

In the late spring, gentle breeze blows back and forth,

The sun is shining brightly on the mountain gardens.

The green branches seem to gather green color,

Yellow flowers seem to be scattered gold.

The beautiful flowers and plants are indeed worth watching,

But it seems that they can’t be entertained for long.

Looking around, there is no good way to go,

So I stop to walk in the deep forest.

Glory fades with youth,

Humbleness comes with old age.

No trace of joy can be seen on face,

Mournful sorrows are uttered.

Singing and sighing is useless,

Only the ancients can comfort my soul.

~~~~~~

王赞，生卒年不详，字正长，义阳（今河南桐柏东）人，西晋诗人。博学有俊才。太康中为太子舍人，工诗，锺嵘《诗品》将其列入。《隋书·经籍志》著录有集五卷，已佚。今存诗五首。

Wang Zan, whose birth and death year is unknown, Zhengchang, was born in Yiyang (now east of Tongbai, Henan Province). He is a poet of the Western Jin Dynasty, and is knowledgeable and talented. He took up the post of Taizi Sheren in Taikang Period. He was good at poems. His poems are included in Zhong Rong's *Shi Pin*. In *Sui Shu · Jing Ji Zhi* he has five volumes, which have been lost. There are five poems in existence today.

《杂诗》诗歌赏析：

这是一首思归的诗，表达了诗人厌弃官场生活、向往隐归林园的心情。诗歌首两句的景物描写，自然入妙，有很强的艺术概括力，成为一时传诵的名句。不少人将这两句作为这首诗的代表，进而作为王赞诗歌最高成就的代表。

A Miscellaneous Poem

This is a poem that has been thinking about returning for a long time. The poem also expressed the poet's feelings of abandoning official life and yearning to return to the pastoral. The scenery description in the first two lines is natural and wonderful. They have a strong artistic generality and become well-received sentences. Many people regard these two lines as the representative of this poem, and then as the representative of Wang Zan's highest achievement.

朔风动秋草，边马有归心。

胡宁久分析，靡靡忽至今？

王事离我志，殊隔过商参。

昔往鸧鹒鸣，今来蟋蟀吟。

人情怀旧乡，客鸟思故林。
~~~~~~

师涓久不奏，谁能宣我心。

The north wind blows the declining autumn grass,

The horses in the border have intenions of returning home.

Why has it been so long since separation,

So long and still, has it come to this day?

Working hard for state affairs is contrary to my ambition,

Far away from hometown,

More than two stars of commercial ginseng.

The yellow oriole screamed happily when he was away from home,

But now the crickets groaned in mourning.

It is natural for people to miss hometown.

Birds also miss homeland in foreign field.

Shi Juan hasn't played a wonderful song for a long time,

Who can vent my sullen aspirations?

~~~~~~

曹摅（？—308），字颜远，谯园（今安徽亳州）人，西晋诗人。初任临淄令，后入为尚书郎，转洛阳令。惠帝末，任襄城太守。永嘉二年（308），为征南司马，因镇压流民兵败而死。《隋书·经籍志》著录有集三卷，已佚。今存诗九首。

Cao Shu(?—308), Yan Yuan, was from Qiao Guo (now Bozhou, Anhui Province). He is a poet of the Western Jin Dynasty. At first he took up the post of Linzi Ling and was transferred to Luoyang Ling later. At the end of Emperor Hui, he served as satrap of Xiangcheng. In the second year of Yongjia (308), he took up the post of Zhengnan Sima. He died due to suppression of refugees and being defeated. In *Sui Shu · Jing Ji Zhi* there is his three volumes, which have been lost. There are nine poems in existence today.

《思友人》诗歌赏析：

这是一首感情真挚的怀友诗。所怀之人为欧阳建。欧阳建，字坚石，渤海南皮
~~~~~~

（今属河北）人，是当时重要的玄学理论家。诗句即是对其作为玄学家的思维和语言活动的绝妙刻画。

Missing Friends

This is a poem about cherishing friends with deep feelings. The cherished person is Ouyang Jian. Ouyang Jian, Jianshi, a native of Bohai Nanpi (Hebei Province), was an important metaphysical theorist at that time. The poem is a wonderful portrayal of Ouyang Jian’s thinking and language activities as a metaphysician.

密云翳阳景，霖潦淹庭除。

严霜凋翠草，寒风振纤枯。

凛凛天气清，落落卉木疏。

感时歌蟋蟀，思贤咏白驹。

情随玄阴滞，心与回飙俱。

思心何所怀？怀我欧阳子。

精义测神奥，清机发妙理。

自我别旬朔，微言绝于耳。

褰裳不足难，清阳未可俟。

延首出阶檐，伫立增想似。

Thick clouds blocked the sun,

Water flooded the yard after the rain.

Severe frost destroyed the wild green grass,

Cold wind moved thin leaves andbranches.

The weather was getting colder and clearer,

The vegetation was sparse and withered.

Feeling the passing of time, I sang “Cricket”,

Chanted “White horse” in memory of friends.

With the winter solstice, I felt uncomfortable,

Thinking and the whirlwind were swirling together.

Who on earth was I thinking about?

It was my dear brother Ouyang.

Inquisitive study to the wonderful state,

Elucidation of the cardinal has profound truth.

No one to speak about subtle words since separated.

It's not difficult to lift clothes and walk.

But it's impossible to meet him.

I went down the steps and looked far away.

It was harder to move while standing still and thinking.

《感旧诗》诗歌赏析：

这首诗以浑厚质朴的语言、对比的手法，抒写了对看重故旧情义的乡人的感念之情，而对世态人情作了抨击，寓意颇为深刻。诗歌既写出了诗人痛切的人生感受，也概括了封建社会重要的本质特征，颇能引起某些人感情上的共鸣。据《晋书》传，曹摅曾被长沙王司马乂任为骠骑司马，司马乂败落后，曹摅被免官，本诗有可能作于免官家居时。

Folks

This poem uses vigorous and simple language and contrast technique to express the gratitude of the Folks who value the old sentiment. The implication is quite profound. The poem not only writes the poet's painful feelings in life, but also generalizes the important essential feature of feudal society, which can quite arouse the emotional resonance of some people. According to *Book of Jin*, Cao Shu was appointed as Biaoji Sima by Sima Yi, King of Changsha. After Sima Yi was defeated, Cao Shu was dismissed from office. The poem might be written when he was dismissed and stayed at home.

富贵他人合，贫贱亲戚离。

廉蔺门易轨，田窦相夺移。

晨风集茂林，栖鸟去枯枝。

今我唯困蒙，群士皆背驰。

乡人敦懿义，济济荫光仪。

对宾颂有客，举觞咏露斯。

临乐何所叹？素丝与路歧。

People worship him when a man is rich and noble,

When he is poor and humble, relatives will leave.

Lian Po and Lin Xiangru lost power and followers left,

Tian Fen and Dou Ying competed, people went away.

Morning wind likes lush forests,

Roosting birds leaves bare trees.

Today I am in trouble because of ignorance,

The county officials turn away from me.

Only the old villagers who respected righteousness.

Sit around me happily.

Read *You Ke* aloud to me,

Raise the wine glass to sing *Lu Si* together.

What's your sigh for such a scene?

Sigh for the cold and warm of humanity.

~~~~~~

陶渊明（365—427），字元亮，东晋亡后更名潜，字渊明，浔阳柴桑（今江西九江）人，东晋至刘宋时期的文学家。他出身于官僚家庭，曾祖父陶侃做过东晋大司马，祖父陶茂、父亲陶逸都做过太守或县令，至他时家境衰微，但他不慕名利，博学。他青年时有“大济苍生”的壮志，先后做过江州祭酒、镇军参军、建威参军、彭泽令等小官。当时政治黑暗，他不愿同流合污，四十一岁时辞去彭泽令，归隐田园。

陶渊明是我国最早的田园诗人，其成就最高的是田园诗。诗中抒发了对农村风光和淳朴生活的热爱，表现了鄙夷利禄的感情和洁身守志的情操。诗歌的风格自然，
~~~~~~

意境超远，语言简洁含蓄，在古代诗歌中独树一帜；由于长期隐居农村，亲自参加农业劳动，他对农民和农村生活有一定的接触和了解，写了很多关于农村的诗歌，诗歌表现了他对农村生活及大自然的热爱，也体现了他不与世俗同流合污的决心。诗风质朴自然，感情率真、形象鲜明，对后世影响较大。但他仍有部分作品，或歌颂坚贞不屈的英雄，或赞扬慷慨牺牲的烈士，说明他并未忘情于世事，体现了他诗歌风格的另一方面。现存有诗歌一百四十多首，散文六篇和辞赋三篇，有《陶渊明集》。

Tao Yuanming (365-427), Yuanliang. He changed his name to Tao Qian. He was from Xunyang Chaisang (now Jiujiang, Jiangxi Province). He was a litterateur from the Eastern Jin Dynasty to the Liu Song period. Tao Yuanming was born in a bureaucratic family. His great-grandfather Tao Kan was once Dasima of the Eastern Jin. His grandfather Tao Mao and his father Tao Yi both took up the posts of satraps or county magistrates. At that time, his family was in decline, but he was not interested in fame and wealth.When he was young, he had the aspiration to "Making contributions to people" . He has successively took posts of small officials such as Jiangzhou Jijiu, Zhenjun Canjun, Jianwei Canjun, and Peng Zeling. At that time, the politics was dark, and he was unwilling to go along in evil deeds. At the age of 41, he resigned from Peng Zeling and returned to the pastoral.

Tao Yuanming is the earliest idyllic poet in our country and his highest achievement is idyllic poetry. The poems express his love for the rural scenery and simple life, and express the contemptuous feelings toward wealth and fame and the sentiment of cleanliness and integrity. The style of the poem is natural. The artistic conception is super far. The language is concise and implicit and the poem is unique in ancient poetry. Due to his long-term seclusion in the countryside, he personally participated in agricultural labor, and had some contact and understanding of farmers and rural life, so he wrote a lot of poems about the countryside. The poetry expresses his love for rural life and nature and also reflects his determination not to go along with the common customs. The style of poetry is simple and natural. The feelings are straightforward and the image is clear, which has a greater impact on later generations. But he also has some works praise the loyal and unyielding heroes, or praise the martyrs who sacrificed generously, which shows that Tao had not forgotten the world and reflects another aspect of his poetic style. There are more than 140 poems, six essays and three Ci Fu and *Tao Yuanming Collection* in existence.

《始作镇军参军经曲阿》诗歌赏析：

东晋安帝元兴三年（404 年），刘裕平收复京邑，可能就在这一年任命陶渊明为镇军参军，此时他刚四十岁，在赴任途中路过曲阿（现江苏丹阳）时写了这首诗。

诗中抒写了作者初任军职时的复杂心态。他本来有宏伟抱负，但因世道黑暗而裹足不前。由于长期生活穷困，他不得不出仕以维持生计，终于因为当时政治异常腐败，门阀制度盛行，加以官场中谄上压下之风极严重，使他无比憎厌仕途生涯，从而陷入出仕与归隐的尖锐矛盾之中。从全诗看，归隐是他在诗中流露的基本情感，第二年他于彭泽令任上弃官归隐正是这种真实的思想感情进一步发展和体现。

A Tour

In the third year of Yuanxing of the Eastern Jin Dynasty (404), Emperor An, Liu Yupingre gained the capital, and Tao Yuanming was probably appointed as Zhenjun Canjun this year. At this time, he was just forty years old and wrote the poem on his way to the post in Qua (now Danyang, Jiangsu Province).

The poem describes the author's complicated mentality when he first took up the military post. He originally had grand ambitions, but he was hesitant to move forward because of the darkness of the society. Due to the long-term poverty, he had to go to officialdom to make a living. Finally, because of the extremely corrupt politics at the time, the prevailing celebrity system, the extreme tendency of flattery and depressiveness in the officialdom, he hated the official career very much, and fell into the sharp dilemma between official career and seclusion. Judging from the whole poem, seeking seclusion is the basic emotion he revealed in the poem. The second year his abandoning Peng Zeling's post is the embodiment of the further development of the true feelings.

弱龄寄事外，委怀在琴书。

被褐欣自得，屡空常晏如。

时来苟宜会，宛辔憩通衢。

投策命晨旅，暂与园田疏。

眇眇孤舟游，绵绵归思纡。

我行岂不遥，登降千里余。

目倦修涂异，心念山泽居。

望云惭高鸟，临水愧游鱼。

真想初在衿，谁谓形迹拘。

聊且凭化迁，终反班生庐。

When I was young, I never thought of being an official,

So I put my feelings on qin and books.

Wearing coarse cloth, content,

I often felt at ease in poverty.

When chance came, I served as the Zhenjun Canjun,

I had no choice but to grievances in the official career.

Putting aside books and ordering my servant to get clothes ready,

I temporarily estranged from the fields.

Sailed in a canoe and slid over the waterfar away,

Looking at the mountain with thoughts in mind.

I went on a trip in foreign lands,

Climbed mountains and rivers for countless journeys.

I was already tired of mountains and waters in other places,

I eagerly missed my old homeland.

I felt ashamed to see birds flying high in the clouds

And fish swimming in the water.

My mind was full of simple thought originally,

How can it be restrained by officialdom.

I would change style at any time,

One day I would return to my hometown.

《辛丑岁七月赴假还江陵夜行涂口》诗歌赏析：

辛丑岁指东晋隆安五年（401）。此年陶渊明三十七岁，他从荆州请假返家，至七月份假期满后，去江陵销假赴任，夜行至涂口时写了这首诗。这首诗记述的就是诗人此次回任途中夜经涂口的所见所闻，表达了诗人归田的愿望。

诗人直陈其事，叙述了平生志趣性情所在。接着由平生性情联系到现实，表现出对过去生活的依恋。诗歌具体描述夜行的情景，凉风将起，江水平平，新月之下诗人告别朋友。诗歌的最后是诗人夜行的感叹，通过比较权衡，诗人做出选择，他决心抛弃功名，挂冠归田。

陶潜在此诗中，抒写了自己对诗书、林园的热爱，对躬耕生活的留恋，和对高官厚禄的淡漠，肯定了在衡门茅屋中修养淳真性情才是美善的人生。由于此诗主题集中，写景清新淡远，而且情景交融，更体现陶诗的特色。诗歌前后呼应，有叙有议，语言自然流畅，景物描写真切形象，感情真挚，增强了诗歌的感染力。

Passing Tukou

Xin Chou Sui refers to the fifth year of Long' an in the Eastern Jin Dynasty (401). Tao Yuanming was thirty-seven years old this year. He asked for leave from Jingzhou and returned home. After spending his holiday in July, he went to Jiangling to report back from leave and take up his post. He wrote this poem when he reached Tukou at night. This poem describes what the poet has seen and heard on the way back to office this time, expressing the poet' s desire to return to the fields.

The poet directly told the story, narrating the ambition and temperament of his life. Then the poem connects from life' s temperament to reality, showing attachment to the past life. The poem specifically describes the scene of walking at night. The cool breeze is about to rise and the river is quiet. The poet bids farewell to his friends under the moon. The end of the poem is the sigh of the poet' s night trip. After comparing, the poet makes a choice. He is determined to abandon his fame and return to the fields.

In this poem, Tao Qian expresses his love for poetry and gardens, his nostalgia for the life of farming, and his indifference to high officials, affirming that the cultivation of honest temperament in the Hengmen hut is a good life. Due to the concentrated theme of this poem, the scenery is fresh and far-reaching, and the scene is blended, which further reflects the characteristics of Tao Poems. The former and the latter of the poem complement each other. There are narratives and discussions in the poem. The language is natural and smooth. The scenery described in the poem is vivid. The feelings are sincere, enhancing the appeal of the poem.

闲居三十载，遂与尘事冥。

诗书敦宿好，林园无世情。

如何舍此去，遥遥至西荆。

叩栧新秋月，临流别友生。

凉风起将夕，夜景湛虚明。

昭昭天宇阔，皛皛川上平。

怀役不遑寐，中宵尚孤征。

商歌非吾事，依依在耦耕。

投冠旋旧墟，不为好爵萦。

养真衡茅下，庶以善自名。

Idling in hometown for six full years,

I completely cut off from the secular for long.

Reading poetry is always my hobby,

No common affairs involvement in pastoral.

Why should I give up and leave,

Head west to Jinzhou, the trip is long.

Under autumn moon I rap the ship's rail with excitement,

Bid farewell to close friends beside the river.

At duskthe autumn wind is infinitely cool,

The empty Kawahara is clear.

How vast it'sunder the clear sky,

And so flat on the fair bank.

Mindful of the official affairs and no time to rest,

I keep walking alone until midnight.

Never do I beg an official in official career,

But the only thing I miss is the pastoral.

One day I will resign and return to my hometown,

The high ranking and wealth are not my haunting.

Cultivate my mind in a shabby room under the thatched eaves,

Living a life like this is considered the best.

《杂诗二首》诗歌赏析：

《杂诗二首》，在《陶渊明集》中归入《饮酒二十首》，分别列第五和第七。《杂诗二首》为陶渊明三十九岁于闲居时所作。两诗皆表现诗人超逸尘俗，将全副身心融入大自然的意趣。

（一）

第一首诗歌为陶诗名篇，是以设问设答的手法表现对尘俗浊世的内心感受，描写诗人心远地偏、悠然看山的情怀，赞颂了田园生活的恬静闲适，突出地表现了诗人心境与大自然相契合的特色。诗人在东篱采菊之时，南山肃穆峻高的形象映现于眼前，连同夕照下山间的云气，觅食归巢的飞鸟，令他心往神驰。于是在对自然景物的直接观照之中，诗人高洁超逸的心灵得到了寄托，达到了物我两忘的境界。这种欣赏大自然的意趣，是直接以心灵感悟的，确实无法用语言说明白。

Two Miscellaneous Poems

Two Miscellaneous Poems, are in *Tao Yuanming Collection* and are included in *Twenty Drinking Poems*, ranking fifth and seventh respectively. *Two Miscellaneous Poems* was written by Tao Yuanming at the age of thirty-nine when he was living in an idle state. Both poems express the poet' s super leisurely state of mind and integrate his whole body and mind into nature.

The first one is Tao' s famous poem, which expresses the inner feelings of the remote world by asking questions and answering. It describes the poet' s feelings of remoteness and leisurely looking at the mountains, and praises the tranquility and leisure of pastoral life. It highlights the characteristics of the poet' s mood and nature. When the poet was picking chrysanthemums under the east fence, the solemn and tall image of Nanshan Mountain appeared in front of him. Together with the clouds in the mountains under the sunset, the birds looking for food and returning to their nests made him excited. Therefore, in the direct observation of the natural scenery, the poet's noble and dignified soul has been entrusted, and he has reached the realm of selflessness. This kind of appreciation of nature is directly inspired by heart, and it really cannot be explained by words.

结庐在人境，而无车马喧。

问君何能尔？心远地自偏。

采菊东篱下，悠然望南山。

山气日夕佳，飞鸟相与还。

此还有真意，欲辩已忘言。

The house built in this complicated world,

But no hustle and bustle of traffic.

How can you do this?

The heart is far away from earthly places.

Pick chrysanthemums under the east fence,

I look up at Nanshan Mountain leisurely.

The scene in the mountains makes me feel better in the evening,

Only the flying birds meet and return together.

It contains infinite natural interest,

I want to express but forget what to say.

（二）

第二首诗歌的意境与第一首大致相同，但隐约地透出了内心的悲哀与不平。酒在陶渊明诗歌的世界中占有突出的地位。在饮酒之中他确立了自我，肯定了个性。因此在群动息、鸟趋林之时，他才啸歌东轩，尽享真朴的人生之乐。

The artistic conception of the second poem is roughly the same as that of the first poem, but it faintly reveals the sadness and injustice in the poet's heart. Wine occupies a prominent position in Tao Yuanming' s poems. He established himself and affirmed his personality while drinking. Therefore, when the flocks of birds were approaching the forest, he sang under the east window and enjoyed the simple joy of life.

秋菊有佳色，裛露掇其英。
泛此忘忧物，远我达世情。
一觞虽独进，杯尽壶自倾。
日入群动息，归鸟趋林鸣。
啸傲东轩下，聊复得此生。

Chrysanthemums have beautiful colors in autumn,
When picked, the flowers are soaked with dew.
Drink the wine in the cup,
Instruct me to be more philosophical.
Although I drink with a cup of wine alone,
I pour it out of the pot.
When the sun goes down, all is quiet,
Returning birds fly back to the forest, singing at ease.
Under the east window I howl proudly,
Live a comfortable life temporarily.

《咏贫士》诗歌赏析：

《陶渊明集》共载《咏贫士》七首诗，此为其中的第一首，以孤云、孤鸟喻贫士，亦以自喻，抒写了诗人不慕荣利的抱负和没有知音的孤独。

《咏贫士》一诗为陶渊明逝世前一年所作。晚年诗人贫病交加，确实是一位贫士。但是，这个贫士精神节操却是高尚、纯洁、坚毅而完美的。他不与污浊的社会苟合，不为庸俗的利禄污染。他甘居困穷，珍重高洁。不怕饥寒，不怕孤立，坚守自己的信仰。这确实是身在乱世的知识分子最可宝贵的品格。诗人就以这种品格自赏自乐。

Chanting on the Poor

Tao Yuanming Collection contains a total of seven *Poems on the Poor*. This is the first of them. It uses lonely cloud and lonely crow to describe the poor, and also uses himself to describes the poet’s disinterest in prosperity and fame, as well as the ambition and Loneliness without a soulmate.

The poem *Chanting on the Poor* was written one year before Tao Yuanming’s death. In his later years, the poet was poor and sick, and he was indeed a poor man. However, this poor man’s moral integrity is noble, pure, persevering and perfect. He does not co-operate with dirty society and does not polluted vulgar profits. He is willing to live in poverty and cherish nobleness. Not afraid of hunger, cold and isolation, he sticks to his beliefs. This is indeed the most precious character of an intellectual who lives in troubled times. The poet enjoys himself with this character.

万族各有托，孤云独无依。

暧暧虚中灭，何时见余辉?

朝霞开宿雾，众鸟相与飞。

迟迟出林翮，未夕复来归。

量力守故辙，岂不寒与饥?

知音苟不存，已矣何所悲。

Everything in nature has its own attachment,

But the solitary cloud has no support.

Silently fading in the sky,

When can we see its brilliance?

The morning glow dispell the heavy night fog,

The birds flock out.

Only the lone bird flies out of the woods slowly,

And returns early before dark.

Don’t you know you will suffer from cold and hunger,

If you live within your means?

If there is no bosom friend in the world,

Then forget it and don't be sad.

《读〈山海经〉》诗歌赏析：

陶渊明《读〈山海经〉》共十三首，组诗各首多以《山海经》所记神话传说中的人或事为歌咏对象，抒发作者对现实和人生的感慨。此诗为第一首，未写任何史事，可以看作是组诗的总序。本诗写耕种之余在静谧环境中浏览《山海经图》的乐趣，实际上是赞颂自己隐居生活的美好。诗人以饱满热情之笔，在诗中描写了归隐之后的乐趣。

Tao Yuanming' s *Reading the Classic of Mountains and Seas* contains 13 poems. Each of the poems in the group poems focuses on the people or things in the myths and legends recorded in the classic of Mountains and Seas as the object of chanting, expressing the author' s feelings about reality and life. This poem is the first poem without any historical facts. It can be regarded as the general preface of the group poems. This poem writes about in general the pleasure of browsing the classic of Mountains and Seas Tu in a quiet environment while farming, and it actually praises the beauty of his living in seclusion. The poet describes full of enthusiasm in his poem the pleasure after returning to seclusion.

孟夏草木长，绕屋树扶疏。

众鸟欣有托，吾亦爱吾庐。

既耕亦已种，且还读我书。

穷巷隔深辙，颇回故人车。

欢言酌春酒，摘我园中蔬。

微雨从东来，好风与之俱。

泛览周王传，流观山海图。

俛仰终宇宙，不乐复何如！

In early summer, in April, vegetation grows,

The house is densely covered by leaves.

The birds are happy to have shelter,

And I like my hut.

After spring plowing and sowing,

I return home to read.

Live in a slum alley,

Friends often turn the front of the cart back.

Drink spring wine happily,

Pick fresh vegetables in my garden.

A light rain came gently from the east,

Accompanied by a gentle breeze.

Feel free to flip through The Biography of Emperor Zhou,

Take a look at the classic of Mountains and Seas.

Know things of the universe instantly,

Why should we not happy!

《拟古诗》诗歌赏析：

《拟古诗》共九首，多为感时伤世、追慕节义之作，约作于刘宋初年。这里所选的一首，以托喻手法，抒写了好景不长、盛年难再的感慨，是作者在晋宋易代之际心境的反映。虽题作“拟古”，却毫无摹拟之迹，与陆机“拟古”相比，显示出迥异的特色。

A Poem Imitating the Ancients

Poems Imitating the Ancients consisted of nine poems, most of which were sentimental to the world and admiring loyalty. The poem is about to be written in the early years of the Liu Song Dynasty. The poem selected here expresses the feeling that the good times will not last long and the heyday is difficult to renew, and it is a reflection of the author' s mood during the turn of Jin and Song Dynasties. Although the title is *Imitating the Ancients*, there is no imitation. Compared with Lu Ji' s *Poems of Imitating the Ancients*, it shows very different characteristics.

日暮天无云，春风扇微和。
佳人美清夜，达曙酣且歌。
歌竟长叹息，持此感人多。
明明云间月，灼灼叶中花。
岂无一时好，不久当如何？

In the evening, the sky is cloudless,
The spring breeze brings a mild warmth.
Beauty likes this clear night,
Drinking and singing all night long.
After singing a long sigh,
This scene is really touching.
The moon is clearly bright in the clouds,
Flowers in the leaves are charmingly brilliant.
Isn't it beautiful for a while,
What will happen soon?

~~~~~~

陆机（261—303），字士衡，吴县华亭（今上海松江）人，西晋著名文学家。祖父陆逊、父亲陆抗都是三国时东吴名将。祖父陆逊为东吴丞相，父亲陆抗为东吴大司马。吴亡，十年不仕。晋武帝太康末，与弟陆云入洛阳，以文章为士大夫所重，名动一时，世称“陆平原”。与潘岳并称“潘陆”，与其弟陆云并称“二陆”。晋惠帝太安二年（303），成都王司马颖与河间王司马颙起兵讨长沙王司马乂，陆机被任命为后将军、河北大都督。陆机兵败受诬，被成都王杀害，死年四十三。

陆机兼工诗、赋和散文，他的诗现存104首，多于同时期各作家，在当时文坛上地位较高。他很注意诗歌的华美，刻意追求辞藻和对偶，开一代之风气。他也有一些文情并茂的佳作，并时有佳句。其辞赋成就较高，《叹逝赋》《文赋》皆为名篇。《文赋》较为系统地论述了文学创作过程中的一系列问题，在中国文学批评史上具
~~~~~~

有极其重要的文学和美学价值。

Lu Ji (261-303), Shiheng, was born in Huating, County Wu (now Songjiang, Shanghai). He was a famous writer of Western Jin Dynasty. His grandfather Lu Xun and his father Lu Kang were both famous generals in Dong Wu during the Three Kingdoms period. His grandfather Lu Xun was the prime minister and his father Lu Kang was the Da Sima of Dong Wu. After the fall of Wu, Lu Ji had not entered the officialdom for ten years. At the end of Taikang, Emperor Jin Wu, Lu ji went to Luoyang with his younger brother Lu Yun. His articles are highly regarded by scholar-officials, and he has been well-known for a while. Later he was called Lu Pingyuan by people.He is also called "Pan Lu" with Pan Yue, and "Er Lu" with his younger brother Lu Yun.In the 2nd year of Tai' an Emperor Hui(303), King of Chengdu Sima Ying and King of Hejian Sima Yong attacked Emperor Changsha Sima Yi. They appointed as Lu Ji as the post-general and the governor of Hebei. Lu Ji was falsely accused of defeat and was killed by King of Chengdu. He died at the age of forty-three.

Lu Ji wrote poems, Cifu and prose. There are 104 poems in existence, more than that of other writers at the same time, and his status in the literary world at that time is high. He pays great attention to the beauty of poetry, deliberately pursues rhetoric and antithesis, and opens up a new style. He also has some well-written works and beautiful lines from time to time. His Cifu has achieved a high level, and *Fu of Sighing* the *Death* and *Wen Fu* are all his masterpieces. *Wen Fu* systematically discusses a series of problems in the process of literary creation, and has extremely important literary and aesthetic value in the history of Chinese literary criticism.

《赴洛道中作》二首诗歌赏析：

《赴洛道中作》二首，历来被认为是陆机五言诗的代表作。第一首写吴亡之后，陆机与弟陆云离开故乡，一起奔赴西晋京都洛阳，沿途所见，无不渗透其悲凉凄恻之情。可见并非主动要去做官，此去前途如何，尚不得知，心中不能没有疑惧。

（一）

第一首诗歌的前四句，诗人写行前与亲友洒泪而别，登上漫漫长路。接下来诗人写此行要去做官，而把官场比做世俗之网，使诗人无法脱身，显然不甚情愿而又心存疑虑，含义深刻；其余数句，则是路上所见所感。既是所见，又是所感。离开故乡，到举目无亲的陌生的洛阳，诗人自然会有顾影自怜的孤独感。诗句将诗人凄凄楚楚、黯然神伤的情景描绘得淋漓尽致。

Two Songs on the Way to Luoyang

The two poems *Two Songs on the Way to Luoyang* have always been regarded as the representative works of Lu Ji' s five-character poems. The first song was written about after the fall of Wu, Lu Ji and his brother Lu Yun left their hometown and rushed to Luoyang, the capital of the Western Jin Dynasty. What they saw along the way, all permeated sadness and compassion. But it is not his initiative to be an official. The future is still unknown, and there are doubts and fears in his heart.

In the first four lines of the poem, the poet shed tears with his relatives and friends before the trip, and walked for a long way. Then the poet writes that he would be an official, and compares the officialdom to a secular web, making the poet unable to get away, obviously reluctant and suspicious, with profound meaning; the remaining few sentences are what they saw and felt on the road. When he leaves his hometown to the unfamiliar Luoyang, he will naturally feel self-pity and loneliness. The verse depicts the poet' s sorrow and sad scenes vividly.

总辔登长路，呜咽辞密亲。

借问子何之？世网婴我身。

永叹遵北渚，遗思结南津。

行行遂已远，野途旷无人。

山泽纷纡余，林薄杳阡眠。

虎啸深谷底，鸡鸣高树巅。

哀风中夜流，孤兽更我前。

悲情触物感，沈思郁缠绵。

伫立望故乡，顾影凄自怜。

Holding the horse rein to leave home,

I felt sad and bid farewell to relatives.

Why did I go far away?

I had no choice but to leave.

With a long sigh I started my way northward,

My mind was still on the southern shore.

My trip went farther and farther,

There was wilderness in the open fields.

The mountains and the marshes were chaotic,

Trees and weeds extremely lush green.

A tiger growled in the depths of the ravine,

A rooster crowed on the top of the trees.

In the midnight sad wind blew over the wasteland,

Lonely animals passed before me.

Heavy sadness filled my chest,

I lingered with deep worries.

Stand for a long time looking at my hometown far away,

I feel sorry for my loneliness.

（二）

第二首诗歌则进一步述说旅途之艰辛和内心的哀伤，将孤寂忧郁的感情推向更高层次。诗歌点明题意，描绘了诗人跨马扬鞭，风尘仆仆奔赴洛阳的形象。诗人以凝炼的笔墨写出了旅途的情思。诗人白天提心吊胆，晚间坐卧不宁。几个连续的动词的使用，将诗人孤寂难安、坐卧不宁的心情表现得细致入微。诗句对其意识动作的描写，将他忧念前途、忐忑不安的心态更是刻画得入木三分。明朗的月亮挂在天空，它洒下的光辉投射到露珠上，在皎洁的月色下，诗人的思绪又回到了故乡，于是披衣而起，独坐畅想。

诗歌层次分明，辞藻华丽，寓情于景，交相呼应，确实是一篇情景相融的佳作。对陆机诗颇多贬词的沈德潜，对此诗也不得不肯定。可见此诗的感染力是谁也无法否认的。

The second song further talks about the hardships of the trip and the poet' s sadness, pushing the lonely and melancholy feelings to a higher level. The poem pointed out the meaning of the title, and portrayed the image of the poet rushing to Luoyang on a horse. The feelings of the journey are written with condensed style. The poet is frightened during the day and restless at night. The use of several consecutive verbs expresses the poet' s loneliness and restlessness in details. The description of his conscious movements in the verses portrays his worrying about his future and his uneasy state of mind. The bright moon hung in the sky, and its brilliance shone onto the dewdrops. Under the bright moonlight, the poet' s thoughts returned to his hometown. So he got up with his clothes on and sat alone, thinking.

The poems are well-structured, gorgeous in rhetoric, embodying feelings in the scene, and echoing each other. It is indeed a masterpiece that blends scenes and emotions. Shen Deqian, who has a lot of derogatory words about Lu Ji' s poems, has to affirm this poem. It can be seen that no one can deny the appeal of this poem.

远游越山川，山川脩且广。

振策陟崇丘，案辔遵平莽。

夕息抱影寐，朝徂衔思往。

顿辔倚嵩岩，测听悲风响。

清露坠素辉，明月一何朗！

抚几不能寐，振衣独长想。

Travel over mountains and rivers in the distance,

Mountains and rivers are long and broad.

I ride up the high hill,

With whip and bridle across the plain.

When I go to bed at night, I go with my shadow,

When I depart in the morning, I go with my sorrow.

Rely on the high rock wall,

Listen to wind echoing from the plain.

Moonlight in the clear dew pendant shining silver,

How clear the moon in the sky.

Touch the pillow on the bed, awake,

I get up and think deeply alone.

《吴王郎中时从梁陈》诗歌赏析：

此诗为陆机在赴任吴王郎中令时，于梁（今河南开封）陈（今河南淮阳）途中所作。陆机在元康四年（294）秋天由太子洗马迁任吴王司马晏的郎中令。陆机于太康十年（289）入洛后，颇为晋朝掌权者器重，尤其是在文坛上地位更高，这些都使他引以为慰；这次又是去吴（现江苏苏州）任职，吴地离他故乡极近。这一切因素，使他写此诗时，内心充满欢欣鼓舞的感情，这感情洋溢在字里行间。

On the Way of Liang Chen

This poem was written by Lu Ji on the way to Liang (Kaifeng, Henan Province) and Chen (Huaiyang, Henan Province) when he was on his way to the post of Langzhong Ling of King of Wu. In the fall of the fourth year of Yuankang (294), Lu Ji was appointed as from Taizi XiMa to Langzhong Ling of Sima Yan. After Lu Ji entered Luoyang in the tenth year of Taikang (289), he was highly regarded by those in power in Jin Dynasty. He especially enjoyed higher status in the literary world, which comforted him greatly. This time he went to Wu (now Suzhou, Jiangsu Province) to take office.Wu is very close to his hometown. All these factors made him full of joy when he wrote this poem, which is permeated between the lines.

在昔蒙嘉运，矫迹入崇贤。

假翼鸣凤条，濯足升龙渊。

玄冕无丑士，冶服使我妍。

轻剑拂鞶厉，长缨丽且鲜。

谁谓伏事浅？契阔逾三年。

薄言肃后命，改服就藩臣。

夙驾寻清轨，远游越梁陈。

感物多远念，慷慨怀古人。

In the past, I had been lucky enough,

Stepped into the gate of Chongxian.

Spreaded and soared towards the top of the phoenix trees,

Stepped forward to the dragon palace.

Only wise men wore the crown,

Colorful clothes made me more refreshed.

Wearing a light sword with a large waistband,

Beautiful and glamorous.

Who said my time for national affairs was short?

It had been more than three years.

Respectfully accepted the subsequent edict,

Appointed Langzhong Ling as an official of vassal state.

In the morning I drove along the road,

Went to the southeast through the land of Liang and Chen.

Touched by the scenery and dreamed endlessly,

I sighed with regret to miss the ancient sages.

《园葵》诗歌赏析：

晋惠帝永宁元年(301)，赵王司马伦谋篡位，以陆机为中书郎。不久，齐王司马冏、成都王司马颖、河间王司马颙等共同起兵讨伐司马伦，迎惠帝返朝，赐司马伦死。齐王司马冏以陆机职在中书，疑上司马伦的《九锡文》及禅文为陆机所作，遂逮捕了陆机等九人，交付廷尉，赖成都王司马颖及吴王司马晏救助，得以减死徙边。

陆机遇赦后，即作了这首《园葵诗》，以向日的园葵自喻，表达了对司马颖的倾慕感激之情。但后来陆机终因军败而为司马颖所杀，这不能不说是诗人的人生悲剧。

Sunflowers

In the first year of Yongning Emperor Jin Hui (301), Sima Lun, the King of Zhao, sought to usurp the throne, and Lu Ji was appointed as Zhongshu Lang. Soon the King of Qi, Sima Ying, the King of Chengdu, Sima Ying, and the King of Hejian, Sima Yong joined forces to defeat Sima Lun, welcome Emperor Hui to return, and gave death to Sima Lun. The King of Qi Sima Jie thought of Lu Ji's post in Zhongshu and suspected that Sima Lun's *Jiuxi Wen* and *Zen* texts were written by Lu Ji. He arrested nine people including Lu Ji and handed them over to the court. Sima Ying and Sima Yan rescued Lu Ji, saved Lu Ji's death penalty and exiled him to the frontier.

After Lu Ji was pardoned, he wrote the poem in which he used sunflowers to describe himself,expressing his admiration and gratitude to Sima Ying. But later, Lu Ji was finally killed by Sima Ying because of his defeat in the army. This is said to be a tragic life for the poet.

种葵北园中，葵生郁萋萋。

朝荣东北倾，夕颖西南晞。

零露垂鲜泽，朗月耀其辉。

时逝柔风戢，岁暮商猋飞。

曾云无温液，严霜有凝威。

幸蒙高墉德，玄景荫素蕤。

丰条并春盛，落叶后秋衰。

庆彼晚凋福，忘此孤生悲。

Plant sunflowers in the north garden,

How they lush and keep alive.

In the morning, the flowers head toward the northeast,

In the evening, their heads turn back southwest.

The dewdrops present bright,

Moon shines with joyful brilliance.

Spring has passed and the breeze disappears,

Autumn wind blows all the year round.

No dew on the clouds,

Thick white frost condenses into a majestic atmosphere.

Thanks to the virtue of high wall shelter,

Shadow shelter flourishes.

The branches flourish with spring,

Fallen leaves decay in the autumn.

Fortunately, it has the blessing of late withering,

So that people forget the sorrow of this solitary life.

《招隐诗》诗歌赏析：

陆机的《招隐诗》共二首，《文选》只录其一。诗作大意是说诗人仕途坎坷，富贵难求，与其因此而终日郁郁不欢，不如隐遁山林，去寻求那清静无为的乐趣。

A Poem of Seeking Seclusion

There are two poems in *Poems of seeking Seclusion* by Lu Ji, and only one of them is recorded in *Wen Xuan*. The main idea of the poem is that the official career of the poet is bumpy. Wealth and honour is hard to find. He should not be depressed all day long because of this. It is good to hide in the mountains and forests to seek the quiet pleasure.

明发心不夷，振衣聊踯躅。

踯躅欲安之？幽人在浚谷。

朝采南涧藻，夕息西山足。

轻条象云构，密叶成翠幄。

结风伫兰林，回芳薄秀木。

山溜何泠泠，飞泉漱鸣玉。

哀音附灵波，颓响赴曾曲。

至乐非有假，安事浇醇朴？

富贵苟难图，税驾从所欲。

It's hard to sleep all night,

At dawn dressed to wander around.

Lingering and thinking where to go?

There is a scholar living in seclusion in deep mountains.

He catches aquatic plants in the south stream of the morning light,

And rests at night at the foot of the Xishan Mountain.

The branches are as light as a mansion,

Leaves are green and dense as curtains.

Gusts of cool breeze sway gently and slowly,

Mixed with the fragrance overflowing the forest.

The mountain stream hits the mountain and the rocks gurgling,

Splashing jade and flying beads dazzle our eyes.

The trend along the valley is like a dragon crooning,

With the sound of twists and turns to the distant mountains.

Realize that the pursuit of bliss in life depends on disgrace,

Why bother to lose simplicity?

Wealth and rank are so difficult to obtain,

It would be better to retreat in mountains.

《于承明作与士龙》诗歌赏析：

陆云，字士龙，陆机之弟。陆机与陆云入洛阳是在太康（280—289）末年。陆机从吴地到洛阳，在万始亭与弟陆云分手，于暂驻承明亭时写此诗赠给陆云，以述思念之意。诗中回顾了告别时的情景，表达了别后的眷顾依恋之感，手足之情跃然纸上。

A Poem to Shilong

Lu Yun, Shilong, is the younger brother of Lu Ji. Lu Ji and Lu Yun entered Luoyang at the end of Taikang (280-289). From Wu to Luoyang, Lu Ji bid farewell to his younger brother Lu Yun at Wanshi Ting Pavilion, and wrote this poem to Lu Yun when he was temporarily lived in Chengming Pavilion to express his missing. The poem recalls the scene of the farewell, expressing the feeling of attachment after the farewell. Brotherhood between them is vividly described in the poem.

牵世婴时网，驾言远徂征。
饮饯岂异族，亲戚弟与兄。
婉娈居人思，纡郁游子情。
明发遗安寐，寤言涕交缨。
分涂长林侧，挥袂万始亭。
伫眄要遐景，倾耳玩余声。
南归憩永安，北迈顿承明。
永安有昨轨，承明子弃予。
俯仰悲林薄，慷慨含辛楚。
怀往欢绝端，悼来忧成绪。
感别惨舒翮，思归乐遵渚。

Entangle by the vulgar idea of entering the officialdom,
So I traveled away from home.
People who set the banquet,
They are all relatives and brothers.
Family members are often sentimentally concerned,
The wanderer feel homesick and affectionate.
Just before dawn, I no longer sleep peacefully,
I wake up with tears that wet my lapels.
Next to Changlin is the intersection of the breakup,
In Wanshi Pavilion I wave hands to say goodbye.
Stand long time gazing at your distant figure,
Listen carefully to the remnants of your voice from afar.

You rest in Yongan on the way back south,
I stay at Chengming on the way north.
Yesterday's tracks remains on Yong'an Road,
You have abandoned me on Chengming Road.
The grass and forest make me feel more desolate,
I wailand weep.
The pain and bitterness is unbearable.
Nostalgia for the past,
The joy of getting along has been cut off.
I lookforward to the future alone.
Just like weaving sadness.
My heart is too sad to spread the wings,
But you are full of joy like a returning bird.

《赠尚书郎顾彦先》二首诗歌赏析：

顾荣，字彦先，与陆机兄弟同入洛。顾家与陆家是世交，又都是吴国的重臣。吴亡后，顾荣到洛阳去做官，与陆机陆云一样是迫于王命，并非自愿。他们志趣相投，又同在王宫中做官，在尚书省任职，长期相处，友情日密。元康八年 (290) 九月，荆、豫、徐、扬、冀五州洪水泛滥，京洛一带苦雨连绵，遍地成灾。陆机与顾荣虽同在尚书省为官，却萧墙阻隔，不通音讯，于是有此赠诗。

Two Poems to Shangshu Lang Gu Yanxian

Gu Rong, Yanxian. He went to Luoyang with Lu Ji brothers. The Gu family and the Lu family are family friends, and both are important ministers of the Wu state. After the fall of Wu, Gu Rong went to Luoyang to take position. Like Lu Ji and Lu Yun, he was forced by the king's order, not voluntary. They were like-minded and both served as officials in Shangshu Sheng of the royal court. Because they got along for a long time, they became closer day by day. In September of the eighth year of Yuankang (290), five states Jing, Yu, Xu, Yang and Ji were flooded, and the area of Luoyang suffered continuous rain, causing disasters everywhere. Although Lu Ji and Gu Rong were both officials in Shangshu Sheng, they couldn't visit with each other. So Lu wrote the poem.

（一）

第一首诗歌写怀友，此诗写因久雨与顾荣不能见面的思念。先述天时不正，苦雨不晴；次述忧患之感；后抒怀友情深。

The first poem is about missing friends.This poem is about the longing for Gu whom he cannot meet because of the rain. The poem states the bad weather at first. It always rains. Then it writes about the poet's worry. Then the poet expresses their deep friendship.

大火贞朱光，积阳熙自南。
望舒离金虎，屏翳吐重阴。
凄风迕时序，苦雨遂成霖。
朝游忘轻羽，夕息忆重衾。
感物百忧生，缠绵自相寻。
与子隔萧墙，萧墙隔且深。
形影旷不接，所托声与音。
音声日夜阔，何用慰吾心。

When the Great Mars moves to mid-heaven summer,
The heat accumulated is most intense in the south.
The encounter between the moon and the western white tiger star,
Indicate thick clouds begin to grow on the long rainy day.
It was an inopportune time for the wind to blow,
Bitter rain keeps falling continuously.
There is no need to take a fan when going out during a day,
A quilt is still needed to protect from the cold at night.
Feeling this makes me worried,
Continuous sorrow really makes me worried.

Although you and I are only separated by a palace wall,

The palace wall is actually so deep.

I haven't seen you for a long time,

So I have to place my longing in letters.

But letters cannot be sent for a long time.

How can I comfort my feelings of missing?

（二）

第二首诗歌描述诗人思虑故乡的心情。先铺叙迅雷惊电振风暴雨之夜景，回应前诗之“凄风”“苦雨”句意。后抒写对灾区流民与家乡百姓苦难的同情。诗歌用词典雅明畅，可为陆机现实主义诗歌之代表作。

The second poem writes about the poet's mood of missing his hometown. First, the poet narrates the night scene of thunder on a night with storm and rain, and responds to the meanings of the "bitter wind" and "bitter rain" in the previous poem. Later, he expresses his sympathy for the suffering of the refugees in the disaster area and the people in his hometown. The poem is elegant and smooth in language and can be a masterpiece of Lu Ji's realist poems.

朝游游层城，夕息旋直庐。

迅雷中宵激，惊电光夜舒。

玄云拖朱阁，振风薄绮疏。

丰注溢修溜，黄潦浸阶除。

停阴结不解，通衢化为渠。

沉稼湮梁颍，流民溯荆徐。

眷言怀桑梓，无乃将为鱼？

Travel in the Imperial Capital during the day,

Return to the duty room to rest at night.

In the midnightthere was a thunderstorm,

Bolts of lighting crackledthrough the sky.

Long black clouds lay on the roof,

The wind rattled against the windows.

Heavy rain overflows the gutters,

Water on the ground overflows the steps.

The dense clouds condense in the sky for a long time,

The streets are flowing like channels.

Crops in the areas of Liang and Ying were flooded,

Jingzhou and Xuzhou were full of refugees.

Seeing this scene, I miss my hometown,

I am afraid it is already a vast ocean.

《赠顾交阯公真》诗歌赏析：

顾秘，字公真，时任交州刺史。诗题中的“交趾”是沿用古称，实际上是指交州。交州辖境包括今越南一部分及广西钦州地区、广州、雷州半岛。顾秘与陆机都做过吴王司马晏的郎中令，后改授交州刺史。他是在南部边疆发生叛乱的紧急时刻受命前往的，他完成了使命，取得了平叛的胜利。陆机赞美他既有“远绩”，又有“明德”，与《晋书》对他的评价是一致的。在诗歌里陆机怀念远在万里之外的朋友，表现了对重逢的渴望。

To Gongzhen in Jiaozhi

Gu Mi, Gongzhen, was Jiaozhou Cishi at that time. The “Jiaozhi” in the title of the poem still uses the ancient name, which actually refers to Jiaozhou. Jiaozhou’s jurisdiction is part of present-day Vietnam and the Qinzhou area of Guangxi, Guangzhou, and Leizhou Peninsula. Both Gu Mi and Lu Ji had served as Langzhong Ling of King of Wu, Sima Yan, and were later re-appointed as Jiaozhou Cishi. He was ordered to go there at a time of emergency when a rebellion broke out in the southern border. He completed his mission and won the victory of defeating the rebellion. Lu Ji praised him for his “achievements” and “virtue”, which is consistent with the evaluation of him in *The Book of Jin*. In the poem Lu Ji missed his friends thousands of miles away and expressed his desire to meet again.

顾侯体明德，清风肃已迈。
发迹翼藩后，改授抚南裔。
伐鼓五岭表，扬旌万里外。
远绩不辞小，立德不在大。
高山安足凌，巨海犹萦带。
惆怅瞻飞驾，引领望归旆。

Earl of Gu has good morals and high style,
Rigorous and lofty.
You were originally assigned to assist the King of Wu,
But now you are a general in southern frontier region.
Now appointed as Zhenfu of Nanjiang.
A majestic drum sounded outside five ridges,
The flag fluttered thousands of miles away.
The establishment of career does not care about remote places,
The establishment of virtue does not pursue wealth and high-ranking officials.
Beyond mountains and valleys,
You see the sea as a belt as if you are waiting for leisure.
Looking at your cart flying off,
I am full of melancholy,
Look forward to your return.

《赠从兄车骑》诗歌赏析：

这首诗是陆机写给他的堂兄陆士光的。陆晔，字士光，吴郡华亭（今上海松江）人，陆机的堂兄，陆机对他有很高的评价。

这首诗确切的写作时间已不可考，但从内容看，是陆机入洛以后的作品。在诗里，陆机以“孤兽”“离鸟”自比，表现出了一种很深的孤独感。虽然做官为臣，但时时不忘回归故乡，故乡的山山水水，父祖的旧居和坟茔，常常出现在脑际，简直到了魂不守舍的程度。他欲归而不得，痛苦得难以自拔，无法排除使他日夜不得安宁的思乡之情。其感情真挚、深沉，动人心弦。

To Brother Shiguang

This poem was written by Lu Ji to his cousin Lu Shiguang. Lu Ye, Shiguang, was born in Huating of County Wu (now Songjiang, Shanghai), and he was the cousin of Lu Ji. Lu Ji praises highly of him.

The exact writing time of this poem is no longer available, but judging from the content, it is Lu Ji’s work after living in Luoyang. In the poem, Lu Ji compares himself with “lonely beast” and “stray bird”, showing a deep sense of loneliness. Although he is an official, he never forgets to return to his hometown. The mountains and rivers of his hometown, the old homes and tombs of his father and grandfather, often appear in his mind. It’s hard to get rid of the homesickness that makes him restless day and night. The feelings are sincere, deep and touching.

孤兽思故薮，离鸟悲旧林。
翩翩游宦子，辛苦谁为心。
仿佛谷水阳，婉娈昆山阴。
营魄怀兹土，精爽若飞沉。
寤寐靡安豫，愿言思所钦。
感彼归涂艰，使我怨慕深。
安得忘归草，言树背与衿。
斯言岂虚作，思鸟有悲音。

Lonely beasts miss their homeland,

Stray birds mourn for the old woods.

Officials have been away from hometown for a long time,

For whom are they so painstaking.

The northern hometown of the valley often appears in front of me,

The beautiful scenery in the northern part of Kunshan is so fascinating.

My thoughts of native land make me dream,

My thoughts of native land make me uneasy.

I'm restless whether I sleep or wake,

always thinking of those whom I admire.

The road of return is full of difficulties,

It makes me resent and miss more deeply.

How can I get the nepenthes?

Plant in front of and behind the house to comfort my heart.

And it is true that even a bird that misses companions makes a mournful song.

《答张士然》诗歌赏析：

这篇诗作描写了诗人终日埋头文案，未得闲暇，幸得出游，见农田风光，不觉引起了强烈的怀乡之情。

A Reply Poem to Zhang Shiran

The poem writes that the poet buried his head in writing all day long, and had no time to rest. He was fortunate to travel and saw the scenery of the farmland. He felt great nostalgic.

洁身跻秘阁，秘阁峻且玄。

终朝理文案，薄暮不遑瞑。

驾言巡明祀，致敬在祈年。

逍遥春王圃，踯躅千亩田。

回渠绕曲陌，通波扶直阡。

嘉谷垂重颖，芳树发华颠。

余固水乡士，总辔临清渊。

戚戚多远念，行行遂成篇。

Promoted to Shangshu Sheng after behaving myself,

How majestic and deep the bureau is.

I was busy dealing with official documents all day,

No time to rest and sleep until the evening.

Visit with the emperor to in the cart to worship the Heaven,

Respectfully pray the Heaven and the Earth to bestow a good harvest.

Take a leisurely tour in Chunwangpu,

Slowly walk in the suburbs to inspect the farming.

The crooked canal surrounds the tortuous path in the field,

The canal shimmers along the straight path.

The millet hung down the heavy ears,

Flowers bloomed beautifully and charmingly on the treetops.

I originally came from that Jiangnan water village,

Ride a horse and face the clear current, feeling homesickness.

Sorrow arose from my heart,

And as I walked,

I chanted this poem to the old ones.

《为顾彦先赠妇》二首诗歌赏析：

诗题为顾彦先而作，第一首诗歌是赠妇，写丈夫思归之情。顾彦先入洛，同迫于王命，外界环境已足忧苦，因而勾起内心对妻子的感念，心曲烦乱，思绪难理，愈不可摆脱。

第二首诗歌是妇答，写妻子闺怨之情。思妇之叹，充溢幽闼，以见盼归之切、怨思之苦。以山川之阻，写空间相距之远，时间相隔之久，把妻子对久别的丈夫之哀怨苦思，化作连绵的意象，意象情思浑然合一。末尾再以温情的祝愿宽慰饥渴的思念，以表答意。

Two Poems to Gu Yan's wife

The title of the poem is written for Gu Yanxian. The first poem is a written to the wife, about the husband's feelings of returning home. Gu Yanxian's trip to Luoyang was also forced by order. In Luoyang the environment was full of distress. As a result, it evokes the gratitude of his wife in the heart. He is upset, and the missings are difficult to get rid of.

The second poem is a reply poem, which writes about the grievances of the wife. The sigh of the woman is overflowing with quietness, to see the singularity and the bitterness of resentment. With the obstacles of mountains and rivers, the distance between the spaces, and the long time of separation, the wife's grievances for the husband who has been gone for a long time are transformed into a continuous image.The image and emotion are unified. At the end, the poet comfort deep missing with warm wishes, and express his intentions.

（一）

辞家远行游，悠悠三千里。

京洛多风尘，素衣化为缁。

修身悼忧苦，感念同怀子。

隆思辞心曲，沉欢滞不起。

欢沉难克兴，心乱谁为理？

愿假归鸿翼，翻飞浙江汜。

Travel far away from home, the official lives in a different place,

Three thousand miles away from hometown.

Luoyang, the capital city,

Is so dusty that white clothes are dyed black.

Leaving homeland makes people feel depressed,

They often miss their deeply loved ones.

Numerous thoughts disturbed my mood,

I was so upset that I could no longer experience joy.

Happiness is gone and I can't be inspired,

The heart is like a mess, who can sort it out for me?

I want to fly with the help of a bird's wings,

Fly gracefully on the waterfront of my hometown.

（二）

东南有思妇，长叹充幽闼。

借问叹何为，佳人眇天末。

游宦久不归，山川修且阔。

形影参商乖，音息旷不达。

离合非有常，譬彼弦与括。

愿保金石躯，慰妾长饥渴。

A woman in the southeast, full of melancholy,

Sigh again and again in her boudoir.

Ask her why shesighs so much,

Her husband is far away from home.

It's been a long time since he was an official and not returned,

The roads are far away with high mountains and wide waters.

The couple haven't seen each other like businessmen,

News has not been passed on for a long time.

I sigh that the clutches of life are so changeable,

As if an arrow have left the string in a twinkling .

I hope you can maintain good health and longevity,

Live up to my ardent concern.

《赠冯文罴》诗歌赏析：

在冯文罴初调斥丘县任县令的时候，陆机曾有诗相赠。陆机在出任吴王郎中令后，因怀念冯文罴，又写诗相赠，表达思念友人的心情，足见他们友情之深。在诗里，陆机回顾了他们同做太子洗马时的亲密友情，并因怀念冯文罴而慨然长叹。冯是他所钦之人，陆机相信，冯文罴一定会干出一番业绩，诗歌表达了对朋友深切的期望和信任。

To Feng Wenpi

When Feng Wenpi first transferred to Qiu County as the county magistrate, Lu Ji wrote a poem as a gift. After Lu Ji took office as Langzhong Ling of the King of Wu, he missed Feng Wenpi and wrote poems to express the feeling of missing friends, which shows the deep friendship between them. In the poem, Lu Ji recalled the close friendship they had when they were Taizi Xima, and sighed with sadness because of his missing. Feng is the person he admired, and Lu Ji believes that Feng Wenpi will definitely make great achievements, expressing his deep expectations and trust in his friends.

昔与二三子，游息承华南。

拊翼同枝条，翻飞各异寻。

苟无凌风翮，徘徊守故林。

慷慨谁为感？愿言怀所钦。

发轸清洛汭，驱马大河阴。

伫立望朔涂，悠悠迥且深。

分索古所悲，志士多苦心。

悲情临川结，苦言随风吟。

愧无杂佩赠，良讯代兼金。

夫子茂远猷，款诚寄惠音。

In the past friends and I serve the Prince in the East Palace together.

It is like the birds that dwell in the same tree and then fly apart.

If there is no wings to fly high in the wind,

They can only be trapped in the old forest.

Who can make me feel excited?

Then you are good friends I respect.

When you set out from Luoyang by cart,

You go to Chiqiu to take office.

I stand and look northward,

The road is so long and deep.

Parting is always sad,

People with lofty ideals will inevitably worry.

Facing the river, I only feel sad and depressed,

Chant the poems that express my missings in the wind.

I'm ashamed not to give you a jade.

Only express affection with good news.

You display your talents in the distance,

Never forget to send me a message to express inquiry.

《赠弟士龙》诗歌赏析：

这是一首描述赠别的诗歌。诗中记述了诗人的离别之苦，希望兄弟二人能够生活在一起。

To Brother Shilong

This is a farewell poem. The poem narrates the pains of parting, and hopes that the two brothers can live together.

行矣怨路长，惄焉伤别促。

指途悲有余，临觞欢不足。

我若西流水，子为东跱岳。

慷慨逝言感，徘徊居情育。

安得携手俱，契阔成騑服。

I resent the long journey when leaving hometown,

My heart is full of sadness in the hurried separating.

There is endless sadness in the long road,

It is always not happy enough to face the wine cup.

I am like the flowing water to the west,

You are like the mountain on the east side, guarding hometown.

What you say is very emotional,

People miss the homeland more deeply.

When will we walk hand in hand,

Like a horse driving on the road?

~~~~~~

郭璞（276—344），字景纯，河东闻喜（今山西闻喜）人，晋代文学家。时中原即将大乱，郭璞南渡，晋元帝授以著作佐郎，不久又迁尚书郎。他曾多次上疏主张宽缓刑罚，减轻赋役，又对腐败的政治提出警告。后因劝阻大将军王敦谋反，被王敦所杀，时年四十九岁。

郭璞为两晋之间的重要作家，他学问渊博，博学广识，造诣极高。郭璞诗赋皆有名，《游仙诗》十四首是他的代表作，萧统选录的《游仙诗》七首影响较大。诗歌文采华丽，抒情性强，尤其是景物描写，极富特色。对郭璞《游仙》之作，历代品评甚多。虽云游仙，实则咏怀，这是其显著特色。郭璞著有《尔雅注》《方言注》《穆天子传注》《山海经注》等，至今传世，为士林所重。

Guo Pu (276-344), Jingchun, was born in Wenxi, Hedong (now Wenxi, Shanxi Province). He is a litterateur of Jin Dynasty. When the Central Plains is about to be in chaos, Guo Pu went to the south, Emperor Yuan of Jin awarded him to Zhuzuo Zuolang, soon promoted to Shangshu Lang. Guo Pu had repeatedly advocated on wide suspension of punishment and reduced tax. And he warned court about the corruption of the politics. Later, at the age of 49, he was killed by a great general Wang Dun for dissuading him from plotting a rebellion.
~~~~~~

Guo Pu was an important writer between Jin Dynasty. He was knowledgeable and accomplished. Guo Pu's poems and Fu are all famous. Fourteen *Poems of Wandering Immortals* are his representative works.Seven of them collected by Xiao Tong have a greater influence. The poetry is gorgeous and lyrical, especially in the description of scenery. There have been many comments on Guo Pu's *Poems of Wandering Immortals* in the past. Although it is immortalized, it is actually chanting, which is its distinctive feature. His works include Annotations to *Er Ya*, Annotations to Dialect, *Annotations to Emperor of Mu*, and *Annotations to the Classic of Mountains and Seas*, which have been handed down from generation to generation and are valued by scholars.

《游仙诗》三首诗歌赏析：

郭璞创作《游仙诗》时，是否有整体的构思，现在难以确考；但从萧统所选七首的编排上，却能看出其内在联系。第一首诗歌总写供选择的两条道路——从政与隐居。第七首，为七首之结。中间五首，反映诗人在选择隐逸道路过程中，思想里充满着矛盾和斗争。郭璞是个具有政治敏感和远大抱负的人，因此对时局的动荡不可能漠不关心。想出世，尘缘未了；想入世，又怕身陷藩篱。内心进退的矛盾斗争，便构成了组诗的波澜。

Poems of Wandering Immortals

It is difficult to ascertain whether Guo Pu's *Wandering Immortals* had an overall idea when he composed them. However, from the arrangement of the seven songs selected by Xiao Tong, we can see their inner connection. The first poem is generally about the two alternative paths—entering the officialdom and seeking seclusion. The seventh is the end. The middle five poems reflect that the poet's thoughts are full of contradictions and struggles in the process of choosing the road of seclusion. Guo Pu is politically sensitive and ambitious, so it is impossible to be indifferent to the turmoil of the current situation. He wants to seek seclusion, but the affinity is not yet finished; he wants to enter the officialdom, but afraid of being trapped. The inner contradiction and struggle of officialdom and seclusion constitute the waves of the poem.

（一）

本篇诗歌列为《游仙诗》的第一首，诗歌用对比的手法，通过两种生活的对比，表达了对仕宦生活的蔑视和隐逸生活的向往。作者运用多层次的结构方式，集中地表现了这一主题。这首诗颇有文采，隐居生活的描写形象生动、引人入胜。情感的表达直接、坚决，有理有据，表达了诗人高蹈风尘之外的理想和对世俗的彻底否定。

This poem is listed as the first one of *Poems of Wandering Immortals*. Through the contrast of two kinds of life, the poem expresses the contempt for official life and the yearning for the reclusive life. The author uses a multi-level structure to highlight this theme. The poem is very literary, and its depiction of life in seclusion is vivid and fascinating. The expression of emotion is direct, firm and reasonable, which expresses the poet' s ideal beyond the world and his thorough negation of the reality.

京华游侠窟，山林隐遁栖。
朱门何足荣，未若托蓬莱。
临源挹清波，陵岗掇丹荑。
灵溪可潜盘，安事登云梯。
漆园有傲吏，莱氏有逸妻。
进则保龙见，退为触藩羝。
高蹈风尘外，长揖谢夷齐。

The prosperous capital city knights,
The mountains and forests outsiders.
Glory and wealth is not enough,
It's better to live in the fairy mountain.
Drink in the clear spring,
Climb mountains and eat ganoderma lucidum.
Ling stream for seclusion,
No need to be dedicated to the official career.
The arrogant official Zhuang Zhou,
And Laiyi's wife were eloquent.
If you return to seclusion, seek immortality into the fairy,

If you retreat, live in the secular world.

Live in seclusion beyond the mundane world,

It is the highest and most clean, surpassing Bo Yi and Shu Qi.

（二）

这首诗是《游仙诗》中的第二首。奇特之构思，丰富之想象，是这首诗突出的特点。亦虚亦实的描写，将人带入亦真亦幻的境界。山美，水美，仙更美。写山高，写水秀，写仙俏，构成一幅令人神往的画面，表现了诗人的理想追求。然而他毕竟是现实中的人，没有忘记这是并不存在的幻境，故最后不能不发出叹问。

It is the second poem of *Poems of Wandering Immortals*.The peculiar idea and rich imagination are the outstanding features of the poem. The true mingled with the false description brings people into the realm of the true and the unreal. The mountain is high. The water is delicate. The fairy is beautiful. They constitute a fascinating picture, expressing the poet's ideal pursuit. But after all, he was a man in reality, and he had not forgotten that this was a land of illusion which did not exist. So he could not help sighing in the end.

青溪千余仞，中有一道士。

云生梁栋间，风出窗户里。

借问此何谁，云是鬼谷子。

翘迹企颍阳，临河思洗耳。

阊阖西南来，潜波涣鳞起。

灵妃顾我笑，粲然启玉齿。

蹇修时不存，要之将谁使？

Qingxi Mountain is high,

The Taoist priest lives on the cloud.

Smoke of clouds roll between the pillars,

The breeze pierces the joy of happiness.

To ask who the Taoist priest is,

Mr. Guiguzi is famous.

I raise my feet in hope of catching up with Xu You.

A breeze came from the southwest,

The water is sparkling and the waves are far away.

Concubine Ling, the Goddess of the Luoshui River, came,

Her jade teeth and heavenly appearance are fascinating.

Unfortunately,Jian Xiu doesn't come anymore,

I want to seek immortality,

Who will introduce?

（三）

本诗描写隐士纵情山林，与仙人为伴的隐逸生活，表达了诗人对名利的鄙弃和对悠闲生活的向往。如果说第二首还是向往仙境，那么这首则是置身于仙境了。在七首《游仙诗》中，这是色彩艳丽、潇洒飘逸的一首。诗歌先从隐士所居的山林写起，通过对景物的描摹，从环境这个侧面展现隐士生活的美好。接着，诗人描写隐士的生活状况：在幽静的山林里，隐士纵情长啸，手抚清弦，十分悠闲。其后数句，诗歌紧扣诗题，写隐士与游仙一起神游四海，十分逍遥。最后诗歌以比喻作结，把追名逐利的小人比作蜉蝣，用能活千年的龟鹤来比喻幽居山林的隐士，藉以表明自己的高洁之志。

This poem describes the hermit's reclusive life in the mountains and forests and with the companions of immortals, expressing the poet's disdain for fame and wealth and his yearning for a leisurely life. The second poem is written for the desire of wonderland, this one is in the wonderland. Among the seven poems of *Wandering Immortals*, this is one with bright colors, natural and elegant. The poem starts from the mountain and forest where the hermit lives. Through the description of the scenery, it shows the beauty of the hermit's life from the aspect of the environment. Then the poet describes the living conditions of the hermit. In the secluded mountain forest, the hermit is indulgent in howling and playing strings, which is very leisurely. In the next few lines, the poem is closely related to the title of the poem and writes about the hermit and the wandering fairy travel around happily. In the end, the poem end with metaphors, comparing the villains who seek fame and fortune to the mayflies, and comparing the tortoises and cranes that live for a thousand years to the hermits who live in seclusion, so as to show the poet' s lofty aspirations.

翡翠戏兰苕，容色更相鲜。
绿萝结高林，蒙笼盖一山。
中有冥寂士，静啸抚清弦。
放情陵霄外，嚼蕊挹飞泉。
赤松临上游，驾鸿乘紫烟。
左挹浮丘袖，右拍洪崖肩。
借问蜉蝣辈，宁知龟鹤年。

The jade orchid and vetch are radiant,
The appearance is fresher and more beautiful.
The green radish climbs the pine forest,
The verdant green covers the mountain.
There is a hermit in the mountain,
Howl and stroke strings.
Indulge in the joy of reaching the clouds,
Chew the flower buds and drink the spring.
See the immortal Chisong Zi,
Soar to the sky and drive crane in purple smoke.
Hold Fuqiu with left hand,
Stroke Hong Ya with right hand.
It is a pity to ask mayfly generations,
Whether know the immortal lives for thousands of years.

南北朝诗歌 南朝宋

Poems of Northern and Southern Dynasties (the Southern Song Dynasty)

鲍照（414—466），字明远，东海（今山东郯城）人。南朝宋代的著名文学家。出身寒微，少时治学勤奋，才华出众，因献诗临川王刘义庆，得到赏识，擢为国侍郎。宋明帝泰始二年（466），刘子顼谋反，战败被诛，鲍照亦死于乱军之中。

鲍照在门阀特权盛行的时代，处处受人压制，这种遭遇使他清醒地认识到当时社会的腐朽。他的作品深刻揭露了当时社会上的黑暗现象，反映了动乱的现实，抒发了自己怀才不遇的愤懑情绪，表现了寒门对世族大地主政治的不满。作品感情充沛，形象鲜明，风格清新。他的文学创作以诗为主，赋与散文也有一定成就。

Bao Zhao (414-466), Mingyuan, was from Donghai (now Tancheng, Shandong Province). He is a famous litterateur in the Southern Song Dynasty. Born from a humble background, he was diligent when he was young, and had outstanding talent. He was appreciated for offering poems to the King of Linchuan, Liu Yiqing, and promoted to Guo Shilang. In the second year of Taishi, Emperor Ming (466), Liu Zixu conspired and was defeated and sentenced. Bao Zhao also died in the rebellion.

Bao Zhao was suppressed in the era when family privileges prevailed. This kind of experience made him soberly aware of the decay of society at that time. His works profoundly exposed the dark phenomena of the society at that time, reflected the turbulent reality, expressed his resentment of talents being urecognized, and expressed the dissatisfaction of the poor family with the politics of the big landlords.His works are full of emotion and have vivid image and fresh style. His literary works are mainly poems, and he has also achieved certain achievements in Fu and prose.

《出自蓟北门行》诗歌赏析：

本篇诗歌既讴歌了战士从军誓死卫国的壮志，又描写了北方边地的风物和从军的艰苦，是一篇边塞题材的优秀作品。

本诗结构清晰，层次分明，由边境告急到派兵讨伐，再到壮士抒发报国之志，层层递进环环相扣。诗歌首先说明出兵的缘由，交代事件的起因。边境告急，告警的文书、烽火传到了京城，朝廷闻警，即调兵防守救援。对边塞风光的描写则是从自然景况的恶劣衬托出行军的艰辛劳苦。将士们攀越石径，飞渡桥梁，疾风呼啸，战马蜷缩着身子，战士的角弓难以拉开。尽管如此，战士们杀敌卫国的决心却没有丝毫动摇。国家危难之际，才能看出臣子的忠贞贤良，为了报答明主，即使为国捐躯也死而无憾。

Northern Frontier

This poem not only eulogizes the soldiers' ambition to defend the country to death, but also describes the scenery of the northern frontier and the hardships of joining the army. It is an excellent work with frontier fortress theme.

The poem has a clear structure and distinct levels. From the border emergency to sending troops to crusade, from the soldiers expressing their ambitions to serve the country, the layers of the poem are interlocking. The poem pointed out the reason for the dispatch of troops and explained the cause of the incident. The border was in an emergency, and the warning document and beacon spread to the capital. The royal court heard the news and dispatched troops to defend and rescue. The description of the scenery of the frontier fortresses was to set off the hard work of the march from the harsh natural conditions. Soldiers climbed stone paths and crossed bridges. The gust of wind howled,the war horse crouched, and the warrior's horns were difficult to pull away. Despite this, the soldiers' determination to kill the enemy and defend the country did not waver in the slightest shake at all. When the country is in crisis, loyalty and virtuousness of the courtiers can be seen. In order to repay the wise emperor, even if soldiers would die without regret for the country.

羽檄起边亭，烽火入咸阳。

征骑屯广武，分兵救朔方。

严秋筋竿劲，虏阵精且强。

天子按剑怒，使者遥相望。

雁行缘石径，鱼贯度飞梁。

箫鼓流汉思，旌甲被胡霜。

疾风冲塞起，沙砾自飘扬。

马毛缩如猬，角弓不可张。

时危见臣节，世乱识忠良。

投躯报明主，身死为国殇。

Message came from the border pavilion,

Beacon-fire quickly spreaded to Xianyang.

The expeditionary cavalry gathered in Guangwu,

Dispatched troops to rescue Shuofang.

In late autumn bows and arrows were powerful,

The enemy army was excellent and strong.

Hearing the news, the emperor furiously pressed sword,

Told the envoys to dispatch.

Troops marched along the rocky road,

Filing across the alpine bridge.

The flute and drum overflowed with thoughts of family and country,

Flag and armor were covered with hoarfrost.

The gust of wind hit the border,

Sand and rocks fluttered into the sky.

The horse hair shrinked like a hedgehog's spines in cold weather,

Strong bow cannot be opened with a cold hand.

The crisis of the country reveals moral integrity,

The social turmoil shows loyalty.

Dedicated to fight against the enemy to serve the Lord,

Sacrifice for the country and die on the battlefield.

《结客少年场行》诗歌赏析：

这首诗作寄托了鲍照强烈的怀才不遇之感和不满现实的愤慨之情。鲍照这首诗作寄托了他不满现实的愤慨之情。从诗中时间跨度之大和内容的深沉来看，可推断为鲍照的晚期作品。诗歌对官僚贵族的豪奢生活表示了蔑视和嘲讽，同时抒发了自己坎坷遭遇的牢骚。此诗一出，后人拟作纷至，影响颇深远。

An excursion on Youth

The poem embodies Bao Zhao’s indignation of his unrecognized talents and dissatisfaction with the reality.Judging from the time span and the depth of the content in the poem, it can be inferred to be Bao Zhao’s works in later years. The poem expresses contempt and ridicule for the extravagant life of bureaucratic aristocrats, and meanwhile expresses his unsuccessful complaints. As soon as this poem came out, it was imitated by later generations and has a profound impact.

骢马金络头，锦带佩吴钩。

失意杯酒间，白刃起相仇。

追兵一旦至，负剑远行游。

去乡三十载，复得还旧丘。

升高临四关，表里望皇州。

九涂平若水，双阙似云浮。

扶宫罗将相，夹道列王侯。

日中市朝满，车马若川流。

击钟陈鼎食，方驾自相求。

今我独何为？坎壈怀百忧。

The green and white horsewith gold bridle,

With a hook on the brocade belt.

Between the banquets a bit of dissatisfaction,

Fight each other with blades.

The officers and soldiers who were hunting were on the way,

They absconded with swords and flew away.

Leave hometown for thirty years,

Finally returned back.

Ascend to a high place to overlook the Four Gates,

Look at the capital inside and outside.

The roads are as smooth as water,

Palaces hover as high as clouds.

The general's houses listed next to the palace,

Pavilions belong to the lord of the princes.

At noon the city was full of people,

Horses and carts shuttled like endless stream.

Ring the bell and dine out,

Crowded with horses and carts.

What am I doing alone today?

Poors have countless sorrows.

《东门行》诗歌赏析：

诗歌用追叙的手法，写离别情景。诗人先是用“伤禽”作比，点明自己离别时的心情，然后具体述说离别时的情景，离别之声令行人感伤，送行和御车之人都黯然神伤溘然泪下。人们洒泪作别，临去时还时不时地回头告别。依依惜别之意尽在不言中。诗歌淋漓尽致地抒发了诗人对家乡的眷恋，具有普遍的人生意义。诗歌用词清新，饱含深情，可称为古今伤别诗之典范。

A Poem on Parting

The poem describes the parting scene in a retrospective way. The poet first uses “injured birds” as a comparison to point out the poet ' s mood at parting, and then specifically describes the scene at the time of parting. The sound of parting makes the pedestrians sad, and people who saw off and drive the cart were sad and weeping. People shed tears to say goodbye, and looked back from time to time when they left. It was unnecessary to anything to express the meaning of farewell. The poem vividly expresses the poet' s nostalgia for his hometown, which has universal meaning in life. The poems are fresh in language and full of affection, and can be a model of ancient and modern poems.

伤禽恶弦惊，倦客恶离声。

离声断客情，宾御皆涕零。

涕零心断绝，将去复还诀。

一息不相知，何况异乡别。

遥遥征驾远，杳杳落日晚。

居人掩闺卧，行子夜中饭。

野风吹秋木，行子心肠断。

食梅常苦酸，衣葛常苦寒。

丝竹徒满坐，忧人不解颜。

长歌欲自慰，弥起长恨端。

Injured birds fear the bowstrings,

Weary passengers fear the music of parting.

Farewell songs broke the hearts of the guests,

Guests burst into tears.

With tears streaming down the face and a broken heart,

Looked back to say goodbye before leaving.

There was still suspense after a moment of separation,

Let alone far away from home.

The carriages and horses went farther and farther,

The sun was setting and it was late.

Peopleclosed the door and lay down,

Wanderers ate in the mid- night.

The wild wind blew the woods in late autumn,

Sad and heartbroken.

It was bitter to eat plums and cold to wear ko-hemp clothes.

Wanderers played the stringsfor nothing,

They were not happy but worried.

Sang a song to comfort,

But it provoked thoughts of melancholy.

《还都道中作》诗歌赏析：

宋文帝元嘉十七年（440），临川王刘义庆由江州刺史调任南兖州刺史，由浔阳（今江西九江）乘船赴广陵（今江苏扬州）就任。时鲍照在刘义庆幕下任国侍郎之职，随同前往，在途中作了此诗。诗篇描写旅途景色，抒发思念故乡的情绪，境界浑阔，意绪愁惨。诗中用了大量对仗，字句精心雕琢，但不失其流畅。

A Tour

In the seventeenth year of Yuanjia, Emperor Wen of the Southern Song Dynasty (440), the King of Linchuan Liu Yiqing was transferred from Jiangzhou Governor to Nanyanzhou Governor, and went from Xunyang (now Jiujiang, Jiangxi Province) to Guangling (now Yangzhou, Jiangsu Province) by boat. At that time Baozhao served as Guoshi Lang under Liu Yiqing, accompanied him and wrote the poem on the way. The poem describes the scenery of the journey and expresses the emotion of missing hometown. The realm is vast and the mood is sad. The poem used a lot of confrontation and the sculpting of words and sentences is exquisite, but without losing their fluency.

昨夜宿南陵，今旦入芦洲。

客行惜日月，崩波不可留。

侵星赴早路，毕景逐前俦。

鳞鳞夕云起，猎猎晓风遒。

腾沙郁黄雾，翻浪扬白鸥。

登舻眺淮甸，掩泣望荆流。

绝目尽平原，时见远烟浮。

倏悲坐还合，俄思甚兼秋。

未尝违户庭，安能千里游。

谁令乏古节，贻此越乡忧。

I stayed in Nanling last night,

The boat entered Luzhou early this morning.

Cherish time when we were away,

Water cannot stay where they rush.

In the morning headed forward with stars above,

At sunset chase the companion boat.

The scale-like sunset clouds appeared slowly,

Wind blew vigorously and violently.

The dust rose like yellow mist,

Waves rolled up and lifted up only white gulls.

I boarded the bow and looked at the Jianghuai countryside,

Covering my face and weeping at Jingchu River.

Looking at the vast plain with all my eyes,

I saw clouds and smoke floating in the distance from time to time.

Suddenly gathered quickly,

Nostalgia for more than three years.

I have never left my home to go out,

How can I travel thousands of miles away.

Who let me lack the moral integrity of the ancients,

Leave the sorrow far away from my hometown.

《玩月城西门解中》诗歌赏析：

这首诗是鲍照任秣陵县令时所写。诗歌描写六月十五夜宴的情景。诗人首创“蛾眉”“玉钩”两词以状摹新月之形，贴切形象，后人遂沿用不衰。诗歌表现出诗人厌倦宦游，欲借公余宴饮聊以消忧之意。诗歌诗篇琢句精工，气势流贯。

A Banquet

The poem was written by Bao Zhao when he was appointed as the magistrate of Moling County. The poem writes about the banquet on the night of the fifteenth day in June. The poet used two words “crooked eyebrow” and “jade hook” to imitate the shape of the crescent moon, which was suitable and vivid, and later generations continued to use them. The poem expressed the poet’s being tired of offical travel and wanting to take a banquet and chat to alleviate worries. The poem was exquisitely crafted and vigorous and full of sentiment.

始见西南楼，纤纤如玉钩。

末映东北墀，娟娟似蛾眉。

蛾眉蔽珠栊，玉钩隔琐窗。

三五二八时，千里与君同。

夜移衡汉落，徘徊帷户中。

归华先委露，别叶早辞风。

客游厌苦辛，仕子倦飘尘。

休浣自公日，宴慰及私辰。

蜀琴抽白雪，郢曲发阳春。

肴干酒未缺，金壶启夕沦。

回轩驻轻盖，留酌待情人。

The crescent moon first appears in the southwest building,

Like a jade hook.

Finally reflects on the steps of the northeast,

Bright and beautiful like a crooked eyebrow.
The eyebrows are hidden by the gorgeous windows,
The jade hooks are isolated by small windows.
At the Fifteenth and sixteenth nights, the bright moon is right in the sky,
Shine the light all over the world.
As the night goes by, the Big Dipper Milky Way sinks,
The moonlight lingers in the curtains.
Flowers first wither due to dew,
Leaves fall back to their roots due to the wind.
Visitors have enough hard work outside,
Tired of the official career.
Get a free holiday, feast and seize this hour.
Play a Song Bai Xue with Shu Qin,
The Yingzhong song Yang Chunis played again.
After the dishes, there is still a lot of wine left,
The dripping of the copper pot indicates the end of the night.
Back to the carriage to stay for a moment,
Preserve the wine for the lover of my heart.

谢灵运（385—433），陈郡阳夏（今河南太康）人，南朝宋初文学家。谢玄之孙，世称谢康乐。谢灵运少而好学，博览群书。后移籍会稽，傍山带江，尽幽居之美。与隐士王弘之、孔淳之等纵放为娱。远近钦慕，名动京师。卒年四十九，有集二十卷。谢灵运是我国山水诗的鼻祖，作品多描写山川景色，自然逼真，文采丰富。

Xie Lingyun (385-433) was born in Yangxia, Chen Jun (now Taikang, Henan Province). He is a litterateur in the early Southern Song Dynasty. He is grandson of Xie Xuan. People called him Xie Kangle. Xie Lingyun was quick in learning and read a wide range of books. Later he moved to Kuaiji and lived in the mountains and rivers, enjoying the beauty of a secluded residence. He indulged in entertainment with the hermits Wang

Hongzhi and Kong Chunzhi. He was admired by people from far and near and well-known in the capital. He died at the age of forty-nine. There are 20 volumes in his collection. Xie Lingyun is the originator of landscape poetry in China. His works mostly describe mountains and rivers, which are natural and lifelike, and rich in literary talent.

《过始宁墅》诗歌赏析：

始宁墅在始宁县（今浙江上虞东南），又名西庄，是谢灵运的庄园，其祖父、父亲皆葬于始宁县，并有故宅及别墅在此。本诗主要是写作者去永嘉任太守时，经过始宁别墅的游观之乐，并表现自己不久就要归来隐居的心愿。诗中写景精工细腻，诗句清丽自然。

Passing Shining Villa

Shining Villa was located in Shining County (now southeast of Shangyu, Zhejiang Province). It was also called Xizhuang and was the manor of Xie Lingyun. Lingyun’s grandfather and father were buried in Shining County, where there were his old houses and villas. This poem is mainly about when the poet went to Yongjia to serve as the satrap, he visited Shining Villa and expressed his wish to return to live in seclusion soon. The scenery in the poem is exquisite and the verse is clear and natural.

束发怀耿介，逐物遂推迁。

违志似如昨，二纪及兹年。

缁磷谢清旷，疲薾惭贞坚。

拙疾相倚薄，还得静者便。

剖竹守沧海，枉帆过旧山。

山行穷登顿，水涉尽洄沿。

岩峭岭稠叠，洲萦渚连绵。

白云抱幽石，绿筱媚清涟。

葺宇临回江，筑观基曾巅。

挥手告乡曲，三载期归旋。

且为树枌槚，无令孤愿言。

Be honest and simple in childhood,

The pursuit of fame and fortune gradually changed.

The disobedience seems to begin yesterday,

It has been twenty-four years since counted down.

The mediocre people far away from the noble,

The inferior people are ashamed of their firmness.

The clumsy mind and weak body are interdependent,

Fortunately, the benevolent and wise man instructs me.

Wise emperor gave orders to guard the seaside,

Set a light sail around the bay to pass through the homeland.

Climb the coast along the mountain,

Climb the peaks and descend the valleys,

Sail on a flat boat across the clear stream up and down.

The mountains and ridges overlap steeply on land,

The continuous islands and islets linger on the water.

The thick white clouds surround the deep and secluded rocks,

The green bamboo covers the clear ripples.

Build a house facing the crooked river,

The construction of the platform is based on the high peaks,

Wave goodbye to relatives and neighbors,

Return home as an official for three years.

Please plant catalpa trees and white elm for me,

I will never violate this vow of return.

《南楼中望所迟客》诗歌赏析：

南楼在谢灵运的出生地始宁（今浙江上虞）。这首诗抒写在南楼等候佳宾而佳宾迟迟未至的心情。诗歌婉转陈述，感情真挚而急切，语言也不甚雕琢，在其诗作中显得比较突出。

A Late Guest in the South Tower

The South Tower was in Shining(now Shangyu, Zhejiang Province), the birthplace of Xie Lingyun. The poem expresses the feelings of waiting for the guests in the South Tower, but the guests have not arrived. The poem states tactfully. The feelings are sincere and eager, and the language is not very polished, which is more prominent in his poems.

杳杳日西颓，漫漫长路迫。

登楼为谁思，临江迟来客。

与我别所期，期在三五夕。

圆景早已满，佳人犹未适。

即事怨睽携，感物方凄戚。

孟夏非长夜，晦明如岁隔。

瑶华未堪折，兰苕已屡摘。

路阻莫赠问，云何慰离析？

搔首访行人，引领冀良觌。

The gloom of the sun gradually sinks to the west,

The road is long, and I'm sad and distressed.

Whom I miss when climbing up the building and looking into the distance?

The belated guest near the river.

It was agreed when we parted,

The fifteenth day would be the time for gathering.

The moon in the sky has long been round like a jade plate,

But the beautiful woman never returned.

Faced with it, I can't help but leave with resentment,

The scene often lead to grief.

The night in Apirl is not long,

But one night is like a year apart.

Before jade-white flowerscould be picked,

The orchid had been picked again and again.

But the road is too dangerous to be delivered,

How can we comfort this parting feeling?

Scratch the head and ask the pedestrians from the north to the south,

Looking around, hoping to see the lady.

《登江中孤屿》诗歌赏析：

孤屿是永嘉（今浙江温州）奇景，是永嘉江中的一个洲渚。谢灵运游览登临以后，当地人建亭其上。此诗所以能被萧统收入《文选》，与作者善于选择景点，并能描绘其特色有关。孤屿山独立江心，在云日辉映水天一色的背景下，呈现出一种幽静的审美境界。谢灵运以精炼的诗句，将景物的特色摄入诗中，使读者如亲临其境，获得幽静异常、超尘脱俗的艺术享受。

这首诗描写秀美的江中孤屿，同时借景言志，表达了诗人不与世俗相合，欲游仙从道的思想情绪。山水之间汇集了天地的灵气，蕴含着纯真的自然意趣，但是却不能为世人所欣赏，这是世人的悲哀。由此，诗人神游万里，他觉得求仙悟道才是自己真正的归宿所在。

同其他诗歌一样，这首诗也是借助于景物的描写抒写诗人的心志，但实际上，这只是诗人苦闷心情的一种宣泄，是诗人仕途失意后的一种情感寄托，诗人并非真的想这样做。此外，从艺术上讲，瑰丽的景物描写，奇特的想象及精美的语言，也是本诗的特色。

Solitary Island in the River

SolitaryIsland is a wonderful sight of Yongjia (now Wenzhou, Zhejiang Province). It is a continent in Yongjia River. After Xie Lingyun’s boarding, the locals built a pavilion on it. The reason why this poem can be included in “Wen Xuan” by Xiao Tong is related to the poet’s good choice of scenic spots and his ability to describe its characteristics. SolitaryIsl and stands alone in the center of the river, presenting a secluded aesthetic realm under the background of cloudsand the sun which reflects the water and sky. Xie Lingyun takes the characteristics of the scenery into the poems with refined verses, so that the readers can appreciate the quiet and supernatural artistic enjoyment as if they are really on the scene.

This poem describes the beautiful Solitary Island, and expresses the poet' s emotions that he does not conform to the world and wants to travel as immortals. Between the mountains and rivers, the aura of heaven and earth is brought together, which contains pure and natural interest, but it cannot be appreciated by people. This is the people' s sorrow. As a result, the poet wandered thousands of miles away, and he felt that seeking immortality and enlightenment was his true destination.

Like other poems, this poem also uses the description of the scenery to express the poet' s mind. But in fact, this is only a catharsis of the poet' s depressed mood, and an emotional sustenance after the poet' s frustration in his official career. The poet does not really want to do so. In addition, from an artistic point of view, magnificent scenery description, peculiar imagination and exquisite language are also the characteristics of the poem.

江南倦历览，江北旷周旋。

怀新道转迥，寻异景不延。

乱流趋正绝，孤屿媚中川。

云日相辉映，空水共澄鲜。

表灵物莫赏，蕴真谁为传？

想像昆山姿，缅邈区中缘。

始信安期术，得尽养生年。

The famous scenic spots at south of the Yangtze River have been tired of seeing,

But north of the Yangtze River has not been visited for a long time.

Exploring new scenery always makes me feel that the road is long,

Looking for wonders feels that time is short.

Cross the Qingjiang water and board Solitary Island,

Solitary Island Mountain is the most beautiful scene in the middle of the river.

The colorful clouds and the red sun reflect each other,

The clear river and the blue sky stay clean and fresh.

No one appreciates the beauty of SolitaryIsland,

Who knows immortals hidden in the caves.

From Solitary Island, we can imagine the Kunshan fairyland,

Remotely isolated from the worldly edge of the dust.

It is only here that I believe that Anqi Fangshu,

It really makes people prolong life.

《斋中读书》诗歌赏析：

这首诗作于永嘉郡（在今浙江温州）书斋。永初三年（422）七月，谢灵运从太子左卫率出为永嘉太守。因苦闷和忧虑，抵达永嘉不久，即患病卧床，直到第二年春天才算痊愈。至秋，称病去职。这首诗叙写诗人在永嘉养病期间的生活，透露出思想上“仕”与“隐”的矛盾，最后表示要到老庄达生之道的哲理中去寻求解脱，以避免身心的过度操劳。

Reading in the Study

This poem was written in the study room of Yongjia County (in Wenzhou, Zhejiang Province). In July of the third year of Yongchu (422), Xie Lingyun transferred from Taizi Zuowei to Yongjia Taishou. Due to depression and anxiety, soon after arriving in Yongjia, he fell ill and stayed in bed until the next spring. By the end of autumn, he resigned with the excuse of his illness. This poem describes the life during his recovery period, revealing the contradiction between “officialdom” and “seclusion” in ideology, and finally expresses the need to seek liberation from Lao Zhuang’s Taoism to avoid excessive physical and mental stress.

昔余游京华，未尝废丘壑。

矧乃归山川，心迹双寂漠。

虚馆绝诤讼，空庭来鸟雀。

卧疾丰暇豫，翰墨时间作。

怀抱观古今，寝食展戏谑。

既笑沮溺苦，又哂子云阁。

执戟亦以疲，耕稼岂云乐。

万事难并欢，达生幸可托。

When I worked in the capital,

I never forgot to live in seclusion in the future.

Besides, I have returned to the mountains and rivers,

Lonely in mood.

There was no sound of disputes in the premises,

A flock of birds fly in the empty courtyard.

Long term bedridden recuperates a lot of leisure time,

Write poems and essays from time to time.

With books in arms, I survey the past and the present,

Make fun when I sleep and eat.

Not only laugh at drowning in the hard work of farming,

But also laugh at Yang Xiong jumped out of Tianlu Pavilion.

A small official is exhausted all day long,

There is no joy in farming either.

Rare things in the world make people happy.

Fortunately, there is a way of life can be trusted.

《入彭蠡湖口》诗歌赏析：

彭蠡湖即今江西的鄱阳湖。彭蠡湖口在今江西九江湖口西，湖口也就是鄱阳湖与长江的交汇处。这首诗当是谢灵运往临川途中，自长江入彭蠡口所作。诗歌记述了诗人的所见所感，也是他山水诗的代表作之一。

刘宋统治集团出于削弱士族势力的目的，一直对有才能、性情倔强的谢灵运存着戒心，让他归田，觉得失去控制，不能放心；召他入仕，又不予重用，未尽其才。谢灵运处于归田不得，出仕不愿的两难境地。此次赴临川任内史，更非其所愿，但迫于形势，不得不行，以致苦闷忧愁之情，与日俱深。诗中写景叙事，都带上浓厚的忧郁色彩。这些分析，都准确地触及了诗中深沉的忧思愁情。

Entering the Mouth of Pengli Lake

Pengli Lake is Poyang Lake in Jiangxi. The mouth of Pengli Lake is in the west of the mouth of Jiujiang Lake in Jiangxi Province, and the mouth is also the intersection of Poyang Lake and the Yangtze River. This poem should have been written by Xie Lingyun from the Yangtze River into the mouth of Pengli Lake on the way to Linchuan. The poem states what the poet sees and feels, and it is also one of his masterpieces of landscape poems.

For the general purpose of weakening the power of the gentry, the Liu Song ruling clique has always been wary of talented and stubborn Xie Lingyun. If they asked him to return to the fields, it seemed that he was out of control and they can' t rest assured. The Liu Song ruling clique asked him to enter the officialdom, but they didn' t put him in an important position and Xie failed to display his talent. Thus Xie Lingyun was in a dilemma that he could not return to the fields and did not want to hold a post. The appointment to Linchuan Neishi this time was not what he wanted, but due to the situation, he had to do it. So his feelings of depression and sorrow have deepened with each passing day. Scenery and narratives in the poems are full of melancholy. These analyses accurately touched the deep sadness in the poem.

客游倦水宿，风潮难具论。
洲岛骤回合，圻岸屡崩奔。
乘月听哀狖，浥露馥芳荪。
春晚绿野秀，岩高白云屯。
千念集日夜，万感盈朝昏。
攀崖照石镜，牵叶入松门。
三江事多往，九派理空存。
灵物郄珍怪，异人秘精魂。
金膏灭明光，水碧辍流温。

徒作千里曲，弦绝念弥敦。

I am tired of the long voyage by boat.

The wind and waves in the river are hard to talk about.

The huge waves rush across the island and then merges,

Hitting the river bank and collapsing into the center of the river.

Under the moonlightlisten to the wailing of the monkey,

The dewdrops on the vanilla spread the fragrance.

In late spring, the plains lush with green grass,

White clouds gather on the high mountains and rocks.

Thousands of thoughts unsolved day and night,

All kinds of sadness cannot be eliminated in morning and dusk.

Climb the peak of the cliff to contrast with the stone mirror,

Walk through the jungle and pull branches and leaves into the pine gate.

The three rivers are at a loss,

Difficult to determine where the nine tributaries are.

Spiritual objects and immortals are secretive souls,

Unwilling to appear to visitors.

The golden cream extinguishes the bright light,

Blue water condenses its warmth.

I play the famous piece A Thousand Milesin vain,

At the end I miss it more deeply.

《七里濑》诗歌赏析：

此诗是在南朝宋永初三年，谢灵运为永嘉太守，赴任途中路过桐庐县富春江畔的七里濑有感而发，作了此诗。诗歌描绘了沿江的景物，抒发了诗人心中的郁愤和他不与时代同流的情怀。

谢灵运是在怀才不遇的情况下前往永嘉的，其心情之抑郁苦闷可想而知。诗人临江远眺，孤独感油然而生，后来诗人在七里濑自然美的启示下获得了心灵的超越，诗人由景及人，反观自身，抒发感慨，表露心志，写对隐居生活的向往。全诗的重点是淳朴的景色之美。诗歌由景及情，情与景交相辉映，景物描写中也透露着诗人的情思。谢灵运的思想与同时期的陶潜和以后的孟浩然、王维都有所不同，但对大自然的热爱，使他成为我国第一位山水诗人。

Qili Lai

This poem was written in the first three years of Yongchu in the Southern Song Dynasty. Xie Lingyun was appointed as the satrap of Yongjia.He passed by Qili Lai in the Fuchun River in Tonglu County on the way to his post. He wrote this poem to express his feelings. The poem depicts the scenery along the river, expressing the anger in the poet’s heart and his feelings of not keeping up with the times.

Xie Lingyun went to Yongjia under the circumstances of being unrecognized for his talents. His depression can be seen easily. The poet overlooked the river, feeling lonely spontaneously. Later the poet achieved spiritual transcendence under the enlightenment of natural beauty. The poet reflects on himself from the scenery and expresses his feelings and aspirations. He wrote about his yearning for living in seclusion. The focus of the whole poem is the beauty of the simple scenery. The poem writes from scenery to emotion, which complement each other.The description of the scenery also reveals the poet’s sentiment. Xie Lingyun’s thoughts are different from those of Tao Qian at the same time and Meng Haoran and Wang Wei in later periods, but his love for nature made him finally our country’s first landscape poet.

羁心积秋晨，晨积展游眺。
孤客伤逝湍，徒旅苦奔峭。
石浅水潺湲，日落山照曜。
荒林纷沃若，哀禽相叫啸。
遭物悼迁斥，存期得要妙。
既秉上皇心，岂屑末代诮。
目睹严子濑，想属任公钓。

谁谓古今殊，异世可同调。

The traveler is full of melancholy inthe autumn dawn,

He stretched his eyebrows to relieve the melancholy.

The lonely travler feels sentimental when seeing the water passing by,

Feel distressed when he walks in the steep shore and collapses.

The stone in riverbed has clear and shallow water flowing through,

The red light shines on the mountains in the west sunset dusk.

In the wildernesstrees are densely leafy,

The birds in the dense forest fly and scream.

Suffer relegation and go to Yongjia,

Think for long, I hope to get the mystery.

With the sincerity and honesty for the first king,

Why cares the later generations will ridicule?

Saw clear waves of Yan Zi Lai surging,

Think of Ren Gongzi fish in the East China Sea.

Who can say that ancient and modern people have different personalities,

They can still play the same tune.

《富春渚》诗歌赏析：

此诗为谢灵运在永初三年（422）被迫离京都去永嘉经过富阳（今属浙江）时所作。被吴均赞为“奇山异水，天下独绝”的富春江，在此诗中，只有云雾、惊浪和险岸，色彩黯淡，景物险恶。它既有作者当时心情的投影，也具有象征意义，象征作者当时所处的险恶政治环境。诗的抒情部分较长，表现了作者在极端苦闷中求解脱、找出路的心境。有人说此诗中的浓雾、惊浪、险岸是徐羡之等凶险政客的拟物写照，也不无道理。

Fuchun Zhu

This poem was written by Xie Lingyun in the third year of Yongchu (422) when he was forced to leave the capital for Yongjia, passing through Fuyang (now Zhejiang Province). Fuchun River is praised by Wu Jun as "wonderful in the mountains and rivers, unique in the world" . In this poem, there are only clouds and fog, thundering waves and dangerous shores. The colors are dim and the scenery is sinister. It is not only a projection of the author' s mood at the time, but also has a symbolic meaning, symbolizing the sinister political environment the poet was in at that time. The lyric part of the poem is long, which shows the author' s mood of relieving and finding a way out of extreme depression. It is said that the dense fog, thunderous waves, and dangerous shores in this poem are imitations of dangerous politicians such as Xu Xianzhi, which is not unreasonable.

宵济渔浦潭，旦及富春郭。

定山缅云雾，赤亭无淹薄。

溯流触惊急，临圻阻参错。

亮乏伯昏分，险过吕梁壑。

洊至宜便习，兼山贵止托。

平生协幽期，沦踬困微弱。

久露干禄请，始果远游诺。

宿心渐申写，万事俱零落。

怀抱既昭旷，外物徒龙蠖。

I passed by Yupu Lake last night,

Arrived at Fuchun fortress this morning.

Wangding Mountain is covered by clouds and fog,

No ferry to park after Chiting.

Crashing down the current and violent waves,

The dangers of Linqu'an are mixed.

Not as wise as Bohun,

Adventures surpassed Luliang Mountain Gully.

Already familiar with the ups and downs,

I'm contented and happy with my duty.

There is a secret appointment in his life,

Suffer setbacks for a long time.

I expressed my wish to guard the county in early years,

Only now has I fulfilled promise to travel far away.

Although the life history gradually stated,

Good times is wasted, everything is gone.

As long as I'm open-minded and magnanimous,

Why do I care my looking like an inchworm?

《登池上楼》诗歌赏析：

谢灵运被贬为永嘉太守后，心理上受到了打击，在郡一周，就因疾去职，直到第二年初春，才大病初愈，这首诗即是诗人病起登楼的所见所感。诗歌表现了诗人政治上不得意的苦闷及决心隐居的志向。

本诗有叙有议，有写景有抒情，情感的表达真实不空洞。诗人在诗作中发泄了官场失意的牢骚。诗人以潜虬和飞鸿作比，表明自己才志高远和进退两难的境地。接下来诗人追叙了被贬到永嘉，后一病不起，直到第二年春天才大病初愈。然后他把目光投向现在，写病起登楼的所见所闻：初春的阳光赶走了冬风，池畔春草丛生。诗人目睹冬去春来的变化，联想到古代伤春的诗歌，心情又转向了忧郁，尽管如此他还是要效法古人，不移归隐之志。

Chishang Tower

After Xie Lingyun was relegated to the satrap of Yongjia, he was psychologically shocked. After a week in his post, he was resigned because of the illness. It was not until the spring of next year that he recovered from serious illness. This poem is what the poet saw and felt when he got sick and went upstairs. The poem expresses the poet's political depression and determination to live in seclusion.

The poem has both narration and discussion, scene description and lyricism. The expression of emotion is true and not empty. The poet vents the grievances of official frustration in the poem. The poet compares himself to the dragon hiding in deep waters and the flying swan goose to show his high ambition and dilemma. The poet recounted that he was demoted to Yongjia, and he fell into illness. He didn' t recover from serious illness until the spring of the following year. Then he turned to the present and wrote about what he saw and heard in the tower: the sun in the early spring had driven away the winter breeze, and spring grass grew by the pool. The poet witnessed the changes from winter to spring, and thought of ancient poems that grieved spring, and his mood turned to melancholy. However, he still wanted to imitate the ancients and stay in seclusion.

潜虬媚幽姿，飞鸿响远音。

薄霄愧云浮，栖川怍渊沉。

进德智所拙，退耕力不任。

徇禄反穷海，卧痾对空林。

衾枕昧节候，褰开暂窥临。

倾耳聆波澜，举目眺岖嵚。

初景革绪风，新阳改故阴。

池塘生春草，园柳变鸣禽。

祁祁伤豳歌，萋萋感楚吟。

索居易永久，离群难处心。

持操岂独古，无闷征在今。

The dragon lurks in the deep waters to enjoy itself,

The swan goose fly high in the sky and made long sounds.

Lift up the sky with shame,

I can’t live in the deep blue waves.

I want to make a contribution,

But lament my clumsiness and lack of talents,

Return to the pastoral because of weakness.

In pursuit of fame I came to this remote seaside,

In bed facing the desolate forest all day long.

Covered with a quilt, sleeping on a pillow,

Not knowing the changes of the seasons and climate.

Listen to the noise of the sea and the sky in the distance,

I look at the rolling mountains.

The sun in the new year drove off the remaining wind in winter,

Bright spring replaces gloomy winter.

Fresh green spring grass grows on the edge of the pond,

Returning birds chirp on the branches of the garden willow.

People reminds me of sad songs,

The lush spring grass reminds me of melancholy Chuyin.

Living alone is long and difficult to be dispatched,

Away from friends, difficult to get peace.

It seems only ancient people can adhere to moral integrity,,

My living in seclusion without boredomis the proof.

《庐陵王墓下》诗歌赏析：

宋武帝刘裕次子刘义真，封庐陵王。刘裕死后少帝刘义福即位，庐陵王与谢灵运、颜延之等友善。少帝失德，徐羡之等密谋废立，按次序当立庐陵王。徐羡之因嫌以前劝庐陵王疏远谢、颜未听，认为他不能担当社稷重任，遂先奏废为庶人，徙新安郡。后徐羡之等派人杀庐陵王于徙所。谢灵运因为此事亦被谗为欲立庐陵王而迁永嘉太守。宋文帝即位，诛徐羡之等，征谢灵运为秘书监。此诗即召还途中过庐陵王墓作。

Under the Tomb of King Luling

Liu Yizhen, the second son of Liu Yu，Emperor Wu of the Southern Song Dynasty, was named King Luling. After Liu Yu's death, the young emperor Liu Yifu ascended the throne.The King of Luling and Xie Lingyun, Yan Yanzhi are close. The young emperor lost his morals, Xu Xianzhi and others conspired to abolish the establishment and make the King of Luling in order. Xu Xianzhi was suspicious of persuading the king of Luling to estrange Xie and Yan, but he did not obey. Wu believed that King of Luling could not take on the important task, so he first dismissed him as a civilian and ordered him to moved to Xin' an County. Later, Xu Xianzhi and others sent people to kill the King of Luling at the residence. Because of this incident, Xie Lingyun was also relegated to the satrap of Yongjia. Emperor Wen of Song ascended the throne, punished Xu Xianzhi, and ordered Xie Lingyun to be Mishu Jian. This poem is written by Poet in front of the tomb of King Luling on his way to post.

晓月发云阳，落日次朱方。
含凄泛广川，洒泪眺连岗。
眷言怀君子，沉痛结中肠。
道消结愤懑，运开申悲凉。
神期恒若在，德音初不忘。
徂谢易永久，松柏森已行。
延州协心许，楚老惜兰芳。
解剑竟何及，抚坟徒自伤。
平生疑若人，通蔽互相妨。
理感深情恸，定非识所将。
脆促良可哀，夭枉特兼常。
一随往化灭，安用空名扬。
举声泣已洒，长叹不成章。

The morning moon was still in the sky when we set off from Yunyang,
We stop to rest in Zhufang at sunset.
I took a boat across the wide river sadly,
Watched the rolling hills in the distance with tears.

Imissgood friend when looking back on the past,

The deep sorrow has been stuck in heart for a long time.

The era when the villain was in power is so irritating,

The new opening of a nation voices sadness in my heart.

Your heroic spirits remains forever between heaven and earth,

I will never forget your face and voice.

It's so long ago when you're gone,

The tomb is already dense with trees and cypresses.

In those years Ji Zha intentionally presented a sword to Xu Jun,

Chu Lao once mourned over Gong Sheng's death.

How does it matter to give a sword after Xu Jun's death?

Is Gong Sheng mourning the grave in vain?

I've always been puzzled by it in the past.

How could Ji Zha and Chu Lao be in great grief?

Now I have come to understand that the grief of man's heart,

Is definitelybeyond the control of reason.

How sad is your death at young age,

Even more unjust and miserable than the average person's death.

Once you have disappeared in the world,

What is the use of all the posthumous seals!

With a long sightears flowed from my eyes,

The sadness and chaos make me no longer write poems of mourning.

《从游京口北固应诏》诗歌赏析：

公元 420 年，刘裕代晋称帝，建立南朝宋王朝，在位三年。此诗是谢灵运跟从刘裕游京口北固山时所作。因为是应诏之作，所以一开始便是颂扬之词，诗歌的中间部分写景，最后以愧食君禄为由而有隐归之意，实际上反映了谢灵运以东晋士族入侍刘宋新王朝的疑惧心理。京口，今江苏镇江。北固，山名。

A Tour to Beigu Mountain in Jingkou

In 420, Liu Yu proclaimed himself emperor in the Jin Dynasty and established the Southern Song Dynasty and reigned for three years. This poem was written by Xie Lingyun when he followed Liu Yu to visit Beigu Mountain in Jingkou. Because it was a work of the edict, it was full of praise at the beginning, and the scene was written in the middle part of the poem. The poem shows the poet's intension of seclusion on the grounds of being ashamed to the salary in the end. It actually reflected Xie Lingyun's fear to serve the new Liu Song Dynasty as the Eastern Jin gentry. Jingkou is in Zhenjiang, Jiangsu Province. Beigu is the name of a mountain.

玉玺戒诚信，黄屋示崇高。

事为名教用，道以神理超。

昔闻汾水游，今见尘外镳。

鸣笳发春渚，税銮登山椒。

张组眺倒景，列筵瞩归潮。

远岩映兰薄，白日丽江皋。

原隰荑绿柳，墟囿散红桃。

皇心美阳泽，万象咸光昭。

顾已枉维縶，抚志惭场苗。

工拙各所宜，终以返林巢。

曾是萦旧想，览物奏长谣。

White jade alert subjects loyal and trustworthy,

Golden cart cover the symbol of lofty status.

The use of the two things originates from the etiquette,

People's cultivation is soul edification.

In the past, Emperor Yao was heard to travel to the south of Fenshui,

Today, I see the holy emperor driving outside the dust.

The flute resounds on the water island in spring,

Cross the cart to follow the saint emperor to step up.

The big curtain overlooks the reflection in the river,

The feast is set as far as possible to send the horizon to the tide.

Light distant mountains, blue forest in smoke,

Bright daylight makes river bank more beautiful.

Plachou lowland willow spit new green,

Rural village burns its light.

Saint emperor praise the heaven and the earth,

Just like the sun shines the sky.

Considering my grace of occupying a high position,

I'm so ordinary to serve for servants.

There is a difference between craftiness and clumsiness,

Each should take his own place andit is better for me to retreat in mountains

I always think of the mountainsl hover over,

The beautiful scenery reminds me of the long song.

《晚出西射堂》诗歌赏析：

刘宋永初三年（422）七月，谢灵运出为永嘉太守，在永嘉任上一年，称疾去职。此诗当作于永初三年深秋。诗作前半写景，后半发泄被迁出都，与友人相离的牢骚。谢灵运在朝廷不被容纳，出京做永嘉太守，很感到不得意而苦闷。这首诗就是他独处西射堂，排遣内心郁积而作。射堂，在永嘉郡（今浙江温州）西。西射堂，即永嘉郡射堂，今西山寺。谢灵运善于从时空的流动去描写景物，诗中选择的物象都是他心绪情思的写照。

Out of Xishe Tang

In July of the third year of Yongchu (422) in Liu Song Dynasty, Xie Lingyun took up the post of the satrap of Yongjia. He served in Yongjia for a year and then was resigned for illness. This poem is written in the late autumn of the third year of Yongchu. The first half of the poem describes the scenery, and the second half vents the grievances of being moved out of the capital and separated from friends. Xie Lingyun's talent was not recognized by the royal court, and he was very disappointed and depressed when he went out of the capital to be the satrap of Yongjia. This poem was written by him alone in Xishe Tang, expressing his depression in his heart. Shetang is in the west of Yongjia County (now Wenzhou, Zhejiang Province). Xishe Tang, namely Yongjia County Shetang, is Xishan Temple today. Xie Lingyun is good at describing scenery from the flow of time and space, and the objects selected in the poem are all reflex of his emotions.

步出西城门，遥望城西岑。

连障叠巘崿，青翠杳深沉。

晓霜枫叶丹，夕曛岚气阴。

节往戚不浅，感来念已深。

羁雌恋旧侣，迷鸟怀故林。

含情尚劳爱，如何离赏心。

抚镜华缁鬓，揽带缓促衿。

安排徒空言，幽独赖鸣琴。

Walk out of the west gate,

Look at the west ridge far away.

The mountains roll up and down,

Green and dark.

Morning frost dyes maple red,

Evening haze gradually from the scene faint.

Sorrow grows deeper as time goes by,

Sadness strikes a person.

The female bird loses and misses its couple,

The lone bird loses way in the forest.

If birds are so kind,

How they make a man separate.

On the mirror the hair turns grey,

Haggard and worn, I am much thinner.

The past is arranged into empty talk,

Only to solve the loneliness by playing lute.

《游南亭》诗歌赏析：

此诗作于景平元年（423）初夏。诗作写久雨初霁时的欣悦，继而抒发岁月流逝，老病侵寻的感伤和归隐之志。是年秋，谢灵运即“称疾去职”。

此诗是继《登池上楼》之后，游南亭（在永嘉郡，今温州）而作。情志与前一首是贯通的。两首都是抒写外界物象的更替演变从而触发内心感慨。不过，前诗观照的物象都带有冬去春来的特征，此诗观照的物象则带有春夏之交的色调。

谢灵运对于节令时序的演变，具有一种特殊的艺术敏感，善于捕捉那些特征性鲜明的物象，准确地再现这种演变推移。他诗中的山水、草木、虫鱼，无不处在节令时序的演变推移之中，处在时间的流转之中。

A Tour to Nanting

This poem was written in the early summer of the first year of Jingping (423). The poem writes about the joy at the beginning of the rain stops, and then he expresses the sentimentality and his ambition of seclusion with the years passed by, old age and illness invaded. In the autumn of the year, Xie Lingyun was “resigned for illness” .

This poem was written by visiting Nanting (in Yongjia County, Wenzhou) after writing Chishang Tower. The emotion is connected with the previous Poem. The two poems describe the inner feelings triggered by the change and evolution of external objects. However, the objects observed in the previous poem all have the characteristics of winter’ s going and spring’ s coming, while the objects observed in this poem have the tones of the turn of spring and summer.

Xie Lingyun has a special artistic sensitivity to the evolution of seasons, and he is good at capturing those distinctive objects and accurately reproducing this evolution. The landscapes, plants, woods, insects, fishes in his poems are all in the evolution of the seasons, and in the circulation of time.

时竟夕澄霁，云归日西驰。

密林含余清，远峰隐半规。

久痗昏垫苦，旅馆眺郊歧。

泽兰渐被径，芙蓉始发池。

未厌青春好，已睹朱明移。

戚戚感物叹，星星白发垂。

药饵情所止，衰疾忽在斯。

逝将候秋水，息景偃旧崖。

我志谁与亮？赏心惟良知。

Days of continuous rain finally stops in a late spring evening,

Dark clouds dissipate and the sky reveals the slanting westward sun.

Thick forest after rain looks particularly refreshing,

The sun had sunk half behind the mountains, half hidden and half visible.

The long hours of rain makes me sick.

I look out the road in the countryside frequently in my guest house.

The path is gradually covered with lush green orchids,

The lotus in the pond is just beginning to bud.

I have not yet been able to enjoy the fun of spring days,

Summer comes in a hurry.

Time passes quickly, I often feel unceasinglysad,

Spotted grey hair has crept up cheek.

Songs, dances and feasts comfort my solitude,

I had been invaded by old diseases.

It is better to go back by boat when the autumn water rises,

Go to the old cliff to cultivate morality.

Who knows what I am thinking of?

The confidant is only the like-minded old friend.

《游赤石进帆海》诗歌赏析：

诗作写海上泛舟遨游的乐趣，结尾几句，在谈玄说理中也反映出谢灵运与刘宋王朝不相融洽，但又惮惧祸患的心理。

A Tour to Chishi

The poem writes about the pleasure of going boating on the sea, and the last few sentences also reflect the disharmony between Xie Lingyun and the Liu Song dynasty, showing hisfeelings of fearing disasters.

首夏犹清和，芳草亦未歇。

水宿淹晨暮，阴霞屡兴没。

周览倦瀛堧，况乃陵穷发。

川后时安流，天吴静不发。

扬帆采石华，挂席拾海月。

溟涨无端倪，虚舟有超越。

仲连轻齐组，子牟眷魏阙。

矜名道不足，适己物可忽。

请附任公言，终然谢夭伐。

Early summer was still cool and warm,

Grassy was alive.

I have slept in a boat on the sea for several days,

I have seen many changes between cloudy and sunny days.

I was tired of looking at the coastal scenery,

Not to mention coming to this remote border.

From time to time the turbulent current was stabilized behind the waves,

Waters and waves also quiet down.

I set sail and went out to the sea to pick onyx,

I hung up the tent to pick up the sea and moon.

The vast sea is boundless,

The canoe flies away from the coast to cruise freely.

Lu Zhonglian despised the title of Qi State,

But the son of Mou was in Jianghai but he missed the royal family.

Advocating famewill inevitably lead to the loss of Taoism,

Self-pleasing things outside the body can be forgotten.

Please remember the words Mr. Rensaid,

Don't be sawed by an axe like that early tree.

《石壁精舍还湖中作》诗歌赏析：

谢灵运在始宁县（今浙江上虞）有庄园，名始宁墅，傍巫湖，石壁精舍即在附近。这首诗描写的是始宁书斋附近的景色。诗歌的前半部分侧重描绘自然景色，后半部分侧重叙写人生哲理。诗作由光线的明暗写时间的推移，由时间的推移写物色的变幻，显示出诗人对大自然细微的观察力，对自然美准确的表现力。哲理由景色抽绎而出，说明人只有清心寡欲，超脱名利的纠葛，才能有本性的解放与自由，达到乐道长生。其实，这正是通过诗的形式来表现诗人对最高统治者不合作的态度。

Wuhu Lake

Xie Lingyun had a manor in Shining County (now Shangyu, Zhejiang province), named Shining Shu, next to Wuhu Lake, and Shibi Jingshe is nearby. This poem describes the scenery near Shining Study. The first half of the poem focuses on depicting natural scenery, and the second half focuses on narrating the philosophy of life. The poem writes the passage of time by the shade of the light, and then writes the change of colors by the passage of time, showing the poet's subtle observation of nature and the accurate expression of natural beauty. The philosophy is drawn out from the scenery, which shows that only with a pure heart and a lack of desire, detached from the entanglement of fame and fortune, can people have the liberation and freedom of nature and achieve longevity. In fact, it is precisely through the form of poetry to express the poet's uncooperative attitude towards the supreme ruler.

昏旦变气候，山水含清晖。
清晖能娱人，游子憺忘归。
出谷日尚早，入舟阳已微。
林壑敛暝色，云霞收夕霏。
芰荷迭映蔚，蒲稗相因依。
披拂趋南径，愉悦偃东扉。
虑澹物自轻，意惬理无违。
寄言摄生客，试用此道推。

The weather is so changeable in morning and evening,
The mountains and rivers are colorful and clear.
Beautiful mountains and rivers make people happy,
Those who enjoy the scenery indulge in it and forget to return.
The sun had just risen when the valley first came out,
It was already sunset on the back of the boat.
The twilight in the dense forest and valley gradually increases,
The flying sunset slowly disappears in the western sky.
The lotus leaves are bright and green,
Calamus and barnyard grass closely surround the lake shore.
Push aside the grass to find the way to the south and walk briskly,
Rest in the corridor and reminisce about the pleasure of this trip.

Think indifferently and naturally and never value trifles,

Satisfied that nature is in harmony with me.

There is a saying that people who keep in good health should listen,

Try this principle to cultivate nature in order to seek eternal life.

谢惠连（407—433），祖籍陈郡阳夏（今河南太康），南朝宋文学家。幼年聪颖，十岁能文。因居父丧时作诗赠会稽郡吏杜德灵，受到非议，长期不得入仕。元嘉七年（430），尚书仆射殷景仁爱其才，向宋文帝说情，为法曹参军。卒时年仅二十七岁。工诗赋，深得族兄谢灵运嘉赏，时人称“大小谢”。其诗赋《隋书·经籍志》著录有集六卷，已散佚。《宋书》《南史》有传。

Xie Huilian (407-433) was born in Yangxia, Chen Jun (now Taikang, Henan Province). He was a writer in the Southern Song Dynasty. He was clever at a young age and was able to write at the age of ten. Xie Huilian was criticized for composing a poem for Du Deling at the funeral of his father and was not allowed to enter the officialdom for a long time. In the seventh year of Yuanjia (430), Shangshu Pushe Yin Jingren appreciate Xie’s talent, and interceded with Emperor Wen of Song. Then Xie got a position as Facao Canjun. He was only twenty-seven years old when he died.He was good at poems and Cifu. His poems were praised by the family brother Xie Lingyun, and people called them “Junior Xie and Senior Xie.” His poetry Sui Shu · Ji Ji Zhi is recorded in six volumes, which has been scattered and lost. There are biographies in Song Shu and Nan Shi.

《秋怀》诗歌赏析：

谢惠连才思敏捷，却一生坎坷，曾被流放废黜，英年早逝。本诗当为后期所作，抒发平生忧患之怀。这是以政治前途为人生最终追求的古代诗人于压抑失意中的典型心理。时不我待，只有及时行乐，才是人生价值的真实体现，这是欲有所作为又不能有为的个性欲望的必然发泄之途。诗作因秋感怀，前半部分先通过寒蝉、唳雁、秋风、孤灯等景物的描写，渲染悲秋气氛，借以烘托自己对世事险恶、人生艰难的感慨。后半部分表明自己豁达的人生态度，是本诗题旨所在。

Chanting on Autumn

Xie Huilian was talented and quick in thinking. But he had a rough life. He was exiled and deposed and died in young age. This poem should be written in his later period, expressing his worries. This is the typical psychology of suppressing frustration of ancient poets whose political future is the ultimate pursuit of life. Time does not wait for people and only having fun in time is the true manifestation of the value of life. This is the inevitable way to vent the individual desires that want to do something but cannot do it. The poem is sentimental because of autumn. The first half of the poem expresses the sadness of autumn through the description of chilly cicadas, wild geese, autumn breeze, and lonely lanterns, so as to express feelings about the dangers of the world and the difficulties of life. The second half shows his generous attitude towards life, which is the theme of this poem.

平生无志意，少小婴忧患。

如何乘苦心，矧复值秋晏。

皎皎天月明，奕奕河宿烂。

萧瑟含风蝉，寥唳度云雁。

寒商动清闺，孤灯暧幽幔。

耿介繁虑积，展转长宵半。

夷险难豫谋，倚伏昧前算。

虽好相如达，不同长卿慢。

颇悦郑生偃，无取白衣宦。

未知古人心，且从性所玩。

宾至可命觞，朋来当染翰。

高台骤登践，清浅时陵乱。

颓魄不再圆，倾羲无两旦。

金石终消毁，丹青暂雕焕。

各勉玄发欢，无贻白首叹。

因歌遂成赋，聊用布亲串。

I have never had ambitions in life,

I have been entangled with worry since young age.

Why does a sad person like me face the withered late autumn?

A bright moon is shining brightly,

The Milky Way in the night sky is extremely splendid.

Sounds of cicadas in the bleak autumn wind are even more mournful,

The wild geese moving southward are chirping in the clouds.

The breath of cold autumn invads the boudoir,
A lone lamp dimly warms the deep curtain.

It is inevitable to be lonely and worried if not following the customs,

It's difficult to sleep until midnight.

Safety and danger are unpredictable,

But who can predict beforehand?

Although I appreciate Sima Xiangru's generosity,

I don't agree with his arrogance.

I also admire Zheng Jun's abandonment of officialdom,

But not envious of his favored "Baiyi Shangshu".

After allI can't fully understand thoughts of the ancients,

So live according to my own temperament.

When guests come, we toast and drink together,

When friends come, we write to each other.

I visitthe platform many times,

I go boating in the clear river from time to time.

The incomplete moon will not be round again in one month,

The setting sun will not reappear in the east in one day.

Mr.Ji's Zhong Ding stone carvings will eventually wear out,

The portraits of heroes will only be glorious for a while.

May we enjoy ourselves when we are young,

Not leave many regrets in vain when we are old.

Thinking of this, I write this poem,

Give it to relatives and friends to read.

《泛湖归出楼中玩月》诗歌赏析：

诗作描写了诗人湖中泛舟，夜归宴饮之后，觉得意犹未尽，继又出楼赏月，通过猿啼、夜露等物象的细腻描写，生动地烘托出了月夜的清幽。月下之江、月下之风、月下之山、月下之树，是淡远，是和柔，是飘逸，是清纯，是晶莹静穆的月的世界，是自然与人情和谐的意境。因而在诗歌的末尾四句，诗人描述了在玩月之时与月的氛围中，人的身心所接受的净化与洗涤。

Enjoying the Moon

At the beginning of the poem, the poet wrote about going boating in the lake, and after returning to the banquet at night, he was still unsatisfied. After going out to enjoy the moon again, through the delicate descriptions of ape crying, night dew and other objects,it vividly highlighted the quietness of the moonlit night. The river under the moon, the wind under the moon, the mountain under the moon, and the tree under the moon are distant, gentle, elegant and pure. It was a world under crystal clear and quiet moon, and the artistic conception of harmony between nature and human. Therefore, in the last four sentences of the poem the poet wrote that in the time of enjoying the moon and in the atmosphere, people got the purification and washing of inner and outer body.

日落泛澄瀛，星罗游轻桡。

憩榭面曲汜，临流对回潮。

辍策共骈筵，并坐相招要。

哀鸿鸣沙渚，悲猿响山椒。

亭亭映江月，浏浏出谷飙。

斐斐气幕岫，泫泫露盈条。

近瞩袪幽蕴，远视荡喧嚣。

悟言不知罢，从夕至清朝。

Go boating on a clear lake at sunset,

Paddle until the stars are up.

The boat return to rest in the lake side,

Lean on the fence to watch the flow of the bend.

Put down crutches and ascend to the balcony to join the banquet.

You invite me courteous and sit at the table.

On the water island come the sound of grief,

Heard bursts of monkeies crying from the mountain tops.

The moon shine brightly on the lake,

The mountain wind suddenly begins to blow fast.

Light smoke haze over the mountain,

The branches of the dewdrop glitter and translucent to drop .

Under the moon, the landscape near and far has its good place to admire,

Bright or dark, quiet faint far.

It was such a good night to drinke wine with a lot of fun,

Friends and family talked and laughed all night long.

《七月七日夜咏牛女》诗歌赏析：

这首诗即据上述“七月七日织女嫁牵牛”的故事写成。这个故事是我国古代民间传说中最为动人的故事之一，在魏晋时期已经流传得相当广泛。本诗借助“七七”之夜牛郎织女相会的故事，表达了诗人内心的一种体验，一种情思。本诗的魅力在于以巧妙的艺术手法大胆地写出男女之情爱。

Chanting on the Cowherd and the Weaver Girl

This poem is based on the story of “The Weaver Girl Marries the Cowherd on July 7” . This story is one of the most moving stories in ancient Chinese folklore, and it has been widely spread during the Wei and Jin Dynasties. This poem uses the story of the date of the Cowherd and the Weaver Girl on the Night of Seven in July, to express the poet's inner experience and sentiment. The charm of this poem lies in boldly writing the love between men and women with ingenious artistic techniques.

落日隐櫩楹，升月照帘栊。
团团满叶露，析析振条风。
蹀足循广除，瞬目曬曾穹。
云汉有灵匹，弥年缺相从。
遐川阻昵爱，脩渚旷清容。
弄杼不成藻，耸辔骛前踪。
昔离秋已两，今聚夕无双。
倾河易回斡，款颜难久悰。
沃若灵驾旋，寂寥云幄空。
留情顾华寝，遥心逐奔龙。
沉吟为尔感，情深意弥重。

The setting sun faded away in front of the houses,
The moon rose eastward to illuminate the curtains and windows.
The leaves are covered with round drops of dew,
The branches shake and blow through the cool wind.
Stepping down the broad steps,
I look at the high stars.
The Milky River has a pair of immortal couples,
All the year apart can not be reunited.
The wide river blocks intimate love,
Small island long blocks beautiful face.
The bobbin never weaves a piece,
Drive forward along the old road.

Autumn is colder since parting.

Tonight we shall not meet in pairs.

It's easy for the Milky Way to turn it upside down,

But it's hard to keep happy for long.

The horse reins is smooth in hand to drive back,

Lonely void in the clouds.

Looking back in the room,

The Cowherd's Heart Chases the Immortal's ride.

I wander to feel sad,

Lovesickness feeling is deeper.

《捣衣》诗歌赏析：

捣衣，即捣衣帛以缝制衣裳。六朝隋唐间，“捣衣”是诗歌中常咏的题材，诗人往往借此抒写思妇的忧愁和对丈夫的盼归之情。谢惠连的这首诗，则是文人诗中较早吟咏“捣衣”的，对后来的同类作品有一定影响。诗篇不无雕琢辞藻的毛病，但描写较为细腻生动，情感也比较委婉真挚，不失为精心结撰之作。

Pounding clothes

Pounding clothes, that is, pounding clothes and silk to sew clothes. During the Six Dynasties, Sui and Tang Dynasties, “pounding clothes” was the theme often chanted in poems, and poets often used it to express the loneliness of lovesick woman' s hope for her husband to return. Xie Huilian' s poem was an earlier chant of “pounding clothes” in the poems, which had a certain influence on later similar works. The poems are not without the faults of the rhetoric, but the description is more delicate and vivid, and the emotions are more tactful and sincere. So it can be regarded as a carefully composed work.

衡纪无淹度，晷运倏如催。

白露滋园菊，秋风落庭槐。

肃肃莎鸡羽，烈烈寒螀啼。

夕阴结空幕，霄月皓中闺。

美人戒裳服，端饰相招携。

簪玉出北房，鸣金步南阶。

櫩高砧响发，楹长杵声哀。

微芳起两袖，轻汗染双题。

纨素既已成，君子行未归。

裁用笥中刀，缝为万里衣。

盈箧自余手，幽缄俟君开。

腰带准畴昔，不知今是非。

Seasons passes and never stops,

Time seems to pass so quickly.

The white dew nourishes the chrysanthemums in garden,

The autumn breeze brings piles of fallen leaves.

The katydid fluttered her wings,

The cicadas whistled fiercely in the wind.

The night falls to cover the curtain of emptiness,

The bright moon rises into the sky to illuminate the lonely boudoir.

The beauty solemnly put on clothes,

Groom to invite each other.

She walks out of the north house wearing a hosta,

Walk down the south stairs with a ring of gold ornaments.

The anvil under the high eaves sounds ping-pong,

The pestle on the promenade contained sorrow.

Sleeves flutter with a faint fragrance,

Slight sweat leaks from the foreheads on both sides.

The white silk has been pounded and flattened,

But husband has not returned since his long journey.

Take out a scissor to cut the silk and sew winter coat,

For him who was thousands of miles away.

This suitcase full of clothes is all out of my hands,

Hide it until my husband returns to open it.

The waistband is the same size as before.

I wonder if it fits him now.

颜延之（384—456），字延年，琅邪临沂（今山东临沂）人，南朝宋著名诗人。他出身寒门，颇受阮籍、嵇康的影响，虽官至金紫光禄大夫，但与当权者向来不合。他仰慕屈原，写有《祭屈原文》；他钦佩"正始名士"，赋有《五君咏》。这不仅表现了他的文学观，也是自我情志的抒发。他在文学史上与谢灵运齐名，时称"颜、谢"。他的骈文亦文辞绮丽，铺锦列绣，多用典事。《文选》载有颜文六篇，可见南朝人对颜文评价亦高。

Yan Yanzhi (384-456), Yannian, was born in Langxie Linyi (now Linyi, Shandong Province). He is a famous poet in the Southern Song Dynasty. He was born in a poor family, and was quite influenced by Ruan Ji and Ji Kang. Although he took the position of Jin Ziguanglu Dafu, he has always been incompatible with those in power. He admired Qu Yuan and wrote the *Sacrifice to Qu Yuan*; he admired "Zheng ShiMing Shi" and wrote Chanting Five Monarchs. This not only shows his literary view point, but also expresses his own ambitions. He was as famous as Xie Lingyun in the history of literature, and both of them are called "Yan, Xie" . His parallel essays are also beautiful, and they use allusions. *Wen Xuan* contains six articles of Yan' s, which shows that people in the Southern Dynasty also have a high evaluation to his essays.

《北使洛》诗歌赏析：

自西晋末以来，中原地区迭遭战乱，破坏严重，诗篇描写沿途所见的残破景象，悲歌感慨，充满故国之思。手法和情调颇受陆机《赴洛道中作》影响，但文字较为朴素。

Gong North to Luoyang

Since the end of the Western Jin Dynasty, the Central Plains region has suffered from wars and severe damage. The poem describes the broken scenes along the way, The sad song is full of thoughts of the homeland. The technique and sentiment are quite influenced by Lu Ji' s *Two Poems on the Way to Luoyang*, but the language is relatively simple.

改服饬徒旅，首路踽险难。

振楫发吴州，秣马陵楚山。

涂出梁宋郊，道由周郑间。

前登阳城路，日夕望三川。

在昔辍期运，经始阔圣贤。

伊榖绝津济，台馆无尺椽。

宫陛多巢穴，城阙生云烟。

王猷升八表，嗟行方暮年。

阴风振凉野，飞雪瞀穷天。

临涂未及引，置酒惨无言。

隐悯徒御悲，威迟良马烦。

游役去芳时，归来屡徂諐。

蓬心既已矣，飞薄殊亦然！

I changed clothes to accompany the soldiers,

Bowed down to avoid fear and obstacles.

I paddled the oars and set out from Wuzhou,

The horses were fed to climb the mountains of Chu.

The trip was through the Liang and Song ancestral pasturelands,

Through the road between Zhou and Zheng.

Go forward on the roads in Yangcheng,

See the Yellow River and Yiluo Rivers in the evening.

In the past the country suddenly lost its luck,
There was always a lack of sages to create great causes.
Yishuigu water broke off the river crossing,
The Taiguan Pavilion did not have a one-foot house rafter.
Many nests appeared on the steps of the palace,
Plumes of smoke appeared from the palace gates.
The king's order spreads in all directions far away,
Lament that this trip is at the end of the winter.
The cold north wind blows the countryside,
The blizzard makes the winter dim.
When I came to the side of the road before opening,
My friend was relatively speechless after drinking wine.
The entourage forced to endure the grief,
The long and winding road seemed upset.
Good time was abandoned for long-distance service,
The return date was repeatedly delayed for certain reason.
My heart of following the times has been indifferent,
Wandering back and forth is like Peng Grass drifting in the wind.

《还至梁城》诗歌赏析：

本篇为《北使洛》的姊妹篇，为诗人从洛阳东归途经梁城（今河南南阳）时所作。诗中描写北地的荒凉和行役的艰辛，情调与《北使洛》相同。诗歌因为被残破的现实激发所致，情调较为消沉。诗歌情感真挚深沉，文字朴实无华，在颜诗中属上乘之作。

Going to Liangcheng

This article is a sister article of Going *North to Luoyang*. It was written by the poet when he returned east from Luoyang on the way via Liangcheng (now Nanyang, Henan

Province). The poem describes the desolation of the northland and the hardships of the service. It has the same sentiment as *Going North to Luoyang*. The sentiment is depressed because of the broken reality. The emotions are sincere and deep, and the language is simple and unpretentious, which is the best work in Yan' s poetries.

眇默轨路长，憔悴征戍勤。
昔迈先徂师，今来后归军。
振策眷东路，倾侧不及群。
息徒顾将夕，极望梁陈分。
故国多乔木，空城凝寒云。
丘垄填郛郭，铭志灭无文。
木石扃幽闼，黍苗延高坟。
惟彼雍门子，吁嗟孟尝君。
愚贱同堙灭，尊贵谁独闻。
何为久游客，忧念坐自殷。

It was a distant and long road,
I was tired and haggard.
In the past, when I went to Luoyang, I often surpassed the army,
Today, I return behind the triumphant army.
Wave horse whip to look at the eastbound road,
Lean forward quickly can't catch up with everyone.
Order for everyone to rest,
Look far away and approaching Liang Chen border.
There are many tall trees in the northern homeland,
Clusters of cold clouds are condensed above the empty city.
The high tombs have filled the outside of the city,
The epitaph inscriptions have been obliterated.

The wood and stones close the gate of the dark tomb,

The green millet seedlings extend up to the high tomb.

I remembered what Yong Men Zhou said,

Sigh for sentimental Monarch Meng Chang.

Fools and bitches are annihilated and buried together,

The noble man who only left a name.

I don’t know why I, a wandering stranger, feel so sad for no reason.

《始安郡还都与张湘州登巴陵城楼》诗歌赏析：

永初三年（422）五月，宋武帝刘裕病卒，太子刘义符继位，徐羡之等辅政。颜延之因与庐陵王刘义真亲厚，为徐羡之等所疑忌，出为始安太守（郡治在今广西桂林）。元嘉三年（426）初，徐羡之等被诛，颜延之被征为中书侍郎，在返回建康（今江苏南京）途中，与湘州刺史张邵同登巴陵（今湖南岳阳）城楼，有感而作此诗。诗篇描写巴陵一带景色，融入个人人生体验，境界雄阔，情调悲凉，有一定艺术感染力。对偶工整，讲究雕饰，亦为本篇特色。

Climbing Baling Tower with Zhang Shao

In May of the third year of Yongchu (422), Liu Yu, Emperor Wu of the Southern Song Dynasty died of illness, Prince Liu Yifu succeeded to the throne, and Xu Xianzhi assisted in the administration. Yan Yanzhi was close to Liu Yizhen, the King of Luling, and then was suspected by Xu Xianzhi and others, and took up the post of the satrap of Shi’an (the satrapure is now in Guilin, Guangxi Province). At the beginning of the third year of Yuanjia (426), Xu Xianzhi and others were condemned and Yan Yanzhi was conscripted as Zhongshu Shilang. On the way back to Jiankang (now Nanjing, Jiangsu Province), he went to the Baling (now Yueyang, Hunan Province) Tower with Xiangzhou Cishi, Zhang Shao. He composed this poem. The poem describes the scenery around Baling and integrates into his personal life experience. The realm is magnificent and the sentiment is sad. The poem has a certain artistic appeal. The antithesis is neat and carved, which is also the feature of the poem.

江汉分楚望，衡巫奠南服。

三湘沦洞庭，七泽蔼荆牧。

经涂延旧轨，登闉访川陆。

水国周地崄，河山信重复。

却倚云梦林，前瞻京台囿。

清氛霁岳阳，曾晖薄澜澳。

凄矣自远风，伤哉千里目。

万古陈往还，百代劳起伏。

存没竟何人？炯介在明淑。

请从上世人，归来艺桑竹。

The Han River of the Yangtze River divides the mountains and rivers of Chu,

Hengshan Mountain and Wushan Mountain set the south.

The YangtzeRiver, Xiangjiang River and Yuanjiang River meet and flow into Dongting Lake,

Many lakes are filled with Jingjiao like clouds.

On the way back to the capital I walk along the original road,

Climb the fortress to explore the rivers and plains.

The water country is surrounded by dangerous terrain,

The crisscrossing of rivers and mountains is indeed a repetition of mountains and rivers.

Behind the back are clouds bordering the forest,

Look forward to the Emperor's Forest Garden.

The fresh air is exhausted and the southern part of the mountain is sunny,

The sun shines on the waves of the bay.

Desolation, the wind is from afar,

The eyes looking from afar sadly.

The eternal past will be displayed endlessly,

Generations are tired of endless ups and downs.

Who will live forever and who will die in the change of history?

If a man of integrity shows good virtues, his spirit lasts forever.

I would like to follow the hermit,

Return to nature to plant mulberry and bamboo.

《应诏观北湖田收》诗歌赏析：

本诗作于元嘉十年（434）十月。诗作写南朝宋文帝率领百官前往北湖观望农业丰收的情景。诗歌的前半部分写出行中的声势和气派，后半部分写农事景物，以及抒发随行的感受。因为是应诏之作，故诗中多歌功颂德和祝福吉祥之辞。诗歌的前六句，以残悴之象观照而得勃勃生机，雕琢之中亦见新奇。精气寒烟，攒素积翠，正是秋冬之交的冷峻之美。接着写文帝出行车驾侍卫之盛和初冬景色之美。诗歌的末尾是诗人自述之词。

North Lake Harvest

This poem was written in October in the tenth year of Yuanjia (434). The poem writes that Emperor Wen of the Southern Song Dynasty led officials to the North Lake to observe the harvest. The first half part of the poem is about the vigor during the trip, and the second half is about farming scenery and expressing feelings. Because it is an edict, the poems sing praises and blessings. The first six sentences are full of vitality by observing the dilapidated image, and novelty can also be seen in lines. The cold smoke of essence and the accumulation of greenery are just the cold beauty at the turn of autumn and winter. Then the poem writes that Emperor Wen travels with prosperous carriages and guards. At same time, he describes the beauty of the early winter scenery. The end of the poem is the poet' s own statement.

周御穷辙迹，夏载历山川。

蓄轸岂明懋，善游皆圣仙。

帝晖膺顺动，清跸巡广廛。

楼观眺丰颖，金驾映松山。

飞奔互流缀，缇縠代回环。

神行埒浮景，争光溢中天。

开冬眷徂物，残悴盈化先。

阳陆团精气，阴谷曳寒烟。

攒素既森蔼，积翠亦葱仟。

息飨报嘉岁，通急戒无年。

温渥浃舆隶，和惠属后筵。

观风久有作，陈诗愧未妍。

疲弱谢凌遽，取累非纆牵。

The emperor Zhou Mu once traveled with eight horses,

Da Yu also traveled through the mountains and rivers by boat and cart.

Carriages show the royal style,

Precedents in the past and today are in cruising.

Our emperor wisely respond to the orders of heaven,

Obey the hearts of the people,

Travel and inspect the vast fields.

Ascend to the tower and overlook the harvest of rice from a distance,

Magnificent and splendid driving of the magnificent cart shines on fields.

The vehicles accompanied by civil and military officials are in an endless stream,

Guards and cavalry rush to and fro.

The emperor's patrol is like the red sun moving in the middle of the sky,

Miles of the brilliance miles shines against the long sky.

All things wither in the early winter,

Metamorphosing is present in the pallor.

The wilderness is heated by the sunlight,

The shady valley drags long and cold smoke.

The cold frost on the branches of trees gleam white,

Pines and cypresses are still fresh and lush.

The farm banquet presents an abundant year,

The trade of rice is to prepare for the disaster year.

The emperor's grace is like rain and dew to nourish people,

Also like a spring breeze, soft and warm to all the officials.

It has been long since I searched for poems to observe people's customs.

Weak in talents and unable to write good poems,

How can the slowness of the horse be evasive and entangled in the reins.

《车驾幸京口侍游蒜山》诗歌赏析：

此诗作于宋文帝元嘉二十六年（450）。京口，今江苏镇江。元嘉二十六年二月，颜延年随侍文帝幸京口，并游蒜山。因应诏做诗。京口是晋东迁之地，晋之陵庙所在之所。文帝出生于此。因而，此次巡幸，甚为隆重。

Suanshan Mountain

This poem was written in the twenty-sixth year of Yuanjia, Emperor Wen of the Southern Song Dynasty (450). Jingkou is Zhenjiang, Jiangsu Province. In February of the twenty-sixth year of Yuanjia, Yan Yannian accompanied Emperor Wen to visit Jingkou and Suan Mountain. He composed poems in response to the edict. Jingkou is the place where Jin moved to from west, where Jin's mausoleum and temple were located. Emperor Wen was born here. Therefore, this tour is very grand.

元天高北列，日观临东溟。

入河起阳峡，践华因削成。

岩险去汉宇，衿卫徙吴京。

流池自化造，山关固神营。

园县极方望，邑社总地灵。

宅道炳星纬，诞曜应神明。

睿思缠故里，巡驾匝旧坰。

陟峰腾辇路，寻云抗瑶甍。

春江壮风涛，兰野茂稊英。

宣游弘下济，穷远凝圣情。

岳滨有和会，祥习在卜征。

周南悲昔老，留滞感遗氓。

空食疲廊肆，反税事岩耕。

Yuan Tian Mountain towers high in the northern land,

Riguan Peak stands erect on the coast of the East Sea.

In the past Qin troops crossed the Yellow River to build the Great Wall,

It once defended the steep Huashan as a shield.

The lofty mountains and ridges,

Now the mountains are not barriers to the capital of the Han Dynasty.

Jiangshan is like a belt guarding the capital.

Rivers and lakes are created by nature,

Mountains and dangerous barriers were also created by the heaven.

The emperor came to the mausoleum of the former king to offer sacrifices to the heaven,

Where the earth was filled with spirit.

The auspicious atmosphere of the emperor’s capital was shown in Bull Fight,

Mercury’s shining light coincided with the prosperity of our country.

The wise emperor deeply cherished his former residence,

Took a cart to inspect and patrol the old place.

Gradually ascended along the driveway to the peak,

The peaks and pavilions with jade cornices were high and above the clouds.

Looked down at the Spring River,

The wind and waves were extremely magnificent,

Vast wilderness of luxuriant grass was thriving.

Emperor's visit fully reflected concern for the people,

The impoverished countryside also condensed the royal favor.

Civil and military officials from all directions gathered here,

The trip was only possible when auspicious signs and divination appeared repeatedly.

In the past Sima Tan's family was unable to travel with him,

He was sad that he had to complain about his fate.

I was deeply ashamed of the vegetarian meal,

I'd better return to farming.

《夏夜呈从兄散骑车长沙》诗歌赏析：

从兄散骑，字敬宗，颜延年的一位同族兄长；车长沙，字仲远。颜延年与他们的亲情友谊均颇深厚。此为其在夏末之夜怀念二人所写的一首诗。这首诗的最大特点是将怀念之情寄寓在对自然景物和生活细节的描绘上。既含蓄深沉，也明晓易懂，较之他那些堆砌典故、雕琢晦涩之作颇不相同。

For Elder Brother Sanqi and Che Changsha

Sanqi, Jingzong, was Yan Yannian' s brother of the same clan. Che Changsha, Zhongyuan, is friend of Yan. The affection and friendship among Yan Yannian and them are quite deep. This is a poem written in memory of them in a late summer night. The biggest feature of this poem is that it embodies the nostalgia in the depiction of natural scenery and life details. It is both implicit and deep, but also easy to understand. Compared with piled-up allusions, sculptural and obscure works, this poem is quite different.

炎天方埃郁，暑晏阕尘纷。

独静阙偶坐，临堂对星分。

侧听风薄木，遥睇月开云。

夜蝉当夏急，阴虫先秋闻。

岁候初过半，荃蕙岂久芬？

屏居恻物变，慕类抱情殷。

九逝非空思，七襄无成文。

Thick dust flies everywhere in midsummer,

The dust is not seen until the end of summer.

In the quiet nightI sit alone,

I see only twinkling stars before the hall.

Listen to the cool breeze blowing in the woods,

Look up at the sky,the moon rushes through the evening clouds.

In the summer night cicadas cry loudly and anxiously,

Sounds of crickets can be heard before the autumn.

The seasons of a year have turned nearly halfway,

How can Tsuen and Hui give out fragrance for a long time?

In seclusion I feel changes in the scenery,

Miss friends and relatives deeply.

My heart and soul go back and forth many times during day and night,

Difficult to compose poems all day long.

《直东宫答郑尚书》诗歌赏析：

郑尚书，即郑鲜之，仕晋为御史中丞。性格刚直不阿，人甚敬惮。入宋后，武帝任为太常、都官尚书，此时颜延年为太子舍人，两人情好笃密，时以诗相唱和。该诗是颜延年在东宫值宿时，接到郑鲜之赠诗后作答的一首诗。

全诗分三部分：先写诗人对郑鲜之的思念，次写值宿东宫时的情景，末写读罢郑鲜之诗后的感受。诗歌感情真挚，词语晓畅，且能将深切感情寄寓于对自然景物和自己行动的细节描写之中。

Reply to Zheng Shangshu

Zheng Shangshu, is Zheng Xianzhi, Yushi Zhongcheng in Jin Dynasty. He is upright and frank and people are very respectful for him. After entering the Southern Song Dynasty, Emperor Wu appointed as him as Taichang and Duguan Shangshu. At this time, Yan Yannian was Taizi Sheren. They had a close relationship and often sang poems together. This is a poem that Yan Yannian replyed after receiving a poem from Zheng Xianzhi when he was on duty in the East Palace.

The whole poem is divided into three parts: at first it writes about the poet' s missings of Zheng Xianzhi.Then it writes about the scene when he stayed on duty in the East Palace. And lastly it writes about the feelings after reading Zheng Xianzhi' s poem. The feelings are sincere and the language is smooth. The deep affection is embedded in the detailed description of the natural scenery and his actions.

皇居体寰极，设险祗天工。

两闱阻通轨，对禁限清风。

跂予旅东馆，徒歌属南墉。

寝兴郁无已，起观辰汉中。

流云蔼青阙，皓月鉴丹宫。

踟蹰清防密，徙倚恒漏穷。

君子吐芳讯，感物恻余衷。

惜无丘园秀，景行彼高松。

知言有诚贯，美价难克充。

何以铭嘉贶？言树丝与桐。

The royal palace is like stars orbiting the North Pole,

The guards are like a pilgrimage to the north of one hundred officials.

The road from the East Palace to the Middle Road is blocked,

The gate is relatively tightly guarded and difficult to enter.

It’s hard to expect to stay at night in the East Hall,

Sings rumors and miss people of Nanyong.

It’s very depressing to sleep, so I look at the Milky Way and stars in the sky.

Look at clouds shroud the cyan double faults,

Gaze at the bright moon shining on the red palace.

Linger in silence beside the screen,

I stand there until the clepsydra dripping off.

I receive a poem from you during the day,

The emotion in the poem moved me.

It's a pity that there is a lack of scholars,

It's hard to learn pine's integrity.

I am well aware devoting to the whole poem with sincerity,

Like the priceless treasure to me.

How will I remember this wonderful gift?

I decided to play it with the strings.

~~~~~~

王微（415—453/443），字景玄，琅琊临沂（今属山东）人，南朝宋诗人。少好学，善属文，能书画，兼通医方、阴阳术数。始为司徒祭酒，后任太子中舍人，以父丧去职。后幽居独处，以文籍自娱。

Wang Wei (415-453/443?), Jingxuan, was born in Linyi, Langya(now Shandong Province). He was a poet of the Southern Song Dynasty. When he was young, he was eager to learn and good at calligraphy, writing, medical prescriptions, yin and yang techniques. At first he took up the post of Situ Jijiu. Then he served as Taizi Zhongsheren and resigned for the death of his father. He lived alone and entertained himself with classics.

《杂诗》诗歌赏析：

这首诗写思妇怀念征夫，造语清浅，情辞凄怨，诗歌情景交融。其幽怨的诗风，对后来江淹的创作有一定影响。

A Miscellaneous Poem

This poem writes about wife misses her husband. The language is simple and the expression of love is sad. The scene blends with emotions in the poem. This poetic style of grievance has a certain impact on Jiang Yan' s poems.
~~~~~~

思妇临高台，长想凭华轩。

弄弦不成曲，哀歌送苦言：

箕帚留江介，良人处雁门。

讵忆无衣苦，但知狐白温。

日暗牛羊下，野雀满空园。

孟冬寒风起，东壁正中昏。

朱火独照人，抱景自愁怨。

谁知心曲乱？所思不可论。

The woman climbs up the platform and looks faraway,

Lean against the window to meditate for long.

Play the strings always fails to make a tune,

Utter sighs of distress:

Stay alone on the river bank,

The husband is in the remote Yanmen Pass.

People ignore pains of being unclothed,

But who knows that a fox white fur is very warm.

The sun set, cattle and sheep returned homes,

Wild birds flew over to fill the garden.

Winter's cold wind blows gusts,

It is dusk when the bishop is high above the southern sky.

Only the candle illuminates the lonely,

The single shadow is only sad and resentful.

Who knows this inner grief ?

Infinite lovesickness is not worth talking about.

南北朝诗歌 南朝齐

Poems of Northern and Southern Dynasties(the Southern Qi Dynasty)

谢朓（464—499），字玄晖，陈郡阳夏县（今河南省太康县）人，南齐诗人，出身陈郡谢氏，与“大谢”谢灵运同族，世称“小谢”。建武二年（495），谢朓出为宣城太守，因而又称谢宣城。永泰初迁尚书吏部郎，因又称谢吏部。谢朓曾与沈约等共创“永明体”。今存诗二百余首，长于五言诗，有集已佚。后人辑有《谢宣城集》。

Xie Tiao (464-499), Xuanhui, was born in Yangxia County, Chen County(now Taikang County, Henan Province). He is a poet from the Southern Qi Dynasty and was born in the Xie family of Chen County, who belonged to the same clan as “Senior Xie” , Xie Lingyun. Xie Tiao was called “Junior Xie” .In the second year of Jianwu (495), he was appointed as the satrap of Xuancheng, because of this he was also known as Xie Xuancheng. At the beginning of Yongtai, he took up the post of Shangshu Libu Lang, because of this he was also known as Xie Libu. Xie Tiao once co-created the “Yongming Style” with Shen Yue and others. There are more than two hundred poems in existence today. He is good at five-character poems, and the collection has been lost. Later generations compile *The Collection of Xie Xuancheng*.

《游东田》诗歌赏析：

诗歌是南朝诗人谢朓创作的古诗作品，此诗描写了春末夏初东田的风光以及与友人携手共游东田所见的美景和感受。诗中写诗人健步登临层台累榭，纵目眺望自然风光，其描景生动，造语清新，突出景物的多姿多彩和勃勃生机。全诗语言清新流丽，多工整对句。突出诗人对自然风光的酷爱。谢朓的山水之作，彻底摆脱了玄言诗的影响，此诗即为一例。

Visiting Eastern Fields

The poem is an ancient poem created by the poet Xie Tiao in the Southern Dynasties. This poem describes the scenery of eastern fields in late spring and early summer and the beauty and feelings of visiting eastern fields with friends. It is described in the poem that the poet walks on the terraces and looks at the natural scenery. His description is vivid and the language is fresh, highlighting the colorful and vigorous scenery. The language of the whole poem is fresh and smooth, with many neat sentences. The poem highlights the poet' s passion for natural scenery. The work of landscapes by Xie Tiao completely got rid of the influence of Xuanyan Poems, and this poem is just the example.

戚戚苦无悰，携手共行乐。

寻云陟累榭，随山望菌阁。

远树暧纤纤，生烟纷漠漠。

鱼戏新荷动，鸟散余花落。

不对芳春酒，还望青山郭。

No fun in the sadness,

Invite friends to go out for joy.

Ascend the peak and cross the pavilions step by step,

Look far away from the mountains and see layers of gorgeous pavilions.

Trees lush in the fog,

Light smoke scatter in the wind.

In the pond fish is playing,

The lotus leaves sway gently,

Birds suddenly fly, petals fall.

No need to drink in this beautiful spring,

Looking at the green hills in the suburbs is more joyful.

《同谢谘议铜雀台》诗歌赏析：

诗歌讽刺了魏武帝以姬妾充奉园陵的愚妄奢侈。诗句描写了死后的祭奠之勤，也显出生前的酒肴之盛。人已葬入园陵，而声歌舞乐照例不误。诗句满含讥讽。诗歌对群伎的描写，似述忠爱，实写其悲苦哀怨。君王已化为虚空，群妾身轻位卑，活为殉葬。诗歌的末两句是全诗的重心，既是哭诉，也是义愤。

Bronze Sparrow Terrace

The poem satirizes Emperor Wei Wu' s luxury of filling mausoleum with concubines. The poem writes about the memorial service after death, which also shows the prosperity of wine and food before death. The dead have been buried in the mausoleum, but the singing and dancing are the same as usual. The poem is full of sarcasm. The descriptions towards concubines seem to describe the emperor' s liking, but actually full of sorrow and grievances. The emperor has turned into nothingness. The concubines are humble and buried alive with the emperor. The last two sentences are the focus of the whole poem, which are not only crying, but also righteous indignation.

繐帷飘井干，樽酒若平生。

郁郁西陵树，讵闻歌吹声。

芳襟染泪迹，婵媛空复情。

玉座犹寂漠，况乃妾身轻。

The gauze tents float on the high bronze sparrow platform,

Fill with wine just as before Cao Gong was alive.

Where I hear the instrumental singing on the stage,

In the wooded west tomb cemetery.

The fragrant placket staines with tears,

No grief when take the clothes to wipe the tears and wept.

The king's throne is so lonely,

Not to mention the pity of maidservants!

《郡内高斋闲坐答吕法曹》诗歌赏析：

这是谢朓任宣城太守时写给吕僧珍的一首诗。吕僧珍与谢朓交谊颇深，曾致函问候谢朓，谢作此诗回答。诗中描绘了宣城景色和自己在此的生活情趣，表示对吕僧珍的怀念，还流露了一同归隐的愿望。其中景色描绘萧疏淡远，富有情致。

A Reply Poem

This is a poem written by Xie Tiao to Lu Sengzhen when he took up the post of the satrap of Xuancheng. At this time, Lu Sengzhen had a deep friendship with Xie Tiao, and once sent a letter to greet Xie Tiao. Xie wrote this poem for reply.The poem depicts the scenery of Xuancheng and his life here, expresses the nostalgia for Lu Sengzhen, and also expresses the desire to seek seclusion together. The scenery depicts is distant and sentimental.

结构何迢递，旷望极高深。

窗中列远岫，庭际俯乔林。

日出众鸟散，山暝孤猿吟。

已有池上酌，复此风中琴。

非君美无度，孰为劳寸心。

惠而能好我，问以瑶华音。

若遗金门步，见就玉山岑。

The terrain of this house is so high to compare,

So wide to see the mountains and the water.

The windows is lined with distant peaks,

Front courtyard overlook the deep and wide woods.

Watch the birds fly away in the cloud at sunrise,

Listen to the wailing of the lone monkey in the mountains after dusk.

Sit alone by the pond and drink,

Listen to the wind blowing and the trees ringing.

If not because your inner beauty is speechless,

How can I let long thoughts linger in heart.

Thank you for your deep affection for me,

Also for precious greetings from far away.

If I can leave Jinmen one day,

We meet at the top of Yushan Mountain.

《暂使下都，夜发新林，至京邑，赠西府同僚》诗歌赏析：

南朝齐武帝时，谢朓跟随随王萧子隆镇荆州。由于萧子隆爱好辞赋，对谢非常器重，但因长史王秀之的忌恨，向齐武帝进谗言，于是谢朓被召还都。谢朓对此极为愤懑，虽回京城，但心怀下都，写此诗寄给西府同僚。诗歌表达了留恋不舍的情意，也表达了对王秀之之流的强烈愤慨。全诗沉郁慷慨，音韵铿锵，脍炙人口。

For Colleagues in Xifu

During Emperor Qi Wu of the Southern Dynasty, Xie Tiao followed Emperor Sui, Xiao Zilong to guard Jingzhou. Xiao Zilong liked Cifu. So he thought highly of Xie Tiao. However, because of Changshi Wang Xiuzhi's jealousy, Wang slandered Xie Tiao to Emperor Qi Wu. So Xie Tiao was called back to the capital. Xie Tiao was extremely angry about this. Although he returned to the capital, he missed Jingzhou, wrote the poem and sent it to his colleagues in Xifu. The poem expresses his nostalgia and his strong indignation towards Wang Xiuzhi and his like. The whole poem is depressed and generous with sonorous rhyme and well-known.

大江流日夜，客心悲未央。

徒念关山近，终知反路长。

秋河曙耿耿，寒渚夜苍苍。

引顾见京室，宫雉正相望。

金波丽鳷鹊，玉绳低建章。

驱车鼎门外，思见昭丘阳。

驰晖不可接，何况隔两乡。

风云有鸟路，江汉限无梁。

常恐鹰隼击，时菊委严霜。

寄言罻罗者，寥廓已高翔。

The surging Yangtze River flows day and night,

Like endless resentment and sadness in heart.

See the suburbs of capital approaching,

Get to know that the road back to Jingzhou is long.

The dawn in the autumn sky reveal a faint light,

Cold Zhouzhu is still dark at night.

Look up to see Jiankang,

The palace walls are densely arranged like teeth.

The moon melts in the sky to illuminate the magpie,

Jade rope starlight shimmers.

Cart reaches the south gate of the capital,

The heart is still near the tomb of King Chu Zhao.

The sunlight in Jingzhou hardly shine on me,

Not to mention the people of Jingzhou far away.

Wind and clouds are in the sky, but birds still pass,

Jianghan water obstructs pedestrians with no bridge on it.

Worry about the sudden attack of the eagle and the falcon,

Also worry chrysanthemum the Double Ninth Festival wither in severe frost.

Till now the person who sent the net,

The bird on the branch has spread its wings to soar through the clouds.

《在郡卧病呈沈尚书》诗歌赏析：

这是谢朓在任宣城太守时写给尚书令沈约的一首赠答诗。诗中主要是写其在宣城郡政绩斐然的情况，并抒发对沈约的深切怀念。诗歌对生活状况的描述清畅自然，富有情致。

To Shen Shangshu in the County

This is a reply poem written by Xie Tiao to Shangshu Ling Shen Yue when he took up the post of the satrap of Xuancheng. The poem mainly writes about his outstanding political achievements in Xuancheng County and expresses his deep missing of Shen Yue. In the poem the description of living conditions is clear, natural and sentimental.

淮阳股肱守，高卧犹在兹。
况复南山曲，何异幽栖时？
连阴盛农节，籉笠聚东菑。
高阁常昼掩，荒阶少诤辞。
珍簟清夏室，轻扇动凉飔。
嘉鲂聊可荐，渌蚁方独持。
夏李沉朱实，秋藕折轻丝。
良辰竟何许？夙昔梦佳期。
坐啸徒可积，为邦岁已期。
弦歌终莫取，抚机令自嗤。

The satrap who came from Huaiyang stayed in Xuancheng,
Lying on the top of the board.
Xuancheng County is beautiful.
How is it different from being a hermit in a secluded forest?
In the continuous rainy days,
The farming season is busy,
People are busy with spring ploughing in the fields.
The gate of the satrapure is often closed during the day,
The court famine rarely hears the sound of litigation.
I love bamboo mats only because summer is coming,
I feel a cool breeze when I shake the fan gently.
The taste of bream is delicious to eat,
Luyi wine is fragrant and I pour and drink it alone.

Summer plum fruit floats in the clear stream,

The autumn lotus root at the edge of the pond,silk light.

When will the good days of meeting come?

Miss deep in the morning, dreaming that the best time is coming.

Sit idle in the hall, chanting poems day after day,

For being the satrap to the first anniversary.

No one cherishes stringed singing,

Lean on table alone to laugh at myself.

《敬亭山》诗歌赏析：

诗歌作于建武二年（495）谢朓出守宣城（今属安徽）时。在对山水的刻画中诗人表达了自己既萦心禄位又想栖隐的矛盾心情。谢朓的山水诗大多写得清新秀逸，而本篇落笔遒劲，意境幽峭，气韵凝重，显得别具一格。这主要由于诗人处在仕隐的矛盾中，有意识地接近山水，而宣城四周有高山为屏，诗人将自己企望栖隐的心情旨趣融入其中，故给诗篇涂上了一层清远绵邈、险峭幽深的色彩。全诗布局有序，较熟练地运用了永明声律和骈化修辞。

Jingtingshan Mountain

The poem was written in the second year of Jianwu (495) when Xie Tiao guarded Xuancheng (now in Anhui Province). In the depiction of landscape, Xie Tiao expresses his contradictory mood between seclusion and offcialdom. Most of Xie Tiao’s landscape poems are fresh and elegant, but the writing of this poem is vigorous. The artistic conception is steep and dignified, which is unique. This is mainly due to the fact that the poet is in the contradiction of seclusion and offcialdom, and he consciously approached the mountains and rivers. Xuancheng is surrounded by mountains as a screen. The mood and interest of the poet are integrated into it. So the poem is painted with a clear and steep color. The whole poem is arranged in an orderly way. The Yongming rhythm and the rhetoric of parallelism are used skillfully.

兹山亘百里，合沓与云齐。

隐沦既已托，灵异俱然栖。

上干蔽白日，下属带回谿。
交藤荒且蔓，樛枝耸复低。
独鹤方朝唳，饥鼯此夜啼。
渫云已漫漫，多雨亦凄凄。
我行虽纡组，兼得寻幽蹊。
缘源殊未极，归径窅如迷。
要欲追奇趣，即此陵丹梯。
皇恩竟已矣，兹理庶无睽。

This mountain stretches across for hundreds of miles,
Overlapping and stacking on top equals to floating clouds.
The hermit has entrusted himself here,
The gods have also come here to settle down.
The top of the mountain is covered by the sky,
The sun is completely covered,
The zigzag clear stream surrounds the foot of the mountain.
The vines cover the mountains in a staggered manner,
The curved trees rise and droop.
The lone crane is wailing in this early morning,
The hungry flying is mourning in the middle of the night.
The drifting clouds and mist have been fascinated in the mountains,
The rain in the mountains is even more cold and desolate.
Although I am an official on this trip,
I am able to explore secluded trails at the same time.
The pursuit of the water source is far from reaching the end,
But the way back is far lost.

If you want to pursue great fun,

Climb to the top of the mountain from here.

Royal grace has passed away,

So I hope that this principle will not be violated.

《休沐重还道中》诗歌赏析：

诗歌或作于建武二年（495）春谢朓在朝任中书郎时，诗歌既表达了他罢官归田的愿望，同时又展示了他的隐仕思想矛盾，这是谢朓这一时期诗作的常见主题，生活在一个充满倾轧和杀戮的政治环境中，具有这种想法是不难理解的。景物描写无论静态动态，均细致生动，读来历历可见，切切可感，充分显示了诗人敏锐的观察力、感受力和独到的表现力。

A Tour

The poem was probably written in the spring of the 2nd year of Jianwu (495), when Xie Tiao served as Zhongshu Lang. The poem not only expressed his desire to be dismissed from office and returned to the fields, but also showed the contradictions of hermit. It was a common theme in Xie Tiao's poems during this period. In a political environment full of tumult and killing, it is not difficult to understand this kind of thinking. The scenery description is extremely detailed and vivid, no matter static or dynamic. It is visible and tangible after reading, which fully demonstrates the poet's keen observation, sensitivity and unique expressive power.

薄游第从告，思闲愿罢归。

还邛歌赋似，休汝车骑非。

霸池不可别，伊川难重违。

汀葭稍靡靡，江菼复依依。

田鹤远相叫，沙鸨忽争飞。

云端楚山见，林表吴岫微。

试与征徒望，乡泪尽沾衣。

赖此盈樽酌，含景望芳菲。

问我劳何事？沾沐仰清徽。

志狭轻轩冕，恩甚恋重闱。

岁华春有酒，初服偃郊扉。

Travel for a short time and ask for a vacation,

Think about idleness and wish to return from temporary dismissal.

Go back to Linqiong, the poems are similar,

There is no Yuan Shao riding in Runan on vacation.

The tyrant pool cannot be separated for a long time,

It is difficult for Yichuan to go against it deeply.

Reeds gradually dump with the wind,

The riverside diffusa is also gently blowing.

Wild cranes in the field scream from afar,

The sandbar geese fly suddenly.

Mount Chu is suddenly appears above the clouds,

Mount Wu faintly outside the woods.

Try with followers to gaze with sorrow,

There are tears of homesickness on their clothes.

Fill the cup with this sentiment,

Gaze at the flowers and grass in the spring.

What am It oiling for?

Receive grace and admire integrity.

With narrow ambitions and not value the post,

Nostalgic for royal grace.

In spring there was wine,

Put on old garments and lay down in the country house.

《晚登三山还望京邑》诗歌赏析：

本篇写登山所见春天傍晚景色及因瞻望京城而勾起的怀乡愁绪，可能作于齐武帝永明九年（491）春诗人将离京跟着随郡王萧子隆赴荆州（今湖北江陵）之时，一说作于齐明帝建武二年（495）春出任宣城太守之时。三山，在今江苏南京西南长江南岸，上有三峰，南北相连。诗歌以敏锐细致的观察和高度的艺术概括力，描绘了一幅层次分明、色调缤纷、饶有情趣的春江暮景图。诗歌词句清丽自然，成为谢朓诗中最受推崇的名句。

Climbing Sanshan Mountain in the Evening

This poem writes about the spring evening scenery seen by writer and the nostalgic sentiment aroused by when he looked at the capital. It may be written in the 9th year of Yongming, Emperor Wu of Qi(491), Xie Tiao left the capital and followed Xiao Zilong to Jingzhou (now Jiangling, Hubei Province). It is said that it was written in the spring of second year of Jianwu, Emperor Ming of Qi (495) when he took up the post of the satrap of Xuancheng. Sanshan Mountain is on the south bank of the Yangtze River in the southwest of Nanjing, Jiangsu Province today.There are three peaks connecting north and south. With detailed observation and high artistic generality, the poem depicts a picture of the evening scene of the spring river with distinct layers, beautiful colors and full of interest. The language is beautiful and natural. Some lines are the most popular in Xie Tiao's poems.

灞涘望长安，河阳视京县。
白日丽飞甍，参差皆可见。
余霞散成绮，澄江静如练。
喧鸟覆春洲，杂英满芳甸。
去矣方滞淫，怀哉罢欢宴。
佳期怅何许，泪下如流霰。
有情知望乡，谁能缜不变。

Stand on the shore of Bashui and look at Chang'an,

Live in Heyang, look at Jing County from afar.

The setting sun reflects the towering roof ridge,

All the high and low buildings can be seen.

The sunset glow disperses like brocades,

The river is as clear as white.

Birds noisily cover the small continent in spring,

The fragrant countryside is full of flowers of various colors.

After leaving I will stay in a foreign country for a long time,

I miss the banquet in my hometown.

When will the return date come,

Tears drop like flowing graupel.

People who have passion miss hometown,

Who keeps the color of black hair unchanged.

《京路夜发》诗歌赏析：

本篇写于齐明帝建武二年（495）初夏出任宣城太守时。诗歌描述了诗人天未明时出发的情景，想象到任后的情状，字里行间流露出诗人思乡倦游的心情。

A Night Tour

This poem was written in the early summer of second year of Jianwu，Emperor Ming of Qi (495), when he took up the post of the satrap of Xuancheng. The poem writes about the scene of departure when it is still dark. The poet imagines the situation after his taking position. Between the lines there is a feeling of homesickness and tiredness.

扰扰整夜装，肃肃戒徂两。

晓星正寥落，晨光复泱漭。

犹沾余露团，稍见朝霞上。

故乡邈已夐，山川修且广。

文奏方盈前，怀人去心赏。

敕躬每跼蹐，瞻恩唯震荡。

行矣倦路长，无由税归鞅。

Arrange the night clothes,

Hurriedly prepare for long-distance vehicles.

Morning stars were sparsely scattered at this time,

The morning light was so dim and confused.

There was still dew on the grass,

Slowly see the morning glow hanging in the sky.

My hometown is farther and farther away,

Mountains and rivers look long and wide.

The official documents and files are piled up on the table,

But I miss friend and I am happy to appreciate.

Cautiously bend down and walk in small steps,

Feel royal grace and shock in heart.

I'm tired of the long journey,

But I can't unload the horse and return to my hometown.

《和王主簿怨情》诗歌赏析：

王季哲是谢朓岳父王敬则之子。据《南齐书·明帝纪》，王敬则在建武元年（494）十月为大司马，诗歌可能作于次年春。在诗歌中诗人描述了女子的怨旷之情。

Grievances

Wang Jizhe, son of Xie Tiao' s father-in-law Wang Jingze. According to *The Book of Southern Qi · Ming Emperor Ji*, Wang Jingze was Da Sima in October of the first year of Jianwu (494). The poem may be written in the spring of the following year and writes about women' s grievances.

掖庭聘绝国，长门失欢宴。

相逢咏蘼芜，辞宠悲班扇。

花丛乱数蝶，风帘入双燕。

徒使春带赊，坐惜红妆变。

生平一顾重，宿昔千金贱。

故人心尚尔？故人心不见。

Wang Zhaojun married away to a foreign land,

Empress Chen no longer accompanied Emperor Wu.

When they met by chance, she couldn't help chanting on Mi Wu,

Losing grace was even more sorrowful than Ban Jieyu.

A few butterflies flew among flowers,

The wind moved the curtain off, a pair of swallows flew in.

Clothes belt loosed every day,

It's a pity that her face was haggard day by day.

It is rare to love and cherish in life.

The affectionof the past is no longervaluable.

Is the old man's heart still the same?

The heart is gone now.

《直中书省》诗歌赏析：

建武二年（495）春，谢朓转为中书郎，这首诗即作于在中书省值班时。由于政治风云变幻莫测，自魏晋以迄南朝在统治阶级中兴起了一股归隐之风：一面当官求禄，一面却又向往着山林隐居的闲散生活。这首诗抒发了谢朓既官居台省又向往山泉游赏生活的思想情感。诗人在描写楼宇建筑的同时，写出了极清丽秀美的佳句，将对自然景物的欣赏同诗人官吏生活紧密地结合起来，显示出新的特色，这无疑是同诗人朝隐的人生态度密切相关的。

On Duty in Zhongshu Sheng

In the spring of the second year of Jianwu (495), Xie Tiao was transferred to Zhongshulang. This poem was written while he was on duty in Zhongshu Sheng. Due to the unpredictable political situation, there has been a trend of seclusion among the ruling class since the Wei and Jin Dynasties to the Southern Dynasties: on the one hand, people were seeking positions as officials, but on the other hand they yearned for a leisurely life in the mountains and forests. This poem expresses Xie Tiao' s thoughts of taking office in Zhongshu Sheng and his yearning for leisure life. While describing the building and architecture, the poet wrote very clear and beautiful lines, closely combining the appreciation of natural scenery with the life in office, showing new characteristics, which is undoubtedly close to his seclusion attitude.

紫殿肃阴阴，彤庭赫弘敞。
风动万年枝，日华承露掌。
玲珑结绮钱，深沉映朱网。
红药当阶翻，苍苔依砌上。
兹言翔凤池，鸣佩多清响。
信美非吾室，中园思偃仰。
朋情以郁陶，春物方骀荡。
安得凌风翰，聊恣山泉赏。

The emperor's palace is deep and quiet,
The emperor's palace is bright and spacious.
The breeze blows the Evergreen Tree,
The sun shines brightly on Palace tower.
The windows are exquisitely decorated with beautiful knots,
The deep colors set off the hanging vermilion nets.
Peony grows luxuriantly,
Moss spreads and grows along the steps.
This is the famous Xiangfeng Pool,
Where many jade pendants make sounds.
Though beautiful, it is not suitable for me to live in,

I want to live in a garden.

The friendship is so pleasant,

The spring is also flourishing.

How can I grow feathers to fly in wind,

Enjoy the spring in mountains at will.

《观朝雨》诗歌赏析：

这是一首写景兼抒怀的诗，很能代表谢朓诗在诗中多写隐仕思想矛盾、先写景后抒怀的创作特色。开头两句，气概不凡，足以笼罩全篇。但诗篇情景分咏，既映衬分明，又浑然一体。诗歌的结构和意境是完整、和谐的，不失为谢朓诗中的上乘之作。

Appreciating Morning Rain

This is a poem that depicts scenery and expresses feelings at the same time. It can well represent the creative characteristics of Xie Tiao's poems in which the poems contain more hermit thoughts and the scenery is first described before the emotions. The first two sentences are extraordinary, enough to cover the whole article. However, the poems are divided into scenery and chants, which are clearly contrasted and integrated. The structure and mood are complete and harmonious. It is the best work of Xie Tiao's poems.

朔风吹飞雨，萧条江上来。

既洒百常观，复集九成台。

空濛如薄雾，散漫似轻埃。

平明振衣坐，重门犹未开。

耳目暂无扰，怀古信悠哉。

戢翼希骧首，乘流畏曝鳃。

动息无兼遂，歧路多徘徊。

方同战胜者，去翦北山莱。

The north wind blows the raindrops,

Depression drifts over from the river.

Not only float on the high Baichang Temple,

But also wet the Jiucheng Deck.

Chaos and confusion like a layer of mist,

Diffuse like light dust.

Early morning I'm dressed and ready to go to the royal court,

But the palace gate have not been opened for a while.

Temporarily avoid troubles,

Think about the ancient times leisurely.

Grab the wings and think about holding the horse's head high,

Ride in the stream but afraid of exposing the gills.

Proceedings and seclusions cannot have the best of both worlds,

So much hesitation when encountering forks.

Stand with the victor,

Pick wild vegetable in the North Mountain.

《和徐都曹》诗歌赏析：

徐都曹，即徐勉，南朝梁文学家。谢朓诗当作于任中书郎时，因与徐勉同在台省，联辔赋诗。诗中对景物的刻画清新而细微，敏锐地表现出了景物的瞬间动态。

A Reply Song to Xu Ducao

Xu Ducao, Xu Mian, was a litterateur of Liang Dynasty in the Southern Dynasty. Xie Tiao's poem was written when he served as Zhongshu Lang. Because he took office in Zhongshu Sheng with Xu Mian, they composed poems together. The depiction of the scenery in the poem is fresh and subtle, keenly showing the momentary dynamics of the scenery.

宛洛佳遨游，春色满皇州。

结轸青郊路，迥瞰苍江流。

日华川上动，风光草际浮。

桃李成蹊径，桑榆阴道周。

东都已俶载，言归望绿畴。

Have fun in Luoyang and Wancheng,

The beautiful spring scenery is all over the capital.

Stop on the road in the countryside,

Look at the vast river rushing from the distance.

The brilliance of the sun sways on the surface of the river,

The wind flow the grass off.

A small lane is under peach and plum trees,

Lined with mulberry and elm trees.

Farming begins everywhere outside the Eastern Capital City,

Return home to look at the green fields indulgently.

南北朝诗歌 南朝梁
Poems of Northern and Southern Dynasties(the Southern Liang Dynasty)

江淹（444—505），字文通，济阳考城（今河南民权东北）人，南朝宋代到梁初时期的文学家。他幼而敏悟，六岁即能写诗，自以孤贫，刻苦学习，早年即以文章著名。在仕途上最初很不得意，依附宋建平王刘景素，不仅未受重视，反而被陷害入狱。出狱后为镇军参军。后因以诗对心怀异志的刘景素进行劝谏，遭刘憎恶，又被黜为吴兴令。吴兴边远荒凉，环境艰苦，江淹在此苦熬三年，他一生的代表作品多半写于此时。及刘景素谋反被镇压，萧道成辅政，器重江淹文才，召为尚书驾部郎。从此逐步提升，官至金紫光禄大夫。晚年安富尊荣，加以世故日深，思想保守，故文学才能显著减退。他的著作较多，以诗赋为主，赋的成就较高。原有集，已散佚，后人辑有《江文通集》。

Jiang Yan (444-505), Wentong, was from Kaocheng, Jiyang(now northeast of Minquan, Henan Province). He is a litterateur from Song to Early Liang of the Southern Dynasty. He was quick in mind and able to write poetry at the age of six. Since he was poor, he studied hard and was famous for his articles in his early years. At the beginning, he was unsuccessful in his official career. He was attached to Liu Jingsu, Emperor Jianping of the Southern Song Dynasty. He not only was ignored, but was framed and imprisoned by Liu. After getting out of prison he served as Zhenjun Canjun. Later, because he used poems to persuade Liu Jingsu, he was hated by Liu and deposed again as Wu Xing Ling. Wu Xing is remote and desolate and it is difficult to live. Jiang Yan had lived there for three years. Most of his life’s representative works are written at this time. When Liu Jingsu’s rebellion was suppressed, Xiao Daocheng assisted in the royal court. Jiang Yan was valued for his talent, and he took up the post of Shangshu Jiabu Lang. From then on he was gradually promoted to Jinzi Guanglu Dafu. In his later years he was rich and honorable, and his sophistication was deepened and his thoughts were conservative. Therefore, his iterary talent was significantly reduced. His works are mainly poems and Fu, and his achievements in Fu are even higher. His collection has been scattered and lost, and the *Jiang Wentong Collection* was compiled by later generations.

《望荆山》诗歌赏析：

荆山在今湖北南漳西。本篇约作于泰始三年（467）秋，江淹到襄阳任巴陵王左常侍不久。由于刚刚蒙受冤狱，现在又远适异乡，举目无亲，前途未卜，因此诗中充满悲苦之情。诗熔古朴遒劲与流丽清新于一炉，显示出从“元嘉体”向“永明体”过渡的痕迹。

Looking at Jingshan Mountain

Jingshan is in the west of Nanzhang, Hubei Province today. This poem was written about in the autumn of the third year of Taishi (467), when Jiang Yan went to Xiangyang to serve as Zuochang Shi of Baling King. Because he has just been unjustly imprisoned, he is far away in a foreign land and has no relatives. His future is uncertain yet. Therefore, the poem is full of sadness. The poem integrates the simplicity with freshness, showing the transition from“Yuanjia Style” to“Yongming Style”.

奉义至江汉，始知楚塞长。

南关绕桐柏，西岳山鲁阳。

寒郊无留影，秋日悬清光。

悲风桡重林，云霞肃川涨。

岁晏君如何？零泪沾衣裳。

玉柱空掩露，金樽坐含霜。

一闻苦寒奏，更使艳歌伤。

Admiring morality and righteousness, I come to Jianghan River,

Only then do I know the length of the northern border of Chu State.

The pass to the south goes around to Tongbai Mountain,

The peaks and ridges to the west extend to Luyang.

There is no shade of trees and flowers in the cold countryside,

Only to feel the cool glow of autumn.

The stern north wind bends trees,

Clouds shrink the river so that it no longer rises.

I don’t know how you feel in this year.

Tears soak my clothes.

The instrument is covered with a layer of white dew,

Frost falls from the wine glass in vain.

At first of I heard the song “Ku Han Xing”,

Then I hear the song “Yan Ge Xing”, which makes me even sadder.

《从冠军建平王登庐山香炉峰》诗歌赏析：

庐山，在今江西九江市南。香炉峰，为其诸峰之一。从诗歌最末两句看，刘景素当有诗在先，此诗当为和建平王游庐山诗而作。诗歌主要描写了恍若仙境的香炉峰景色。诗歌的末四句写登临引发出的归隐之志，回应题目，示为应和而作。

Xianglu Peak in Mountain Lushan

Mount Lushan is in the south of today’s Jiujiang City, Jiangxi Province. Xianglu peak is one of its peaks.Judging from the last two sentences of this poem, Liu Jingsu should have written a poem, and this poem should be written in reply to the poem of King of Jianping’s tour of Lushan. The poem mainly describes the scenery of Xianglu Peak, which resembles a fairyland. The last four sentences of the poem write about the ambition of seclusion triggered by the climbing, which responds to the title and shows as a response.

广成爱神鼎，淮南好丹经。

此山具鸾鹤，往来尽仙灵。

瑶草正翕艳，玉树信葱青。

绛气下萦薄，白云上杳冥。

中坐瞰蜿虹，俛伏视流星。

不寻遐怪极，则知耳目惊。

日落长沙渚，曾阴万里生。

藉兰素多意，临风默含情。

方学松柏隐，羞逐市井名。

幸承光诵末，伏思托后旌。

In ancient times the fairy Guangcheng cherished the tripod,

The King of Huainan in the Han Dynasty liked *Dan Jing*.

Phoenixes and white cranes frequently appear in this mountain,

The gods who ride the phoenixes and drive the cranes.

The fairy grass grows luxuriantly and dazzlingly,

The trees are always green.

The red clouds of aura descend from the sky and reflect the jungle,

Smoke from the incense burner go straight up into the sky and turn into white clouds.

Sit on the mountain and see the rainbow flying,

Look down the meteors in the sky.

You don't have to go far to search for strange things.

You can find something new in the mountains.

Looking westward, the red sun sink outside Changsha Isle,

Mountains turn dark, and night gradually falls.

The orchids everywhere make me think of living in seclusion,

My heart is full of complicated feelings in wind.

I want to learn the evergreen pines and cypresses,

Ashamed to chase the vulgar fame.

Today I have the honor to serve with the beautiful poems of the virtuous king,

Secretly think of myself as a follower.

~~~~~~
~~~~~~

徐悱（约495—524），字敬业，东海郯（今山东郯城西南）人，南朝梁诗人。其父徐勉、妻刘令娴均有文名。徐悱诗今存《赠内》《白马篇》及本诗等数首，载《文选》《玉台新咏》。

Xu Fei(approx. 495-524), Jingye, was born in Donghai Tan (now southwest of Tancheng, Shandong Province). He is a poet of Liang from the Southern Dynasty. His father Xu Mian and his wife Liu Lingxian both have literary fame. Xu's poems, including *Zeng Nei*, *White Horse*, and this poem, are included in *Wen Xuan* and *New Ode to Yutai*.

《古意酬到长史溉登琅邪城》诗歌赏析：

"古意"是六朝以来诗歌中的常见主题，乃托言古事以抒今情。溉，为司徒长史。琅邪，郡名。诗作借言汉代之事，抒发诗人投笔从戎，收取北地的雄心壮志。在诗歌结尾，诗人以李广的故事慨叹壮志难酬，诗歌的风格悲壮凄凉。

Langya City

"Ancient meaning" has been a common theme in poems since the Six Dynasties, which express feelings of the present by talking about the past. Gai refers to Situ Changshi. Langya is a county's name. The poem writes from the events in Han Dynasty to express Poet's ambitions to join the army and recapture the Northland. At the end of the poem, the poet uses the story of Li Guang to lament that his aspirations are hard to realize. The style of the poem is tragic and desolate.

甘泉警烽候，上谷拒楼兰。

此江称豁险，兹山复郁盘。

表里穷形胜，襟带尽岩峦。

脩篁壮下属，危楼峻上干。

登陴起遐望，回首见长安。

金沟朝灞浐，甬道入鸳鸾。

鲜车骛华毂，汗马跃银鞍。

少年负壮气，耿介立冲冠。

怀纪燕山石，思开函谷丸。

岂如霸上戏，羞取路傍观。

寄言封侯者，数奇良可叹。

See the beacon in Ganquan Palace,

We know the enemy has invaded,

Shanggu County is located in the border, resisting Loulan.

This wide wavy river is a natural danger,

The mountains here are undulating and overlapping.

From the inside to the outside, the terrain is so dangerous,

Just as the belt surrounded by steep mountains.

Dense bamboo forests extend to the foot of the mountain,

The city tower on the top of the mountain stands up to the sky.

Climb up the city wall and look at it from a high distance,

When we look back on the city wall,We can see, the capital, Chang'an.

The Yu River connects with Ba River and Chan River,

The long corridor leads to the Yuanluan Palace.

The bright and gorgeous carriages are galloping in a staggered manner,

The precious horse is running excited with the silver saddle.

When I was a teenager, I was full of passion,

The heroic ambition to serve the country was inspiring.

I see the ancients taking stone as a model,

I often think of leading the army to conquer dangerous border.

Running an army will never be like conquering an army.

I will be ashamed to let bystanders laugh at me.

There is a saying to those who are made marquis,

When my fate is not going well, I only sigh deeply.

~~~~~~

沈约（441—513），字休文，吴兴郡武康（今浙江德清）人。南朝梁文学家、史学家。沈约幼而孤贫，笃志好学，昼夜不倦。昼之所读，夜辄诵之，博通群籍。时，谢玄晖善为诗，任彦昇工于文章，约兼而有之，然不能过也。

Shen Yue (441-513), Xiuwen, was born in Wukang, Wuxing County (now Deqing, Zhejiang Province). He was a writer and historian of the Southern Liang Dynasty. He was poor at young age, but he dedicated to learning and felt tireless day and night. He recited at night what he read in the daytime. He read wide ranges of books. At that time, Xie Xuanhui was good at poems, and Ren Yanhsheng did well in essays. Shen Yue was good at both of them, but he couldn’t pass Xie and Ren.

《应王中丞思远咏月》诗歌赏析：

诗歌为和王思远咏月之作，紧扣“月华”二字展开铺写，情景如画，清丽流转，用词精美。全诗描绘了月夜光影的变化与人的感受，而光影的变化与对光影的感受相反，并以形状、感觉、色彩形成的对句出之。其手法颇与捕捉外界自然光影瞬间变化的印象派绘画艺术酷似。

A Reply Poem to Wang Siyuan

The poem is a work in reply to Wang Siyuan chanting on the moon, which closely links to the word “moonlight” to write. The scene is picturesque, clear and beautiful. The language is also very exquisite.The whole poem depicts the changes of light and shadow in the moonlit night and the feelings of people. While the changes and feelings of light and shadow have the opposite meanings, and are expressed in pair sentences of shapes, feelings, and colors. The technique is quite similar to the impressionist painting art that captures the momentary changes of natural light and shadow of world.

月华临静夜，夜静灭氛埃。

方晖竟户入，圆影隙中来。

高楼切思妇，西园游上才。

网轩映珠缀，应门照绿苔。

洞房殊未晓，清光信悠哉。
~~~~~~

Moonlight descended on the quiet night,

Quiet night swept away the scattered dust.

The glow filled the square portal,

Light shone in from the cracks in the wall.

In the building the women was in brilliance,

Moonlight shone in the Western Garden.

Radiance reflected the red lattice on the window,

Shone on the green moss outside gate.

The bedroom was deep before dawn,

The sky was so clear and lovely.

《咏湖中雁》诗歌赏析：

永明体诗人沈约、谢朓、王融等都写过不少咏物诗，尤以沈约为多，但总体成就不高。这首《咏湖中雁》诗，意思比较平浅，但刻画精致，大雁的种种情态跃然纸上，有一定的美学价值。

Chanting on Wild Geese in the Lake

Yongming poets such as Shen Yue, Xie Tiao, and Wang Rong have written many chanting poems, especially Shen Yue, but the overall achievements are not high. The meaning of this poem *Chanting on Wild Geese in the Lake* is relatively simple, but the portrayal is delicate. The various movements of the wild goose are vivid on the paper, which has a certain aesthetic value.

白水满春塘，旅雁每回翔。

唼流牵弱藻，敛翮带余霜。

群浮动轻浪，单泛逐孤光。

悬飞竟不下，乱起未成行。

刷羽同摇漾，一举还故乡。

In spring the pond is filled with clear water,

A swarms of geese fly in circles.

Forage in water moves slender green algae,

The condensed wings are covered with thin hoarfrost.

Float together and set off gentle waves,

Float alone chasing the solitary light in water.

Hovering in the air will not fall,

Scattered takeoffs has not yet arranged in line.

The whole wings fly together, swaying,

Fly back to the distant hometown through clouds and fog.

《三月三日率尔成篇》诗歌赏析：

三月三日，即农历的上巳日。古人于每年三月上旬的巳日临水祭祀，并用浸泡了香草的水沐浴，认为这样可以祓除不祥。这种风俗起源于周代，汉魏以后相沿，魏以后，大概为了便于记忆，将节日固定为每年农历三月初三。春天正是风和日丽、鸟语花香的季节，三月三日逐渐成为人们春日到水边郊游踏青、饮宴游玩的节日。宴饮时，人们把酒杯放到水中任其漂流，漂到谁面前就由谁取饮。骚人墨客还免不了要吟诗作赋，这就产生了一系列以“上巳”和“三月三日”为题的作品。沈约的这首诗，虽以长安、洛阳为背景，实际描写的是江南的春禊活动，刻画了青年男女纵情游乐的情态。

Shangsi Festival

March 3rd is on the third day of the third month of the lunar calendar. The ancients used water soaked in vanilla water to have a bath and make rituals in early March every year. They thought that this would eliminate the ominousness. This custom originated in Zhou Dynasty and followed in Han and Wei Dynasties. After Wei Dynasty, the festival was fixed on the third day of the third month of the lunar calendar for the sake of memory. Spring is the season of breeze, beautiful birds and flowers. March 3rd is gradually becoming a festival for people to go to the water for outings and banquets in spring. When in banquets, people put their wine cups in the water and let them drift in front of whoever takes the drink. It is inevitable for poets to write poems and compose Fu. Thus they wrote a series of works titled "Shangsi" and "March 3rd" . Although Shen Yue's poem is about Chang' an and Luoyang, it actually describes the Chunxi activities in the south of the Yangtze River. It portrays the indulgence and pleasure of young people.

丽日属元巳，年芳具在斯。

开花已匝树，流嘤复满枝。

洛阳繁华子，长安轻薄儿。

东出千金堰，西临雁鹜陂。

游丝映空转，高杨拂地垂。

绿幘文照耀，紫燕光陆离。

清晨戏伊水，薄暮宿兰池。

象筵鸣宝瑟，金瓶泛羽卮。

宁忆春蚕起，日暮桑欲萎。

长袂屡以拂，雕胡方自炊。

爱而不可见，宿昔减容仪。

且当忘情去，叹息独何为。

The good day belongs to Shangsi Festival,

A whole year's bloom concentrats at this time.

Trees are full of colorful flowers,

Tactful birds stand on branches.

Luoyang's young teenagers are in groups,

Chang'an's frivolous men echo each other.

To the east comes the Qianjin bam in Luoyang,

To the west is the Yanjiao Pi in Chang 'an.

The gossamer floats in the sky against spring light,

Branches of willows are hanging high.

The green silk shine under the sun,

The purple swallows shine in spring breeze.

Play freely by the Yishui River in the morning,

We camp by the orchid pond in the evening.

The sumptuousness of the banquet soundes the treasure,

The golden feather bottle floats on the water.

How can we think of the hunger of spring silkworms,

Mulberry leaves are about to wither when the sun sets.

Constantly cover face with long sleeves,

The rice is cooking.

The lover hides and couldn't meet,

Appearance changes overnight.

Or should we forget about love and leave,

What is the use of sighing alone?

《游沈道士馆》诗歌赏析：

《游沈道士馆》是南朝诗人沈约创作的一首五言诗。全诗以古喻今，夹叙夹议，讽喻与游仙统一，显出构思之妙，是沈诗的五言压卷之作。

本诗写作背景、主旨与《宿东园》相同，皆表达了诗人入梁后有志台司终不见用的失意心情。诗作借秦皇汉武故事发端，抒发自己诚心向道的思想感情。诗人想象自己从道后神仙般的逍遥自在生活，表达了诗人自甘淡泊的愿望。

Taoist Shen's Pavilion

Shen Taoist Pavilion is a five-character poem written by the Southern Dynasty poet Shen Yue. The whole poem uses the past to metaphor the present. There is narration and discussion in the poem. The unity of Satire and immortals shows the poet' s wonderful idea. It can be a five-character masterpiece work of Shen Yue' s Poetry.

The background and theme of this poem are the same as those in *Staying in Dongyuan*, and both express the poet' s frustration that he would never be valued. The poem is based on the story of Emperor QinShihuang and Emeperor Han Wu, expressing his sincere thoughts and feelings to Tao. The poet imagines that he will live a life like a fairy after studying Taoism, expressing the poet's indifferent desire.

秦皇御宇宙，汉帝恢武功。
欢娱人事尽，情性犹未充。
锐意三山上，托慕九霄中。
既表祈年观，复立望仙宫。
宁为心好道，直由意无穷！
曰余知止足，是愿不须丰。
遇可淹留处，便欲息微躬。
山嶂远重叠，竹树近蒙笼。
开衿濯寒水，解带临清风。
所累非外物，为念在玄空。
朋来握石髓，宾至驾轻鸿。
都令人径绝，唯使云路通。
一举陵倒景，无事适华嵩。
寄言赏心客，岁暮尔来同。

Emperor Qin Shihuang unified the land of China,
Emperor Wu of the Han Dynasty made remarkable achievements with magnificent force.
As emperors, they enjoyed the joys of the world,
But still felt unsatisfied in their hearts.
Yearn for the life of the immortals in the three mountains on the sea,
Envy immortals on the nine heavens.
The temple was built to pray to the gods for longevity,
The palace of Wangxian was built to hope immortals would protect them.
Where is their behavior out of good ways,

But the endless desire to pursue pleasure!

People need to be content to be carefree,

Never want more in heart.

When I come across a place to stay,

Stay for a long time and stop working hard.

Mountains in the distance are like a screen with overlapping undulations,

Forests and bamboos hazy like smoke.

Untie clothes and bath in the cool spring,

Open chest to welcome the breeze slowly.

How can things outside make me linger and care,

Thoughts are only on the avenue of advocating emptiness.

When friends come, I dedicate the precious chalcedony,

When Guests come, we travel and ride together.

Not take the road of vulgar people at all,

Only come in and out from the sky with white clouds.

Float high in the sky and fly above the sun and moon,

Go to Hua and Song Mountains to rest when there is nothing to do.

Like-minded friends listen to me,

You might as well come here to live together in old age.

《冬节后至丞相第诣世子车中》诗歌赏析：

沈约作此诗感叹人情冷暖、世态炎凉，在当时具有普遍性。本诗有一定典型性，诗歌夹叙夹议，笔调冷峻，感慨深沉。

In the Carriage

Shen Yue wrote the poem to lament the coldness and warmth of humanity and the scorching state of the world, which was universal at the time. The poem pointed to current malpractices and was a typical poem. There was narration and the discussion in the poem. The tone was serious and the emotion was deep.

廉公失权势，门馆有虚盈。

贵贱犹如此，况乃曲池平。

高车尘未灭，珠履故余声。

宾阶绿钱满，客位紫苔生。

谁当九原上，郁郁望佳城。

Once General Lianpo lost power,

The gate suddenly turned from lively to deserted.

From being in power to losing power, people's feelings are changeable,

Not to mention that Quchi is desolate.

The dust raised by the high carriage has not disappeared,

Sounds of the footsteps still linger.

The steps are already covered with moss,

Purple moss has long been growing on the guest seats.

Who came to Jiuyuan Mountain,

Silently look at the tomb of his father and grandfather.

《早发定山》诗歌赏析：

定山，在今浙江杭州东南。诗篇描绘了定山奇特迷人的景色，抒写了诗人对于山川灵秀的深相眷恋之情。诗风颇近似于谢灵运，但无大谢的古奥生涩，具有圆活自然的特色。沈约为“永明体”的创始人之一。诗篇对仗精整，声调谐和，节奏明快，体现了诗人的创作主张。

Setting out to Visit Dingshan Mountain in the Morning

Dingshan Mountain is in the southeast of Hangzhou, Zhejiang Province today. The poem describes the peculiar and charming scenery of Dingshan Mountain, and expresses the deep love for the beauty of mountains and rivers. The style of the poem is quite similar to Xie Lingyun, but is not ancient and jerky like Xie Lingyun’s with bright and natural characteristics. Shen Yue was one of the founders of “Yongming Style”. The poem was well-balanced and had harmonic tones and bright rhythm, reflecting the poet’s creative proposition.

夙龄爱远壑，晚莅见奇山。
标峰彩虹外，置岭白云间。
倾壁忽斜竖，绝顶复孤圆。
归海流漫漫，出浦水浅浅。
野棠开未落，山樱发欲然。
忘归属兰杜，怀禄寄芳荃。
眷言采三秀，徘徊望九仙。

When I was young,I loved remote valleys,
I saw Qishan Mountain again when I came here.
The peaks tower is above the colorful rainbow,
Mountains are surrounded by white clouds.
Steep cliff suddenly stands upright,
The top of the high peak looks like a solitary circle.
Big river flowing eastern into the sea is vast,
Small river rushing out of Pukou is surging.
Wild thorns bloom and have not yet withered,
Wild cherry trees bloom like flames.
Enjoying the bluegrass so much as to forget to leave,
The desire for fame can be entrusted to Fangquan.
After tossing around and picking ganoderma lucidum,
I linger, looking forward to the appearance of the immortals.

《新安江水至清浅深见底贻京邑游好》诗歌赏析：

本篇作于齐隆昌元年（494 年）沈约出任东阳太守时。新安江，源于今江西婺源西北，流经安徽休宁、歙县合练江，始称新安江；再东流入浙江省境，在建德东南与兰江合，东北流至浙江桐庐为桐江，至浙江杭州富阳为富春江，至旧钱塘县境为钱塘江。诗篇前部写江水的澄净清澈，后部展开联想，表示愿以此水为京师友人洗濯冠缨，实则希望京师友人身处嚣尘之中而能洁身自好。

A Tour to Xin'an River

The poem was written in the first year of Longchang in Qi Dynasty (494 年), when Shen Yue took office of the satrap of Dongyang. Xin' an River is originated in the northwest of Wuyuan, Jiangxi Province. It flows through Xiuning, Anhui, and Helian River in She County, and was originally called Xin' an River. Then it flows eastward into Zhejiang Province, joins the Lanjiang River in the southeast of Jiande, and flows northeast to Tonglu, Zhejiang, Tongjiang River. To Fuyang, Hangzhou, Zhejiang, it become the Fuchun River, and to the old Qiantang County, is the Qiantang River. The front part of the poem writes about the clarity of the river, and the back part starts to image, expressing the willingness to wash the crowns of friends from capital in this river. In fact, the writer hopes that friends remain clean and self-conscious when they are in the midst of the crowds.

眷言访舟客，兹川信可珍。

洞澈随深浅，皎镜无冬春。

千仞写乔树，百丈见游鳞。

沧浪有时浊，清济涸无津。

岂若乘斯去，俯映石磷磷。

纷吾隔嚣滓，宁假濯衣巾。

愿以潺湲水，沾君缨上尘。

I keep looking around,

The river is really worth cherishing.

It is so clear regardless of the depth,

Also clean in winter and spring.

The shadows of high trees reflect directly on the bottom of the water,

Swimming fish can be seen in the deep water.

There was also a time when the water of blue waves is turbid,

Although Ji water is clear, it is so dry that there was no drop of water.

Do you want to ride this river flow far away,

Be profiled on the phosphorous rock in the river.

I have left the noisy and dusty capital,

I still use the river to wash clothes.

I would like to use the flowing river to wash the dust off the hat belt.

《和谢宣城》诗歌赏析：

沈约同谢朓俱为"竟陵八友"之一，一生交谊甚厚。隆昌元年（494），沈约由吏部郎出为宁朔将军、东阳太守，明帝即位，进号辅国将军，征为五兵尚书。建武二年（495），谢朓由中书郎出为宣城太守，在宣城作了《在郡卧病呈沈尚书》，这首诗是对其的应和之作。诗篇叙写了诗人虽在朝而若隐的生活，倾吐了对谢朓的思念之情。沈约为"永明体"的创始人之一，讲求平仄对仗，在这首诗中也有体现，但气质厚挚，语言朴茂，仍不乏古诗韵味。

A Reply Poem to Xie Xuancheng

Shen Yue and Xie Tiao are both one of the "Eight Friends of King of Jingling" . They are close friends. In the first year of Longchang (494 年), Shen Yue was appointed as General Ningshuo and Dongyang satrap from Libu Lang. When Emperor Ming ascended the throne, Shen entered the rank of Fuguo Generals and enlisted as Wubing Shangshu. In the second year of Jianwu (495), Xie Tiao was appointed as the satrap of Xuancheng from Zhongshu Lang, and wrote *To Shen Shangshu* in Xuancheng. The poem is a reply poem. The poem tells the story of Shen' scareer life in the royal court, but in fact he seemed to live in seclusion. It also expresses his feelings of missing Xie Tiao. Shen Yue is one of the founders of the "Yongming Style" . He emphasizes flatness and confrontation, which is also reflected in this poem, but the emotions are deep and the language is simple. It still has the charm of ancient poetry.

王乔飞凫舄，东方金马门。
从宦非宦侣，避世不避喧。
揆余发皇鉴，短翮屡飞翻。
晨趋朝建礼，晚沐卧郊园。
宾至下尘榻，忧来命绿樽。
昔贤侔时雨，今守馥兰荪。
神交疲梦寐，路远隔思存。
牵拙谬东汜，浮惰及西昆。
顾循良菲薄，何以俪玙璠。
将随渤澥去，刷羽泛清源。

Wang Qiao flew in a pair of mallards,
Dongfang Shuo escaped at the Golden Horse Gate.
Being an official is different from ordinary bureaucrats,
Not living in seclusion in mountains, but in the royal court.
The king assessed my situation,
I had raised my wings and flew again and again.
In the morning, I went to the gate of Jianli Palace to court,
In the evening, I took a shower and lay down in suburban home.
When guests came, I took off the gray seat,
Asked to serve the green wine bottle.
In the past wise men were like rain in time,
The moral character of satrap of Xuancheng is as fragrant as vanilla.
Meeting frequently in the dream made me feel tired,
The road was far away aparting us.

It is a mistake to enter official career with mediocre qualifications in youth,

In old age, I became disheartened about fame and fortune.

My talent is indeed shallow,

How can it be compared with those in the court?

I would like to follow the birds and float away,

Swim in the clear waves of the East Sea.

《宿东园》诗歌赏析：

这首诗作于齐明帝建武四年（497），是南朝诗人沈约所作的一首五言诗。诗人为国子祭酒，年五十七岁。时掌管东郊祭祀，留宿东郊。当时朝政昏乱，诗人忧虞深郁，故作此诗。诗作描写了东园郊野一带萧索凄冷的况味，抒发时光消逝、人生易老的感叹。据《梁书·沈约传》载，诗人沈约对于萧衍受禅称帝曾起积极促进作用，卓有勋劳。但是入梁以后，官职卑微。诗人心怀不满，萌生隐退之意。

诗歌由曹潘诗引入，描绘荒芜的东郊秋天日落前后景象，笼罩着落寞、衰微氛围，透露诗人迟暮感伤情绪与幻想服药长生、求得精神解脱的愿望。诗歌选取一系列典型物像，铺陈描绘，细密精工，具有鲜明的形象美。今昔之感与自伤之情同黄昏景物浑融一体。诗歌语言流利自然，对仗工整，音调和谐。

Sleeping in Dongyuan

This poem was written in the fourth year of Jianwu Emperor Ming of Qi (497). It is a five-character poem written by the Southern Dynasty poet Shen Yue. The poet was Guozi Jijiu, and was fifty-seven years old. At that time, he was in charge of the sacrifices in the eastern suburbs and stayed at night in it. At that time, the royal court was in a mess, and the poet was worried and depressed, hence write this poem. The poem describes the sad and desolate situation in the suburbs of Dongyuan, expressing the sigh of the passing of time and the tendency of life to grow old. According to the *Liang Shu · Shen Yue Biography*, Shen Yue played an active role in promoting Xiao Yan' s proclaiming emperor, and he was very rewarding. But after entering Liang, his official position was humble. The poet was dissatisfied and wanted to resign.

The poem was introduced by poem of Cao Pan, depicting the deserted eastern suburbs before and after sunset in autumn. It is shrouded in a lonely and declining atmosphere, revealing the poet's late sentiment and fantasy of taking medicine for longevity and wishing for spiritual liberation.The poem selects a series of typical objects to laid out and depict. It is meticulous and exquisite with a good image. The feelings of past and present are blended with the evening scene. The language is fluent and natural. The contrast is neat and the tone is harmonious.

陈王斗鸡道，安仁采樵路。
东郊岂异昔，聊可闲余步。
野径既盘纡，荒阡亦交互。
槿篱疏复密，荆扉新且故。
树顶鸣风飙，草根积霜露。
惊麏去不息，征鸟时相顾。
茅栋啸愁鸱，平岗走寒兔。
夕阴带曾阜，长烟引轻素。
飞光忽我遒，宁止岁云暮。
若蒙西山药，颓龄倘能度。

Dongjiao Road is where King of Chensi holds the cockfight match,
Pan Anren followed to chop wood.
Today Eastern Suburbs is not different from the past,
Take a leisurely stroll and entertain here.
Roads in the countryside circulate to and fro,
Trails in the fields crisscross and appear barren.
Some of hibiscus fences are dense and some are sparse,
Some of farmhouse gate are new, some are broken.
The gust of wind on the top of the tree makes noises,
Still a little bit of frost and dew are on the roots of the grass.

The frightened roe deer runs in a hurry,

Flying birds look back from time to time.

Sorrowful cry of owls is heard from the thatched roof,

Shivering hare runs swiftly on the hill.

Evening haze is like a long belt wrapped around the mountain,

Long mist pulls away the light white silk.

The moonlight falls on me like water rushing down,

It means the year will come to an end.

If I get medicine for immortalityon the West Mountain,

I might be able to fly to the moon in old age.

《学省愁卧》诗歌赏析：

学省，即国子监，为封建时代的教育管理机构和最高学府。本诗作于齐明帝建武初年 (494)。此时朝政混乱，沈约深怀忧虑，故在诗中抒写了这一失意之感。诗歌描写了秋风萧瑟勾人愁思的时令，也描写了荒凉寂寞的景象，表达了诗人欲解脱这种无所作为处境的心志。

A Song on Worry

The Ministry of Education, also names the Imperial College, was an educational management institution and the highest institution in the feudal era.This poem was written at the beginning of Jianwu, Emperor Ming of Qi (494). At that time the royal court was in chaos and Shen Yue was deeply worried. So he expressed this feeling of frustration in the poem.The poem describes the season when the autumn wind is bleak and the desolate and lonely scene, which expresses the poet' s desire to escape from the mediocre State.

秋风吹广陌，萧瑟入南闱。

愁人掩轩卧，高窗时动扉。

虚馆清阴满，神宇暧微微。

网虫垂户织，夕鸟傍檐飞。

缨佩空为忝，江海事多违。

山中有桂树，岁暮可言归。

Autumn wind blew across the solitary and vast countryside,

Bleak air entered the small northern gate of courtyard.

The sad man is lying with the door closed,

High windows slapped by the wind from time to time.

The palace was empty.

The tone was dim and quiet.

Spiders hung webs on the windows,

Birds flew near the eaves in the evening.

I feel ashamed of not display my talents and doing nothing.

And it is different from seclusion life.

The osmanthus in the hills is sweet and graceful,

I had better resign this year.

参考文献

References

[1] 夏征农，辞海 [M]. 上海：上海辞书出版社，1999.

[2] 许渊冲，翻译的艺术 [M]. 北京：五洲传播出版社，2006.

[3]《古汉语常用字字典》编写组，古汉语常用字字典 [M]. 北京：商务印书馆，1998.

[4] 许渊冲，汉魏六朝诗一百五十首 [M]. 北京：北京大学出版社，1996.

[5] 沈文凡，汉魏六朝诗三百首译析 [M]. 长春：吉林文史出版社，1999.

[6] 许渊冲，汉魏六朝诗 [M]. 北京：中国对外翻译出版公司，2009.

[7] 许渊冲，汉魏六朝诗选 [M]. 北京：五洲传播出版社，2012.

[8] 吴小如，汉魏六朝诗鉴赏辞典 [M]. 上海：上海辞书出版社，2016.

[9] 王云路，六朝诗歌语词研究 [M]. 哈尔滨：黑龙江教育出版社，1999.

[10] 傅刚，文选版本研究 [M]. 北京：世界图书出版社，2014.

[11] 张启成，文选 [M]. 北京：中华书局，2019.

[12] 陈宏天，赵福海，陈复兴，昭明文选译注 [M]. 长春：吉林文史出版社，1988.

[13] 胡大雷，韩晖，昭明文选教程 [M]. 桂林：广西师范大学出版社，2016.

[14] 许渊冲，中诗英韵探胜 [M]. 北京：北京大学出版社，1992.

[15] 宇文所安，中国早期古典诗歌的生成 [M]. 北京：三联书店，2012.